I0629459

Mystery by moonlight . . .

All was still and quiet on deck. Even my footsteps on the bleached and sanded boards were drowned by the slap of water against the side of the ship as we plowed through the waves. I walked back toward the rear of the ship ("aft" toward the "stern," I corrected myself mentally, thinking of Gene in the Navy) and drew up short as I realized I was not alone after all.

A man stood at the taffrail holding something in his hands, and as I debated the wisdom of calling a friendly greeting to him, given the lateness of the hour and my own sketchy attire, he dropped his burden overboard and turned away from the railing. Instinctively I drew back into the shadow of a lifeboat mounted overhead, holding my breath lest it betray my presence even as I scolded myself for my own foolishness.

So deep were the shadows that he passed within four feet of me and never even suspected my presence. Consumed by curiosity, I waited only until I heard the door close behind him before I hurried to the spot where he'd stood, and leaned out over the taffrail. Far below, the ship's propellers churned the water into frothing waves of gleaming luminescence. There was just light enough for me to make out the painted smile on the end of a Christmas log before it disappeared beneath the foaming surf.

Moon over the Mediterranean

A Novel of Romantic Suspense

MOON OVER THE MEDITERRANEAN
©2017 by Sheri Cobb South. All rights reserved. No part of this book may be used or reproduced in any manner without written permission from the author, except in the case of brief quotations embedded in critical articles or reviews.

Moon over the Mediterranean

A Novel of Romantic Suspense

Sheri Cobb South

Prologue

Let these describe the undescribable.
GEORGE NOEL GORDON, LORD BYRON,
Childe Harold's Pilgrimage

August 1961
Venice, Italy

T he sunlight reflecting off the water created dappled patterns of dancing light on the ceiling as I sat up in bed and stretched my arms wide. Somewhere out on the canal beyond the window of my hotel room, a gondolier sang a plaintive melody in a minor key. I could only pick out the odd word or two of its lyrics; my very limited Italian, painstakingly gleaned from a phrasebook, was unequal to the task of translation. After all, lyricists in this, the most romantic city in the world, rarely waxed rhapsodic over directions to the Piazza San Marco or the time of the next train to Rome.

Nearer at hand, the hum of an electric razor (a more mundane sound, but one no less romantic, at least to my mind) penetrated the closed bathroom door. Smiling to myself, I threw off the covers and slid my arms into the sleeves of my blue satin robe.

"I'll be outside," I called in the general direction of the bathroom, then pushed aside the curtain, opened the French window, and stepped out onto the tiny balcony overlooking the canal. I leaned forward and propped my elbows on the ornate wrought iron railing, admiring the play of sunlight over the unfamiliar band of gold adorning the third finger of my left hand.

The dark prow of the gondola sliced through the water beneath my balcony, its sleek curve resembling the neck of a great black swan. At that moment the sun disappeared behind a cloud, and I shivered, even though the summer morning was already growing uncomfortably warm. The melancholy song of the gondolier began to fade, and I found myself hoping that, by the time my husband and I left Venice in a week's time, the haunting music and the lapping of water against the side of graceful old buildings would have once more become the quintessential Venetian experience, and no longer the stuff of nightmare . . .

1

Travel, in the younger sort, is a part of education;
in the elder, a part of experience.
FRANCIS BACON, *Of Travel*

Three months earlier
En route to Barcelona, Spain

W hen a boy would rather be at the bottom of the sea than on dry land getting married to the girl he claims to love, something is terribly wrong somewhere."

Those pearls of wisdom, dropped at an altitude of twenty thousand feet, were my first inkling that the purpose of this trip was not, as I had been assured, that of helping my poor widowed aunt (her description, not mine) cope with the loss of her husband, my Uncle Herman, some fifteen months earlier. Unfortunately, it was too late to do anything about it now, as our Boeing 707 would soon be making its final approach into Barcelona with its one hundred and fifty passengers, among whom were my Aunt Maggie and me.

"Gene does love me," I insisted. "Besides, he's on a submarine, not at the bottom of the sea."

Maggie waved one manicured hand in a gesture of dismissal. "He might as well be, as far as you're concerned." She took my hand and squeezed it so tightly that her red-lacquered nails cut into the skin. "Robin, honey, it's not that I don't like Gene. I just hate to see you waste the best years of your life waiting for him to be ready to settle down. Some men never do, you know."

I turned away and fixed my eyes on the window, staring down in apparent fascination at the red clay tile rooftops rising to meet us. In truth, I couldn't think of anything to say to Aunt Maggie; after all, she hadn't said anything that I hadn't thought, however reluctantly, myself. Gene and I had been dating since our sophomore year of high school, and the only question regarding our eventual marriage had not been 'if,' but 'when.' After graduation, he had joined the Navy, and I, having nothing better to do, had enrolled in college. I had been rather puzzled at the time by my mother's insistence that I further my education; after all, in Mother's view, there were only three reasons for higher education for a female. A girl could go to secretarial school and eventually marry her boss, or she could go to a teacher's college and eventually marry the principal, or she could go to nursing school and eventually marry a doctor. Since I'd always been good at English, I chose the teaching route. Mother was disappointed—I suspect she'd hoped to have a doctor in the family—but to my mind, it made very little difference: by the time I earned my diploma, Gene's four-year commitment to the Navy would be complete, and we would marry and settle down to raise a family, without my ever having seen the inside of a classroom, at least not from the teacher's side of the desk.

But Gene had re-enlisted within a month of my graduation from college, and I'd spent the last two years attempting to explain split infinitives, dangling participles, and predicate nominatives to uninterested eighth-graders. And now, halfway through his second tour of duty, I'd learned that Gene had requested—*requested!*—an assignment aboard a submarine, delaying our wedding once again so that he could see the world before settling down to a life of domestic bliss. ("How much does he think he'll be able to see from a submarine?" had been Aunt Maggie's not unreasonable response to this newest postponement.)

"Besides," she continued now, releasing my hand with a final pat, "if he wants to see something of the world first, why shouldn't you do the same? After all, what's sauce for the goose is sauce for the gander."

"We're not barnyard fowl," I protested.

A sudden jolt punctuated my objection, and I realized with some surprise that the back wheels of the plane had touched down. I was in Europe now—Spain, to be exact—but although the big adventure promised by Aunt Maggie might be said to have begun, I didn't feel any different. The

11

bumpy taxiway to the terminal looked very much like the one we'd left back in the States, and the hard lump of pain at what I couldn't help thinking of as Gene's betrayal was still firmly stuck somewhere between my throat and my chest. The plane finally lurched to a stop before the terminal, and Aunt Maggie dragged her patent leather handbag from its resting place at her feet, rummaged inside for her compact, and began to powder her nose.

"Look at it this way," she said. "If your Gene is going to make a career of the Navy, he'll want a wife who can hold her own with the other well-traveled Navy wives. In that case, you'll want to be a credit to him."

Yes, I decided resolutely as I unbuckled my seat belt, rose stiffly from the seat I'd occupied for the last eight hours, and attempted (without visible success) to smooth the creases from my white poplin sailor dress. I was going to have a lovely time, and the next time Gene saw me, I would no longer be a small-town junior high English teacher, but a cosmopolitan woman with a smattering of Spanish, French, Greek, and Italian at my command. He would take one look at the sophisticated creature I had become, and thank his lucky stars that no other man had snapped me up while he'd been dragging his feet. I snatched my round beribboned hat from the rack above me and plunked it firmly onto my head (the better to hide my slightly mussed ash-blond hair), then picked up my purse and followed Aunt Maggie down the aisle toward the front of the plane.

I emerged blinking into the bright sunshine, and made my way down the rollaway stairs and onto the tarmac, where I drew my first breath of European air. The temperature was pleasantly mild, but heat rose from the pavement in visible waves, promising an uncomfortably warm afternoon. Baggage handlers were already at work unloading luggage from the cargo hold, and it was easy to pick out my suitcase and its matching cosmetic case, a gift from Aunt Maggie and Uncle Herman upon my graduation from college. Still unused two years later, they were starkly, pristinely white ("bridal white for the honeymoon!" I had exclaimed delightedly—naïvely—at the time), embarrassingly so amongst all these less beautiful but far more worldly bags bearing labels from London and Paris, Hawaii and Bermuda. I was aware of a certain self-consciousness as I picked them up and followed my aunt to the customs barrier. Aunt Maggie—no believer in traveling light—had collared a skycap to wrestle her four bags through customs and to the taxi stand, where he dumped them (with considerable relief, it seemed to me) into the trunk along with mine. Meanwhile, Aunt Maggie gave instructions to the taxi driver, overcoming the language barrier through a combination of gesticulation and sheer volume. At last we piled into the back seat and the taxi peeled out, tires squealing, into the traffic.

"He reminds me so much of your Uncle Herman," Aunt

Maggie said with a reminiscent sigh.

"Who, the taxi driver?" I glanced in bewilderment at the back of his head, and tried to reconcile the memory of my tall, thin, gray-haired uncle with the dark, somewhat stout Spaniard at the wheel, hurtling us through the streets of Barcelona at a speed that sent the plume of smoke from his cigarette flying out the open window in wispy white shreds. "Why?"

"Because Herman never listened to a word I said, either."

Anything I might have said to this was obliged to wait, for at that moment the taxi turned a corner so sharply that I had to grab the armrest on the door to keep from being flung into Maggie's lap. Once the danger passed, I settled back in my seat and watched as the city flew past, medieval churches juxtaposed oddly with billboards advertising Coca-Cola.

And suddenly there was our ship: the *Oceanus*, her sleek lines blindingly white against the blue of the sky and the still bluer hue of the sea, festooned from bow to stern with brightly colored flags flapping gaily in the breeze. The taxi drew up with a screech of brakes and a cloud of dust, and we climbed out, stretching our limbs gingerly to make sure they were still intact. I took a deep breath of air that smelled faintly of salt and fish while Aunt Maggie paid the taxi driver, a procedure that required yet another round of shouting and gesturing.

At last the matter was settled to the satisfaction of both, and the driver opened the trunk and unceremoniously dumped our suitcases on the sidewalk as if he couldn't be rid of them soon enough. We gathered our luggage—I tucked Aunt Maggie's smallest case under my arm—and we took our places at the end of the line straggling out from the gangplank. This, it soon transpired, wound its way through a maze of vendors' booths, all selling souvenirs to tourists eager to lighten their wallets before boarding the ship. Offerings of chocolate and cured meats reminded me that I'd had nothing to eat but the modest breakfast provided by the airline, but Aunt Maggie pointed out that we would have all we could eat and more, once we'd boarded the ship. I did sigh briefly over a selection of lace mantillas in black, white, or scarlet, but my resolve was strengthened by the daunting prospect of putting down my luggage so that I might rummage through my purse for *pesetas* sufficient to make such a purchase. Another booth caught my eye, a booth festively decorated for Christmas although it was now the middle of May, and I stopped to stare in bewilderment at foot-long lengths of rough log with stubby wooden legs and a happy face painted on one sawn end.

"What are they?" I asked the smiling Spanish woman tending the booth. *"¿Qué es?"*

Her smile grew broader as she picked up one of the logs, and I couldn't be sure whether she detected a potential sale, or she simply thought my accent was funny.

"This, it is the *caga tió*, the, how do you say, the shitting log."

"The *what?*" I hardly knew whether to be shocked or delighted.

"It is a very old tradition in Catalonia," she explained. "Beginning with the Feast of the Immaculate Conception, the children feed the *caga tió* and cover it with a blanket to keep it warm. Then on Christmas Day, they sing to it and beat it with sticks so that it will sh—"

"Will poop," Aunt Maggie put in primly, although I knew that with sufficient provocation, she could air a vocabulary that would make most sailors blush.

"*Si*, will poop, as you say, candy and nuts."

"That does it," I announced, setting my luggage down and fumbling in my purse. "I've got to buy one of these things, or no one at home will believe it. How much? Er— *¿Cuánto?*"

She named a sum—I had no idea whether it was a bargain, or highway robbery—and I counted out the coins into her hand and took possession of my very own *caga tió*. Declining her offer to box it up, I tucked it under my arm and picked up my suitcases—not without some difficulty, as Pooping Pedro kept trying to slide out from under my arm— and Maggie and I headed toward the gangplank and took our places in the slow-moving line of passengers waiting to board.

When we finally reached the top, the reason for the delay became obvious. After we had produced passports and boarding papers and collected our cabin keys, we were commanded to "Smile!" by a dark-haired, bronze-skinned young man whose face was obscured by a large camera. There was a burst of light from the flashbulb—apparently the lifeboats suspended overhead cast enough of a shadow to make the flash necessary in spite of the brilliant sun—and then the photographer lowered the camera.

"One more," he said, and disappeared behind the camera again, but not before I'd had a glimpse of dark eyes, white teeth, and a nose that belonged on a Greek coin. I was suddenly and painfully aware of my wrinkled skirts and shiny makeup, all the more noticeable next to my aunt's polished elegance. I need not have worried, though, for no sooner had the flash popped than he turned his attention to the elderly couple boarding the ship behind us. "Smile!"

I hurried along the deck after Maggie, not quite certain whether to be annoyed by his indifference, or grateful for it.

It was cool and dark below deck. I followed Maggie down the corridor to the narrow doors marked 322 and 324—our side-by-side cabins—inserted the small brass key into the lock of number 324, and pushed it open.

"It's tiny!" I exclaimed.

"It's a ship, Robin, not the Ritz-Carlton," Aunt Maggie

pointed out. "The cabins are not large, but you'll be surprised at how much they manage to cram into such a tight space."

She was right. On the opposite wall, two twin beds were positioned on each side of the curtained porthole with a small nightstand in between, while nearer at hand one corner had been turned into a rudimentary closet. A narrow door to my immediate right opened onto a private bath with its own microscopic shower. My luggage, which had been snatched away by a porter while I waited in line, had arrived before me, and now waited at the foot of one of the beds.

"Not spacious, perhaps, but it has everything you need," Aunt Maggie said, apparently reading my mind. "Still, I thought we might find sharing a single cabin a bit too much togetherness. I'll be right next door, though, if you need anything. And now," She paused long enough to cover a yawn with one hand. "I intend to lie down and take a nap. I never sleep well on planes, and that infant across the aisle who cried all night certainly didn't help. I suggest you do the same. Take a nap, I mean, not cry all night."

I agreed to this plan, but once Aunt Maggie had departed for her own cabin, I found myself too restless to even think of sleeping. I set Pooping Pedro on the nightstand, then hefted the larger of my two suitcases onto the bed and began to unpack, hanging my dresses from the rod that constituted the closet and folding my underwear into the nightstand drawers. The second suitcase contained my cosmetics and toiletries, and these were soon stowed away in the bathroom. Having completed this task, I stepped out into the corridor (noting the "Do Not Disturb" hanger dangling from Aunt Maggie's doorknob), locked the cabin door behind me, and retraced my steps to the deck.

Passengers were still boarding, although the line had slowed to a trickle. Looking at my fellow travelers, I began to understand why Gene had been so encouraging when I'd written to tell him of Aunt Maggie's invitation: there was no one on board for him to be jealous of. The average age of the *Oceanus's* passengers seemed to be about seventy, the only exceptions being the Greek god with the camera (who couldn't really be said to count, since he was a member of the crew) and a slender young woman standing at the rail and looking out to sea, her long black hair hanging halfway to her waist beneath the wide brim of her hat. Someone's daughter, I guessed, only to be proven wrong a moment later when she was approached by one of the older passengers, a well-preserved man with silver hair who stole an arm about her waist and planted a most unfatherly kiss on her scarlet lips. As she turned toward him, the sun caught her full in the face, and I realized she was older than I'd thought—forty if she was a day, although she was carefully and heavily made up to look at least a decade younger. *The mistress*, I thought, and abandoned any half-formed hope of making a female friend nearer my own age.

Any further inspection of my fellow passengers was interrupted by the loud blast of the ship's horn announcing the "all aboard." A flurry of activity followed, as the last stragglers came running up the gangplank, only to meet the hastily departing visitors running down after seeing their loved ones safely on board. Fifteen minutes later, the gangplank was lifted and the ropes that tethered *Oceanus* to her berth were cast off. Slowly, very slowly, the ship began to move away from the pier. Far below, the unfortunate souls left behind stood on the dock waving a final "bon voyage" to their friends and relatives. I leaned over the railing and waved back at them madly even though I didn't know a single soul.

As the pier shrank from view, the long night of flying finally caught up with me, and I realized how sleepy I was. Resolving to follow Aunt Maggie's example, I returned to my stateroom for a nap. I turned the key in the lock and pushed the door open—and saw a face grinning maniacally at me through the gloom.

2

Look for me by moonlight.
ALFRED NOYES, *The Highwayman*

I n the next instant, the sinister face resolved itself into the cheerful features painted on the end of a holiday log.

"Oh, Pedro!" I scolded, pressing a hand to my pounding heart. "You scared me half to death!"

Predictably, the *caga tió* said nothing, but continued to smile happily from the nightstand. I took off my hat and tossed it over Pedro's painted face to prevent a similar scare when I awakened, then kicked off my shoes and collapsed onto the nearer of the two beds.

A light yet persistent tapping on the door eventually awoke me from a deep and dreamless sleep. "Robin, honey, are you awake?" my aunt called. "It's almost time for the lifeboat drill, and then we'll need to get dressed for the Captain's Bon Voyage Reception."

"I'm awake," I called back, and tried hard to believe it. I rolled off the bed, noting how the lighting in my stateroom

21

had changed since I'd been so startled by Pedro; apparently I had been asleep for some time. I staggered to the door and opened it as proof of my wakefulness.

At that moment the ship's horn began emitting short, loud blasts, and if I hadn't been awake already, that would have been more than sufficient to do the job. A requirement for sea-going vessels for almost fifty years—ever since the sinking of the *Titanic*—the lifeboat drill was mandatory for all passengers and crew. It was impossible *not* to know where we were supposed to go; the nearest muster station was clearly marked on a diagram just inside my cabin door, and similar diagrams were posted at intervals up and down the length of the passageway.

We arrived to find quite a crowd already gathered, and once the last stragglers had reported in to the crew member who checked off their names on a list of passengers, the exercise began. Two elderly ladies listened intently to the instructions as if quite certain their lives depended on their committing the procedure to memory, while one man with an anchor tattooed on his forearm was obviously annoyed at having to take time out of his vacation to listen to information he'd no doubt committed to memory during his days in the navy. Most passengers fell somewhere between the two extremes, my aunt and I among them.

After learning how to put on the bulky life jackets (not a flattering look by any means, but I suspected in a real emergency we would put them on eagerly enough with no thought for appearances), we were given instructions as to how to board a lifeboat ("One at a time, and with each person taking a seat quickly so as not to block the way for passengers behind") and how to abandon ship, in the unlikely event that it should become necessary ("Put one hand over your mouth and pinch your nostrils shut with thumb and forefinger, then step—don't jump—off the deck"). I couldn't help wondering if anyone would actually remember any of this information in case of an actual emergency.

At last the drill was done, and we were dismissed to prepare for the reception.

"I'll be ready in half an hour," I promised Aunt Maggie when we parted company at the door of my stateroom. Once inside, I turned my attention to the task of transforming myself. A quick shower (there was really no point in lingering beneath the halfhearted trickle of hot water, since I could barely turn around in the tiny space allotted to it) made me feel human again, a feeling enhanced once I'd put on a long, full-skirted dress of periwinkle blue with a sheer overskirt of embroidered silver net and a wide, shallow scoop neck. By the time I'd slipped my feet into silver spangled pumps, the bathroom mirror had de-fogged sufficiently for me to put on makeup. I didn't pile my hair up, but teased it into a pouf at the crown and fastened a silver bow in the front. Twenty-four minutes later—well within the half-hour I'd promised—I grabbed my small silver clutch bag, locked the door to my stateroom behind me, and tapped at Aunt Maggie's door.

My aunt had cautioned me in advance that evenings aboard ship tended to be formal affairs, and I had packed accordingly; still, I was taken aback by the vision that stood in the corridor. Although Aunt Maggie was well into her fifties, her figure was still good, and she clearly intended to make the most of it. She wore a strapless number in shades of blue and green whose full skirt had been split from waist to hemline, revealing close-fitting slacks made of the same fabric. Her red hair had been piled up on her head, the better to draw attention to the emeralds that dangled from her ears.

"Oh, Maggie!" I breathed. "You look amazing!"

"Well, I did my best—although it's difficult, when one is shown up by a beautiful young niece."

I smiled in acknowledgment of the compliment, but made no comment. I would have looked ridiculous in anything even half so sophisticated—like a twelve-year-old playing dress-up—and she knew it as well as I did. Still, I was grateful for the first time that the fact I still lived with my parents meant I had few expenses, and therefore sufficient funds to buy plenty of new clothes for the trip. I hadn't worn a formal gown since the senior prom, and it would have been too humiliating to accompany my stylish aunt to dinner dressed like a teenager.

"Don't you look lovely!" she exclaimed, waving one hand in a circular motion that gave me to understand I was to turn around so she could inspect me from all angles. "Perfect," she pronounced at the completion of this exercise. "That shade of blue just matches your eyes. Gene is an idiot."

I rolled my eyes, but made no attempt to defend him. I hadn't thought of Gene since I'd woken up, and realized to my surprise that I didn't want to think of him now.

"But enough about him," Maggie said quickly, apparently sensing my mood. "Let's go dazzle our shipmates, shall we?"

The Captain's Bon Voyage Reception—the brochure described it exactly like that, capital letters and all—was to be held on the Europa deck, which told me absolutely nothing about exactly where it was on the ship. All the decks had names calculated to evoke images of exotic ports of call. I'll admit they were more glamorous than simple numbers, like hotel floors, but also considerably less informative. Thankfully, a framed diagram mounted next to the stairs indicated that Europa was down three decks from our present location on Capri Deck.

"By the time we dock in Venice, we'll know this ship like the back of our hand," my aunt predicted confidently, and started down the stairs.

We reached the Europa deck to find many of our fellow passengers there ahead of us, all talking with voices raised to make themselves heard over the splashing from a three-tiered fountain prominently located in the middle of a spacious atrium whose wide floor-to-ceiling windows looked out over the sea. A waiter in a crisp white dinner jacket appeared at Aunt Maggie's elbow, proffering a tray of goblets filled with champagne. Maggie took two and handed one to me.

"Eat, drink, and be merry, for tomorrow we d—"

"Dock in Livorno," put in a deep masculine voice.

We both turned and beheld our captain, resplendent in a starched white uniform bristling with gold braid. He smiled at Aunt Maggie, teeth white against a suntanned face.

"Surely you don't mean to suggest that I would fail to deliver two such lovely ladies safely to their destination?" he continued, dismissing the waiter with a glance. The man all but genuflected—no small feat while balancing a tray of champagne glasses—then took himself discreetly off.

"You don't mean to tell me *you're* the one in charge of this tub!" Maggie exclaimed. "Why, you're no more than a boy!"

"Hardly a boy, madam," he objected in charmingly accented English. "I am forty-two."

"Is that supposed to make me feel better?" she challenged with exaggerated dismay. "Why, I'm old enough to be—no, not your mother, but certainly old enough to have been your babysitter."

He laughed at that, a deep rumble that shook his chest and made his gold braid sparkle under the lights. "I could only wish to have had so charming a babysitter in my youth. And this"—he turned to me—"this young lady must be your sister?" He meant "daughter," of course, but I had to admire the man's diplomacy.

"My niece," Maggie put in with the indulgent smile of one who intends to enjoy such shameless flattery while she can, without for one moment taking it seriously. "She has never been abroad before, so I persuaded her to accompany me."

"Excellent!" the captain declared, rubbing his hands together. "I look forward to the opportunity of sharing my beautiful country with you."

"Oh, but I've been to Italy before," Aunt Maggie corrected him. "My husband liberated Rome in '45—not all by himself, of course, he had a little help from the rest of the Allied forces—and several years after the war he took me to Italy to show me some of the places he'd seen."

"Of course," the captain said, and after exchanging a few platitudes on the glories of the Coliseum and the Trevi Fountain, he turned away to speak to a couple of newcomers. For the first time it occurred to me that our captain might well have begun his maritime career with the Italian Navy, and I wondered if it was the mention of the war or Aunt Maggie's having a husband that had caused him to beat a hasty retreat.

Deprived of the captain's company, we took our places in the line at the buffet table, where a selection of savory finger foods was on offer. We filled our tiny plates, and as we looked about for somewhere to set our glasses down, I saw a couple of people I recognized: a distinguished-looking older man in a tuxedo, and a raven-haired woman in slinky red satin, cut low in both front and back.

"Oh, look!" I breathed in an undervoice. "It's the Mistress and her Sugar Daddy!"

"*Who?*" Delightfully scandalized, Aunt Maggie turned to look in the direction I indicated, just in time to see The Mistress plunk a grape into her benefactor's mouth.

"At least, I think that's who they must be. He's definitely *not* her father, and I don't think she looks like the marrying kind, do you?"

"Let's find out, shall we?"

Maggie headed purposefully in their direction, and I, burdened with a plate in one hand and a champagne glass in the other, could do nothing to stop her. I hurried after her, not quite sure whether I hoped to prevent her from doing anything embarrassing, or to prevent *me* from missing anything interesting the pair might say. To my surprise (and yes, relief), my aunt did not approach them directly, but turned at the last minute as if to pass them by. Just as she drew abreast of the man, her cocktail napkin slipped from her fingers and fluttered to the floor.

"Oh dear!" she exclaimed helplessly, shifting plate and glass back and forth as if trying to decide how to reclaim the napkin without littering the carpet with canapés and/or champagne.

"Allow me." The Sugar Daddy interrupted his low-voiced conversation with the woman long enough to balance his plate atop his champagne glass while he stooped to retrieve the errant napkin.

"Oh, thank you!" Aunt Maggie gushed. The man (who was seventy years old if he was a day) brushed aside her protestations with a smug smile, while the Mistress regarded Maggie with a tightening of her scarlet lips.

"Not at all," he assured her. "Anything for a fellow passenger. Allow me to introduce myself: Graham Grimes, at your service, and my traveling companion, Sylvia Duprée."

"Margaret Watson—Maggie, to my friends."

Miss Duprée's lips grew thinner. "Charmed, I'm sure."

"And who is this lovely young lady?" The smile he bestowed on me was so avuncular I half expected him to pat me on the head.

"My niece, Robin Fletcher."

"Miss Fletcher." He acknowledged me with a nod. "Tell

me, is this your first trip to Europe?"

"It is, Mr. Grimes, but I can't tell you how chagrined I am that it's so obvious!"

"Not at all," he assured me, laughing. "Every young person should visit the Old World at least once, if for no other reason that it gives them a deeper appreciation of the New. Do you plan to spend tomorrow in Livorno?"

The question was addressed to both of us, but since Maggie had planned the details of our trip, I let her answer. "Actually, we planned to spend the morning in Florence, with a side trip to Pisa in the afternoon—see if we can straighten up that tower for them, you know."

Mr. Grimes laughed as if this quip were wonderfully funny; I supposed it must be the champagne making him particularly jovial. Unfortunately, it didn't seem to be having the same effect on Miss Duprée, who looked as if steam were about to start coming out her ears. I was a bit surprised that she considered Maggie a threat, since she must have been younger by a decade. I wondered if perhaps she wasn't quite so certain of Mr. Grimes's affections as she would have liked.

"Have you been to Livorno before?" Maggie was asking. "Can you tell me how to find the bus station?"

"Oh, surely there's no need for that," put in a new voice. All four of us turned *en masse* to regard the newcomer, a tall man of about sixty with silver hair and blue eyes behind horn-rimmed spectacles. I glanced at my aunt, and noticed an appreciative gleam in Aunt Maggie's eyes. Beyond her, Miss Duprée's eyes narrowed appraisingly, as if she were comparing her present situation with the possibility of future prospects.

"I've hired a car for the very same route," the man continued. "Why not come with me? I'm afraid I can't show you the sights—I have a meeting with a colleague—but I can give you a lift there and back. My name is Paul Hurley, I live in Virginia, I'm a surgeon—semi-retired—and I have a clean driving record. Is there anything else you'd like to know?"

"All right, Dr. Hurley, you've convinced me," declared Aunt Maggie, laughing. "I can't say I was looking forward to squeezing aboard a crowded bus, especially if we do much shopping."

"I also happen to be a dab hand at carrying parcels," the doctor assured her. "But won't you call me Paul?"

"Only if you call me Maggie."

"Smile!"

All five of us turned as one, just in time to be blinded by a flash of light. Most of the culprit's face was hidden behind his camera, but the gleam of white teeth below the lens and the thick waves of black hair above were sufficient for me to identify the same photographer who'd snapped my photo as I'd boarded the ship travel-stained and jet-lagged. I glared at him, or at least in his general direction, as near as I

31

could tell from the spots dancing in front of my eyes.

"Do you have to do that?" I grumbled under my breath, as the others returned to their interrupted conversation.

"Do what?" he asked with an innocent air that didn't fool me for a minute.

"You know what," I accused. "Sneaking up and taking pictures when people are least expecting it."

"You will have a chance to pose for formal portraits later on the cruise," he promised with just a hint of a foreign accent I couldn't place. "In the meantime, I like to capture the ship's passengers unawares, before they have a chance to put on the masks they show to the world."

I glanced over my shoulder at Maggie talking animatedly to Paul, at Miss Duprée cooing at Mr. Grimes as she stroked his arm. Was it possible that he was right, and there was more to the pair than I'd thought? "Who do you think is wearing a mask?" I asked, intrigued by the idea in spite of myself.

He waved one hand in a gesture clearly meant to encompass everyone on the ship. "We all have masks we wear in public, concealing from the world the secrets we wish no one to see."

"All of us? Tell me, what deep, dark secret do you think I'm hiding?"

He regarded me with a long, steady look that made me profoundly uncomfortable, although I could not have said why. "You," he pronounced at last, "are trying to present to the world the picture of a young woman deeply in love, and yet you are not as happy as you would have everyone believe."

"That's the most ridiculous thing I ever heard!" I scoffed, although my cheeks burned.

"Is it? You wear a diamond engagement ring, and yet you are not accompanied by your fiancé, but your mother."

I shook my head. "I'm afraid I don't think much of your theory. Maggie is not my mother, but my aunt, and while it's true that I'm engaged to be married, I'll have you know that Gene is—" I reminded myself that I owed no explanation to an impertinent photographer I'd never laid eyes on before today, and would never see again once the ship docked in Venice. "Well, never mind that. Suffice it to say that he and I are very happy together."

"I am pleased to hear it," he said, acknowledging this snub with a knowing grin that made my palm itch to slap him.

"But you said 'we all,' " I reminded him, determined to abandon a topic that had become uncomfortably personal. "Yourself included. Don't tell me, let me guess: the humble ship's photographer who is really a keen student of human nature."

His dazzling white smile deepened, and without the camera concealing his face, I could see the dimple in his left cheek. "You are closer than you realize. I wear the mask of a humble ship's photographer in order to conceal my true identity of an international man of mystery."

"You're going to have to do better than that," I said, rolling my eyes.

"Very well. If you insist, I am wearing the mask of the all-knowing sage while I work up my nerve to ask a beautiful lady to allow me to show her about Livorno in the morning. I have only a few hours' leave, but it should be sufficient for a stroll along the seafront, and perhaps a quick bus ride to the Santuario di Montenero—the Sanctuary on the Hill. Even if you are not interested in the sanctuary itself, it is only five miles distant, and well worth the journey for the views of the city and the coast."

"Oh, but I—that is—" I was a little disconcerted by how disappointed I was to turn him down; it occurred to me that he was easier to dislike when he was being impertinent. "I'm sorry, but I've already made plans. Dr. Hurley offered Aunt Maggie and me a lift to Florence in his hired car."

"Of course," he said, accepting my refusal with a good grace. "You must by all means see the Cattedrale di Santa Maria del Fiore, and be sure to visit the Galleria dell'Accademia for Michelangelo's *David*."

"You seem to be well-acquainted with the sights of Florence."

"The crew takes turns having a few hours of leisure

while the ship is in port."

"So that explains it. I thought perhaps you were Italian."

"In fact, I am Greek: Markos Rondo, at your service," he said, sketching a little bow. "And you are Robin Fletcher, are you not? I'm pleased to meet you."

"Charmed, I'm sure, but if you expect me to be amazed that you know my name, I'm afraid you're doomed to disappointment. I don't doubt you heard Aunt Maggie introduce me only a few minutes ago."

He flashed that white smile at me again. "Actually, I looked you up on the ship's manifest shortly after you boarded." While I struggled not to appear surprised—much less flattered—he continued. "May I hope to show you about my own country when we dock in Piraeus?"

I reminded myself sternly that my presence on this trip was supposed to be as company for Aunt Maggie. "I—I'll have to see what my aunt has planned," I answered vaguely, and turned my attention back to the group.

"Why, Robin, it appears you've made a conquest," Maggie observed, as Markos bore down on another cluster of passengers with camera at the ready.

"Hardly that," I protested.

"You know, Robin, you may be engaged, but you're not dead. It wouldn't hurt Gene to suffer a few pangs of jealousy. In fact, it might light a fire under him."

I would be lying if I said the thought hadn't crossed my

mind. Thankfully, Miss Duprée spared me the necessity of putting Aunt Maggie off with a blatant falsehood or, perhaps worse, offering her any encouragement.

"Graham, darling, I have the most *crushing* headache!" Miss Duprée drooped against him like a wilting flower, the back of one hand pressed dramatically to her forehead. "If we are to go ashore tomorrow, I must go and lie down at once."

"Of course," he said hastily, setting his empty champagne glass down on a side table. "If you will excuse us, ladies—Dr. Hurley—"

We all murmured goodnight, and watched as Mr. Grimes led his "traveling companion" off in the direction of the stairs.

"Now, there goes a man who's firmly under a woman's thumb," remarked Aunt Maggie. "And if she's only his 'traveling companion,' I'm Queen Elizabeth. You'd better watch yourself, Paul. She looked as if she wouldn't mind trading in our friend Graham for a newer model."

"You terrify me!" the doctor said, making a big show of mopping his brow with his cocktail napkin. "But I think she's probably right about turning in early. Shall we go up to our cabins for a good night's sleep, and then meet in this same spot tomorrow morning at, say, eight o'clock? That should give us time for a quick breakfast on board ship before starting out."

Maggie readily agreed to this proposal—no one asked me, I noticed with some amusement—and the doctor bade us both goodnight as we crossed the still-crowded atrium and headed toward the aft stairs. It wasn't until I was back in my stateroom that I recalled seeing Mr. Grimes leading Miss Duprée up the midships staircase and wondered fleetingly what sort of accommodations the Sugar Daddy had arranged for his Mistress—something more luxurious than my tiny compartment with its little round porthole, I was willing to bet. Still, the bed where I'd taken my nap was comfortable, and at the moment that was good enough for me. I kicked off my high-heeled shoes and padded in stocking feet to the closet to hang up my dress. Slip, stockings, and bra followed, then I pulled my nightgown over my head, turned out the light and finally, after a last look out the porthole at the ship's lights reflecting off the dark waves, collapsed into bed.

Unfortunately, my body was still several time zones behind; I awoke some time later to find my cabin still dark. I'd left the curtains open, and through the porthole I could see the moon rising just over the horizon, spreading a broken trail of silver across the water.

"Oh!" I breathed, reaching for the camera I'd left on the nightstand. I framed the tranquil scene in the viewfinder, then pressed the button—and all but blinded myself when the flash reflected off the glass of the porthole.

"Blast," I muttered. If I wanted a picture, I would have to go up on deck, where I wouldn't have to shoot through glass. I'd left my watch on the nightstand, and its glowing hands informed me that the time was almost three o'clock in the morning. I grabbed my robe for modesty's sake— although I thought it unlikely that anyone would be lingering about at so late an hour—and left my cabin, locking the door securely behind me.

All was still and quiet on deck. Even my footsteps on the bleached and sanded boards were drowned by the slap of water against the side of the ship as we plowed through the waves. I walked back toward the rear of the ship ("aft" toward the "stern," I corrected myself mentally, thinking of Gene in the Navy) and drew up short as I realized I was not alone after all. A man stood at the taffrail holding something in his hands, and as I debated the wisdom of calling a friendly greeting to him, given the lateness of the hour and my own sketchy attire, he dropped his burden overboard and turned away from the railing. Instinctively, I drew back into the shadow of a lifeboat mounted overhead, holding my breath lest it betray my presence even as I scolded myself for my own foolishness.

So deep were the shadows that he passed within four feet of me and never even suspected my presence. Consumed by curiosity, I waited only until I heard the door close behind him before I hurried to the spot where he'd stood, and leaned out over the taffrail. Far below, the ship's propellers churned the water into frothing waves of gleaming luminescence. There was just light enough for me to make out the painted smile on the end of a Christmas log before it disappeared beneath the foaming surf.

3

Lump the whole thing! say that the Creator made Italy
from designs by Michael Angelo.
MARK TWAIN, *The Innocents Abroad*

I don't remember returning to my stateroom, although I must have done so, for I awoke the next morning in my own bed. The curtain was open, just as I'd left it, and beyond the porthole, the sunlight sparkled on the water like diamonds. Closer at hand, Pedro grinned at me from the nightstand.

"What do you think, old boy?" I asked him. "Was it only a dream? Who would buy you—well, one of your siblings, anyway—only to throw you overboard? I've heard of buyer's remorse, but that's ridiculous."

As usual, Pedro kept his opinions to himself, and a glance at my tiny travel alarm clock informed me that I didn't have time to linger in one-sided conversation. I threw back the covers, then went through my morning beauty routine before donning a pink striped cotton sundress. I snatched up my big straw bag and wide-brimmed straw hat, then locked my stateroom behind me and rapped on Maggie's door. She opened it at once, and it seemed to me that my always immaculate aunt had taken special pains with her appearance. Not that she was overdressed; Aunt Maggie would never commit such a sartorial sin. No, she was perfectly dressed for sightseeing in a full skirt and crisp short-sleeved blouse, both in a shade of green that just matched her eyes. Her bright hair was covered with a chiffon scarf in varying shades from peridot to emerald. Apparently she had high hopes for Dr. Paul Hurley; I made a mental note to leave them alone as much as possible.

We made a quick breakfast at the buffet on the Firenze Deck, and tucked a couple of apples into my bag for a snack later in the morning before returning to the atrium, where we found Dr. Paul waiting for us. After a brief review to make sure we hadn't forgotten anything important—Passport? Stateroom key? Camera? Extra film? Flash bulbs?—we made our way down the gangplank, and I set foot on Italian soil for the first time. Maggie and I waited while Paul approached the service counter, and soon returned with the key to his rented Fiat.

"I apologize for its small size," he said, opening the passenger's-side door and raising the seat so I could climb into the back. "When I reserved it, I did not expect to have such charming passengers."

"Talk to us like that long enough, and we'll soon be

begging you for the privilege of folding ourselves in half," Maggie assured him as he pushed the passenger's seat back into place for her.

"Still, if I had known I would have company, I would have arranged for something larger—a Ford, perhaps."

"We can ride in Fords any day," I said, shifting on the back seat to smooth my skirt beneath me.

"Exactly," Maggie agreed. "If we're going to see Italy, we might as well do it in an Italian car. 'When in Rome' and all that, you know."

Paul slid behind the wheel, turned the key, and the engine sputtered to life. Most of the cars we met on our way were no larger than our own little Fiat, and as we wound through the narrow streets of old Livorno, I no longer wondered at their small size: two of the tiny vehicles could barely meet to pass, and anything as large as a Ford would have taken up more than its fair share of the pavement.

At last, we left the city behind us in favor of the open highway and my first look at the Italian countryside. I lost interest in Maggie and Paul's conversation and pressed my nose to the window, mesmerized by the silver-green of olive trees that whizzed past and the hillsides striped with tiered rows of grapevines. Occasionally, we passed houses whose plaster had faded to soft yellow or cream, with red clay tiled roofs and, more often than not, a tall, narrow cypress tree planted by the door, thrusting its spear-pointed tip toward the sky. According to the guidebook I'd tucked into my bag, the cypress by the door denoted hospitality and a welcome to travelers.

Recalling something else in my bag that needed my attention, I rooted out my billfold and counted the colorful lira notes, all printed in purple and green and orange, like Monopoly money. I reminded myself that just because they ranged in denomination from five hundred to five thousand didn't mean they were worth that much in American dollars. I would have to be careful shopping—assuming, of course, that I found something I wanted to spend them on. If the Italians had any equivalent of the *caga tió*, I would give it a pass; besides taking up far too much room in my luggage, one nightmare-inducing souvenir was quite enough.

An hour's drive brought us to Florence, and I could tell when we approached the old section of the city by the narrowing of the streets. Paul found a place to park the little blue Fiat—although not without difficulty—and we all climbed out of the car, stretching arms and legs cramped from the tight squeeze.

"Make a note of the location," he cautioned us, pointing out various street signs and shops that might serve as landmarks. "We'll meet back here at, shall we say, two o'clock? That should give you time to see the major sights of Florence before we head to Pisa."

If Aunt Maggie was disappointed that he hadn't

changed his mind and decided to accompany us, she never let on. She thanked him effusively for giving us a lift into town, and promised him we wouldn't keep him waiting. "Now, Robin, which way do we go to get to the cathedral?" she asked when he'd gone on his way.

I fumbled in my big straw bag for the guidebook, and opened it to the map of Florence. "Which cathedral?" I asked. "The city seems to be full of them."

After much discussion and consulting of maps, we decided to try and find "Florence's Westminster Abbey," the Basilica of Santa Croce. According to the guidebook, it was the final resting place of Michelangelo, Machiavelli, Rossini, and Galileo; more to the purpose, it appeared to be the nearest landmark to where we stood, which meant, at least in theory, that it should be the easiest to find. A ten-minute walk (during which we only had to retrace our steps twice) brought us to the Piazza Santa Croce, a large paved square dominated by the basilica on its western end. At least, the map said it was on the western end; I was so completely turned around by this time that I could hardly have said which end was up.

After pausing to catch our breath and snap a photo, we crossed the square, and I became increasingly grateful for my rubber-soled espadrilles; Aunt Maggie had opted for high-heeled pumps, and consequently had a hard time navigating the uneven cobblestones. The slow pace gave me plenty of opportunity to survey the vendors' stalls dotting the square. Besides the usual postcards, refrigerator magnets, and painted china plates, there were dozens of long-nosed wooden marionettes in red and white costumes and tall pointed hats, all dangling from hooks in the roofs of the stalls like so many executed felons. One vendor apparently noticed my interest, for he grabbed one of the puppets down from its hook and shook it in my direction, making its jointed arms and legs flail wildly as he shouted something to me in incomprehensible Italian. The only word I could understand was "Pinocchio," but this one word was enough to make me realize that Florence had been the home of the wooden boy's creator—not, as my students would have said, Walt Disney, but Carlo Collodi. I was sorely tempted—after all, I taught literature as well as grammar—but my thirteen-year-old students would have rolled their eyes at any suggestion they might enjoy so juvenile a teaching prop. I gave the vendor a regretful smile and shook my head, contenting myself with taking a quick photo before hurrying after Aunt Maggie.

We paid our admission and entered the church, which seemed strangely quiet after the bustle of the square. Michelangelo's tomb was on our immediate right, an immense marble structure topped with a bust of the deceased and fronted by a trio of depressed-looking women.

"It says the three statues represent sculpture,

architecture, and painting," I said, consulting the guidebook. "Why do you suppose they were represented as women?"

"Wishful thinking," Aunt Maggie said. "What about these two?"

She pointed across the nave to the tomb of Galileo, where a pair of marble ladies lounged against the scientist's final resting place.

I ran my finger down the page until I came to a description of the tomb. "One is astronomy, and the other is geometry. There was supposed to be a third, representing philosophy, but for some reason it was omitted. Apparently there's some debate as to why."

"Now, that can't be right!"

"What can't?" I scanned the page, looking for anything I might have misread.

"I remember geometry very well from high school, and I'm quite certain it was male!"

I laughed out loud, clapping a hand over my mouth as the irreverent sound echoed through the church. After looking our fill at the Gothic glories of Santa Croce, we exited the basilica and followed the map to the Arno River, strolling along it until we came to the Ponte Vecchio, the medieval bridge lined with shops that hung over the water seemingly in defiance of gravity.

"Even the Nazis thought it was too beautiful to destroy," I said, referring once more to the guidebook.

"I remember hearing something about that at the time," Maggie said. "I'll bet it didn't stop them for long, though."

"No. They just blew up the buildings on either end instead."

"It figures. But enough about the Nazis! While we're this close, why don't we wander through the Uffizi for an hour or so? We can satisfy our appetite for Renaissance art before we set out in search of the Cattedrale di Santa Maria del Fiore."

"The what?" I asked, thumbing through the guidebook. I thought the name sounded familiar; Markos, the ship's photographer, had recommended that we not miss it.

"In English, the Cathedral of Saint Mary of the Flowers. Even the city's name means 'flower,' which is why you see them everywhere—on its flag, its coat of arms—"

"Oh, here it is! 'The city's most recognizable landmark, noted for its massive dome engineered by Filippo Brunelleschi,' " I read aloud.

By this time my feet were beginning to ache in spite of my comfortable shoes, and I was all for visiting the Uffizi museum, especially if it offered a few benches where we could sit down. But one hour stretched into two as we surveyed works by Botticelli, Leonardo da Vinci, and the ubiquitous Michelangelo. As we exited the museum and headed northward toward the cathedral, Aunt Maggie noted that we were going to have to hurry if we wanted to see

Michelangelo's *David* before meeting Paul at two o'clock.

We had no trouble finding the cathedral; even if we hadn't had a map, we could have found it simply by following the other tourists. If I'd thought the Basilica of Santa Croce was impressive, it was only because I hadn't yet seen the cathedral. An enormous building of white marble lavishly ornamented in pink and green, it looked like nothing so much as a giant wedding cake topped, not with a tiny ceramic bride and groom, but with a red brick dome so massive that the dome atop the U. S. Capitol—my only real point of reference—was dwarfed by comparison. Unfortunately, the line for climbing the stairs into the top of the dome was too long to be feasible, in the light of our promise to meet Paul back at the car at two. The line to climb the bell tower wasn't much shorter, so I was forced to be content with taking photos of the cathedral's elaborate exterior, or what I could of it: the whole thing was too large to fit into the frame, and the buildings across the street from it pressed too closely to allow me to back up far enough that the entire building would be visible. Aunt Maggie collared a fellow tourist—German, from the sound of his speech—and after much gesturing, gave him to understand that he was requested to take a picture of the two of us with the cathedral in the background. Smiling and nodding, he reached for my camera, and after pointing out the button he should press, I handed it over and took my place beside Aunt Maggie, both of us smiling brightly as the German tourist snapped away.

From the cathedral, we bore northeastward until we reached the Galleria dell'Accademia, where *David* awaited us. By this time, I'd seen enough artwork to understand what made Michelangelo's interpretation unique: the other representations we'd seen presented Goliath's slayer in his moment of victory, holding the giant's severed head aloft in triumph. Michelangelo's *David* gazed pensively over the heads of his admirers, apparently focused on the task before him. Nor was he alone in his contemplation: I saw the same rapt concentration on the faces of the many art students seated around the statue with sketchpads on their laps, trying with varying degrees of success to reproduce the sculptor's masterpiece in charcoal. With a start of recognition, I realized one of the aspiring artists was no stranger.

"Markos?" I asked incredulously. He wasn't wearing the knife-creased white trousers and starched white shirt he'd worn on the ship, but dungarees and a red knit polo shirt open at the neck. He looked different, and somehow younger, out of uniform. "I thought you were spending the day in Livorno."

He looked up from his work and gave me a rueful smile. "I meant to, but I couldn't get a date."

I chose to ignore this remark, gesturing instead at the sketchpad on his lap. "Can I—may I see?"

After what seemed to me a moment's hesitation, he

turned it around. At the sight of his sketch, the sudden and (if I were honest) not unwelcome suspicion that he might have followed me to Florence died. He was good. More than that, he was *very* good.

"You're very talented," I told him.

"Thank you."

"So what are you doing photographing tourists on a cruise ship?"

"It's hard to make a living as an artist," he said, dismissing the notion with a shrug before continuing in a very different voice, "So, since we both find ourselves in Florence, why not have lunch with me? I know a little *ristorante* near the Ponte Vecchio with outdoor tables overlooking the Arno."

Much as my feet protested the very idea of retracing my steps all the way back to the river, I was sorely tempted. I glanced around for Aunt Maggie, but she'd disappeared; either she had decided to give me the opportunity to talk to a good-looking young man in privacy, or she'd gone behind the statue to investigate *David*'s posterior. Knowing Aunt Maggie, it could have been either one.

"I'm sorry, but I'm supposed to be meeting someone at two," I said.

"And so, I'm too late again," he said with an exaggerated sigh.

"It isn't that," I began, then remembered that I owed

neither apology nor explanation to a chance-met stranger on a ship. "I don't want to keep him waiting, so I'd better be going. I'm sure I'll see you again back on the ship."

I waggled my fingers at him in farewell, then circled around the statue in search of my aunt. Just as I'd suspected, she stood behind *David*, staring up at his marble buttocks.

"What a guy!" she remarked appreciatively.

I shrugged. "If you say so," I said without enthusiasm.

"Robin?" She tore her gaze away long enough to look at me. "Is something wrong?"

"Can we go now? We'll need to meet Paul soon, and I'd like to grab a bite to eat somewhere."

As it turned out, we didn't have time for a restaurant meal. We stopped at a curbside market and bought bread, cheese, and figs, and these—together with the apples I'd secreted away in my bag at breakfast—constituted our lunch, eaten balanced on our knees in Paul's rented Fiat as he drove westward toward Pisa. I tried not to think about sipping Chianti at an intimate table for two overlooking the River Arno.

We arrived in Pisa at just past three-thirty. Thankfully, finding a parking space proved easier than it had in Florence, and after a short walk, we emerged onto the broad green space known as the Campo dei Miracoli—the Field of Miracles. If I'd thought Florence's cathedral looked like a wedding cake, the Field of Miracles boasted three of them, all brilliantly white against the thick green carpet of grass. Nearest at hand was the round, barrel-like baptistry; beyond it, and by far the largest of the three, was the cathedral itself, whose tiers of arcades were reflected in those of its famous bell tower—the Leaning Tower, which did indeed lean out as if peeking out from behind its parent cathedral like a precocious child, too shy to call attention to itself yet determined not to be ignored.

Not that it would have been possible to ignore it in any case. Streams of tourists passed us on their way to seize a place in the line to climb the tower.

"What do you think?" Paul asked doubtfully, eyeing the long queue snaking out from the base of the tower. "They'll be sounding the 'all aboard' at six. Can we make it in time?"

Maggie shook her head. "We'd better not risk it. What do you think, Robin?"

"Oh, it would be a shame to be so close and not even try to get in," I protested. "We might never have another chance."

"Go ahead and get in line, Robin," Paul urged. "Maggie and I will keep an eye on the time, and if you haven't returned by the time we need to head back to the ship, we'll motion for you to come down."

He didn't have to work very hard to convince me. As I'd said, I might not have another chance. I paid for my ticket and stood in line, glancing at them occasionally in case they were signaling to me. As I watched, Paul threw back his head and laughed at something my aunt had said, and it occurred to me that they might have their own reasons for wanting me to attempt the climb.

There were almost three hundred steps from bottom to top, many of which had been worn uneven by the footsteps of eight hundred years' worth of tourists, and the spiral staircase grew narrower the higher I climbed. Furthermore, the tower was dark, lit only dimly from the small windows spaced at intervals. And, as the tilt was almost fifteen feet from vertical—with no handrails—I had no more thought to spare for Maggie and Paul; I had all I could manage just putting one foot in front of the other.

At last I reached the top, and emerged into the sunshine. I waved at my ant-like aunt eight floors below, then took a couple of photos of the panoramic view from the top. Finally, determined not to linger until they had to flag me down, I retraced my steps down the stairs to the ground.

"I'll admit, I'm glad you're back on terra firma," Maggie said. "Then again, if this 'terra' was very 'firma,' the tower wouldn't lean the way it does."

"It's quite safe, at least for the present," Paul assured us. "Someday it will have to be stabilized, but in the meantime, they only let a few people up at a time—which is why the lines are so long. If we're all ready, then, let's head back to the ship."

Aunt Maggie and I agreed to this program, with one caveat: on our way out, we insisted Paul take a photo of us with the Leaning Tower in the background. The three of us located a point far enough away that the whole thing would fit into the viewfinder of my camera, and Paul took the shot, then took one more for good measure. To my surprised delight, he asked me to take a picture of him and Aunt Maggie together, even giving me his business card so that I could mail a copy of the photo to him.

"There's no need for that," I told him, checking the counter on the top of the camera. "I'll have finished this roll of film by the time we return to the ship, so I'll drop it by the camera shop on board for developing."

I took the picture, and another just in case the first one didn't turn out, then handed the camera to Aunt Maggie.

"Would you take one of me? I'd like to send it to Gene."

"Excellent idea! Let him see what he's missing. Say 'Cheese,' " Maggie commanded, giving me no chance to defend my fiancé. I saw her finger move as she snapped the picture, but instead of handing the camera back to me, she glared at something or someone over her shoulder. "Well, drat! I'm going to have to take another one, Robin. Someone walked into the frame just as I snapped the shutter."

I followed her disapproving gaze, and suffered a shock. The man had his back to us now, but I had no difficulty recognizing a muscular man of medium height with tanned skin and jet-black hair. I knew instinctively that when the photos were developed, they would show him to be about forty years old, with a thick mustache and somewhat fleshy cheeks. For I had seen this particular man before, and not just in a dream: it was he who had stood at the stern of the *Oceanus* and tossed Pedro's luckless counterpart overboard.

4

O body swayed to music, O brightening glance,
How can we know the dancer from the dance?
WILLIAM BUTLER YEATS, *The Tower,*
Among School Children

R obin? Honey, are you okay?" Aunt Maggie's voice
pulled me from the recollection of what I'd thought
had been a dream.

"I'm fine," I said, shaking my head as if to banish the
memory. I glanced back at the man's retreating form, and
noticed that he carried a bulging paper bag from one of the
vendors' stalls lined up along the entrance to the Campo dei
Miracoli. I hoped whatever he'd bought here in Pisa would
have a happier fate than his souvenir from Barcelona had.
"It's just that—you know I don't like it when you talk about
Gene that way."

"I know you don't, and I'm sorry," she said with
uncharacteristic remorse. "Here, let's take another photo,
now that there's a break in the tourist traffic. You can get it
developed onboard ship, and mail it to Gene from the next

port."

Actually, Gene was the last person on my mind at the moment, but having kept quiet about my late-night adventures thus far, I felt a bit foolish bringing them up now. I merely nodded, and smiled for the camera. But I had a feeling that particular photo would reveal my smile to be a bit forced.

The drive from Pisa to Livorno was considerably shorter than the trip from Livorno to Florence had been, so we reached the ship fully half an hour before the "all aboard" sounded. I stopped by the ship's camera shop to drop off my film before dressing for dinner, and somehow I wasn't surprised to see Markos back in uniform at the photo counter.

"Good evening, Miss Fletcher," he said. "Did you enjoy your afternoon in Pisa?"

"Yes, I did. Very much, thank you," I said.

"I trust your date did not disappoint."

I thought of Maggie and Paul chatting in the car on the drive back to the ship. Actually, it had been their date, not mine, but that was none of his business. "No, I don't think he disappointed at all. When can I pick up my photos?"

Markos looked as if he might have liked to say something, but whatever it was, he bit it off. "Four days— let's see, that would be Friday, any time after three."

"Thank you," I said again, and started for the staircase

leading up to my own stateroom on Capri Deck.

"Really, Robin, why do you dislike that boy so?" Aunt Maggie scolded as we climbed the stairs.

"I don't dislike him," I said somewhat unconvincingly. "He just annoys me. I don't know why."

Maggie gave me a rather knowing look, but said only, "Be sure to wear something tonight that's easy to move around in. There's dancing on the Lido Deck after dinner."

Which meant, I suspected, that she'd already made arrangements to meet Paul after dinner on the Lido Deck. Oh well, I thought, one of us might as well have a whirlwind romance, and I, I reminded myself sternly, was engaged and therefore unavailable for shipboard dalliance. Still, I dressed for dinner in an evening frock with a full tulle skirt that wouldn't hamper movement, just in case I should happen upon any potential dance partners under the age of forty.

When we reached the formal dining room on Firenze Deck, we were greeted by a smiling individual, resplendent in a white dinner jacket, who introduced himself as the maître d'hôtel and offered to show us to our table. I was a bit taken aback to discover that passengers were assigned to specific tables, and that while on board ship, we would be expected to share our evening meal with strangers. This appeared to be no surprise to Aunt Maggie, however, so I fell in behind her as we threaded our way between tables covered in white linen and laid with fine china, silver cutlery, and crystal goblets. The maître d' led us to a large round table positioned before a window—not a porthole like the ones in our staterooms, but a wide picture window through which we could see the blue waters of the Mediterranean, each wave tipped with gold from the setting sun. Several of our tablemates were already in place, and I realized that some of them were not strangers after all: the Sugar Daddy (really, I must learn to think of him as Mr. Grimes before I said something embarrassing) sat with his back to the window, while the Mistress—er, Miss Duprée— had claimed the chair on his right. I wondered if this was so she might have a better view out the window, or whether it was because it placed her out of the sun's too-harsh rays: given her advanced age, I thought cattily, she would probably be wise to keep out of direct sunlight. Out of pure malice, I took the place at Mr. Grimes's left, allowing the setting sun to fall full on my twenty-three-year-old face; after all, Miss Duprée might be more sophisticated than I would ever be, but there wasn't a thing she could do about the twenty years that separated us. As I sat down, I realized that the gentleman on her right was no stranger, either.

"Maggie, Robin," Paul said. He and Mr. Grimes had risen as we approached the table (a courtesy that, I had to admit, would never have occurred to Gene), and the slightest of gestures brought Aunt Maggie to the vacant chair next to his. Since the maître d' was busy holding my chair for me,

Paul performed the same office for Maggie before he and Mr. Grimes returned to their seats. That left three chairs still empty. Two of the three were soon taken by a couple in their sixties, a red-faced man who looked extremely uncomfortable in a dark suit and tie, and a woman, presumably his wife, wearing an obviously new gown that still managed to look frumpy on her.

"The name's Hollis, Henry Hollis," the man said, reaching across the table to shake hands with Paul and Mr. Grimes. "And this here is my wife, Martha."

He smiled rather self-consciously at Mrs. Hollis as he performed the introduction, and she beamed back at him, blushing rosily.

"I'm pleased to meet you both," Paul said. "If I may do the honors?" He performed the introductions and then, after everyone at the table had been identified, asked the newcomers, "Are you perhaps celebrating your wedding anniversary?"

I had to admire his tact. It was obvious the Hollises were not frequent travelers (I wondered, with some chagrin, if any of my shipmates had formed that immediate impression of me, as well), and that they were ill at ease with the level of formality that prevailed onboard ship in the evening.

"Well, you might say so," confessed Mr. Hollis with another sheepish grin. "In fact, we're on our honeymoon."

"Now, Henry," Martha Hollis protested feebly, as everyone at the table exclaimed delighted congratulations— everyone except Miss Duprée, who offered a thin-lipped smile. I decided the socially awkward Mrs. Hollis was worth ten of her.

Aunt Maggie drew her out by asking questions about how they met and, upon learning that Maggie was herself a widow, Martha Hollis quickly lost her embarrassment in expressions of ready sympathy. It transpired that Mrs. Hollis—Martha Peabody, as she was then—had never been married before. She'd once been engaged, she said, but her young man had been killed in the Great War—the first one, she explained, the one that was supposed to end all wars, and had for a whopping twenty years. In the meantime, Mrs. Hollis—Henry's first wife, that was—had died two years ago, and he'd hired the spinster Miss Peabody to cook and clean for him, as he was so busy with the farm that he came home in the evenings too tired to do more than slap together a sandwich before collapsing into bed to get what sleep he could before getting up the next morning to do it all again. And then one day, he'd realized that it was Miss Peabody's companionship, rather than her cooking, that he most looked forward to at the end of the day.

"To tell you the truth," she confided, flushing pink, "I'd lost all hope of ever marrying. So don't you give up hope, Miss Duprée," she added, directing this last to the Mistress.

"I'm sure it'll happen to you too, as pretty as you are."

"I am in no hurry," Miss Duprée assured her with a smile that would have frozen water. "There are worse things than being single—being obliged to live on a farm, for instance."

There was a moment of shocked silence, quickly filled by Aunt Maggie. "What a romantic story, Mrs. Hollis."

"Just like a fairy tale," I agreed warmly, following my aunt's cue. "I hope you and Mr. Hollis will be very happy together."

Mrs. Hollis gave us both a grateful smile, but lapsed once more into an awkward silence that made it clear she was fully aware of the insult. When our final dinner partner came to take the vacant place between Mrs. Hollis and me, everyone at the table, with the possible exception of Miss Duprée, could have fallen on his neck in gratitude. But as he seated himself, I got a good look at his face. It was the same man who had walked into my photo—the same man I'd seen on deck last night.

"I trust I am not too late," he said with an accent I couldn't place. "I hope you will forgive me."

"Oh, but your tardiness is not my only grudge against you," Aunt Maggie put in brightly.

"Indeed?" He bared his teeth at her in what I supposed must pass for a smile.

"Yes. You ruined the photo I took of my niece Robin

this afternoon in Pisa," she explained, although her playful tone made it clear that she spoke in jest.

He turned to look at me, a cold gaze through eyes that should have been dark, given the rest of his coloring, but instead were pale blue, startlingly so against his swarthy skin. Ice blue, I thought, resisting an urge to shiver.

"If this is so, I apologize," he said, although I'd never heard anyone sound less remorseful.

"It—It's quite all right," I stammered. "We took another one." Feeling something else was called for, I added, "I'm Robin—Robin Fletcher. This is my aunt, Margaret Watson."

"Konstantin Devos, at your service." He gave a little nod, like a seated bow, first in my direction and then in Maggie's. There followed another flurry of introductions, and then the entire table fell silent as the first course was set before us. Given the choice of making labored conversation with our ill-assorted tablemates or devoting our attention to the most succulent oysters I'd ever tasted (not that they had come my way that often), we all chose the latter. So it was all the more surprising that, as I pushed back my chair after the chocolate mousse and rose to my feet, Mr. Devos laid a hand on my arm.

"I understand there is to be dancing on the Lido Deck in half an hour, Miss Fletcher," he said. "I hope you will do me the honor of saving a dance for me."

Suddenly I felt like the heroine of a Jane Austen novel,

having no desire to dance with the gentleman who offered, but knowing I must accept if I hoped for an opportunity to dance with more desirable partners later. After all, it was still bad form to spurn one potential partner only to take to the floor with another. Some things, alas, had not changed in a century and a half.

"I would be happy to dance with you, Mr. Devos—provided I'm able to move, after the meal I just ate."

He bared his teeth again in that feral smile. "All the more reason for a little after-dinner exercise. I shall look for you in half an hour, then." He clicked his heels together and made a stiff little bow, then took himself off.

"Why, Robin, aren't you the *femme fatale!*" exclaimed Aunt Maggie as we repaired to the ladies' room to powder our noses before setting off in search of the Lido Deck. "I believe you've made another conquest!"

"Heavens, I hope not!"

"Nonsense! Every girl deserves a whirlwind romance with a tall Latin lover before she marries and settles down."

"First of all, he's not Latin with a name like that, but Greek. Second, he's forty if he's a day. Third, he gives me the creeps."

Her carefully plucked eyebrows rose. "For heaven's sake, why?"

Too late, I remembered that I'd never confided to Aunt Maggie the midnight encounter on the deck. "It seems silly now," I confessed, "but late last night I saw him behaving—well, oddly." I summarized briefly my midnight wandering, and the strange behavior of Mr. Devos. Her reaction was hardly what I had hoped for.

"Robin, you really shouldn't go wandering about like that alone, and at such an hour," she said, sounding more like my mother than my worldly aunt.

"I know you're right, and I won't do it again," I promised. "Still, I hadn't thought anyone would be about at such an hour, except perhaps the crew. But I can't for the life of me imagine why he would spend good money on a *caga tió*, and then throw it overboard. It seems, I don't know, sinister somehow."

"Only because that thing had a face painted on the end of it," was Maggie's practical observation. "It's amazing how painting human features on an object makes us think of it as somehow human. If it had been a plain, ordinary log, you wouldn't have thought twice about it."

"You may be right," I conceded. "I'll admit, if someone did such a thing to Pedro, I would consider him the next thing to a murderer."

"If it troubles you so much, why don't you just ask Mr. Devos? After all, he can hardly throw *you* overboard."

She made the whole thing sound so simple that I felt foolish for giving it a second thought. "I suppose he could try, but it might be a bit awkward with several hundred witnesses. If he does, promise me you'll sound the 'man overboard.' "

"I promise." Having swiped a lipstick across her mouth, she dropped the tube into her beaded evening bag and snapped it shut. "Now, if you're ready, we'll see if we can find the Lido Deck. Is it up or down, do you think?"

I hadn't the slightest idea, so it was with considerable relief that we found a cutaway diagram of the ship's layout mounted on the wall just outside the ladies' room.

"It looks like we're here, amidships on the Fiesta Deck," I said, pointing to the red arrow on the diagram. "We'll need to go up one level to the Lido Deck, then aft until we reach the club where the dancing will be."

"Useful Robin! I knew I'd brought you along for a good reason."

The club proved not to be an actual club at all, but an open space on the deck with a bar at one end and a raised dais at the other, where a combo comprising piano, string bass, and drums played popular standards from decades earlier. In between, a few couples were already dancing, while other passengers, either singly or in pairs, sat at tiny round tables set up along the perimeter, where they could either watch the dancing or gaze out over the dark water. I wasn't surprised to find Paul waiting to claim Maggie as soon as we came through the door.

"There you are!" he exclaimed, as if he'd been waiting

for weeks instead of minutes. "Shall we?"

"Well, I—" Maggie glanced uncertainly at me.

"Go ahead," I said quickly, earning a grateful smile from Paul. "I'll just find us a table while you two enjoy yourselves."

He led Maggie onto the dance floor as the dance band struck up the opening bars of "You Make Me Feel So Young"—an appropriate choice, I thought—and I located an empty table near the railing. In truth, I felt vaguely like the wallflowers at my junior-senior prom must have, sitting alone while those of us with boyfriends danced the night away. By the time Mr. Devos found me, I was all too ready to oblige him, if only to get away from the wall—er, rail. When he put his arm about my waist and pulled me close enough to crush the front of my full skirt, however, it was only with an effort that I was able to relax in his embrace, resisting the instinct to flinch away from his touch.

"So tell me about yourself, Miss Robin Fletcher," he said, as we swayed to the rhythm of "Embraceable You."

"There's really not much to tell," I said, shaking my head dismissively. "I'm an American, I live in North Carolina—it's on the eastern seaboard, although I don't actually live near the coast—and I teach English to junior high school students. Thirteen-year-olds," I explained, in case he was unfamiliar with the intricacies of American education.

His answering expression was puzzled. "I would have thought they would know English very well by the time they were thirteen years old."

"You'd be surprised," I said with a laugh, thinking of some of the essays I'd graded over the course of my brief career. "But I don't teach them to *speak* English; I teach grammar, composition, and literature."

"I see." He nodded solemnly. "An accomplished young woman, in fact."

I mumbled something, I don't know what. I'd never thought of myself as particularly accomplished; after all, I hadn't yet accomplished the feat of getting Gene to say "I do."

"And yet," Devos continued, baring his teeth at me, "I have a feeling you are uncomfortable with me. Why is that, Miss Fletcher?"

I glanced rather wildly about for Aunt Maggie, but found her sitting at the little table with Paul, both of them laughing over cocktails. *Just ask him*, she'd said. Very well, I thought, and took a deep breath. "Not uncomfortable, Mr. Devos, just curious. You see, when you walked into my photograph at the Leaning Tower, I realized I'd seen you before."

"Here onboard ship, no doubt," he nodded, swinging me in a wide circle to avoid a buxom woman and her stout partner.

"Well, yes, but under rather strange circumstances. Last night I awoke sometime after midnight, and when I saw the moonlight shining so brightly on the water, I knew I had to get a photo. But the flash reflected off the glass in the porthole, so I had to come up on deck."

"Yes?" he prompted, smiling that wolfish smile. I realized he knew exactly what I'd seen, and what I was going to ask, but he didn't intend to make it easy for me. Annoyed, I continued. "As you know, I wasn't the only one on deck. You were there, throwing something off the back of the ship. I'll admit I was curious to know what it was, and so after you'd gone back inside, I went to look."

"And was your curiosity satisfied?"

"Only in part. It was a *caga tió*, a Christmas log just like the one I'd bought in Barcelona."

"Yes, it was. But there is an old English proverb about curiosity and the cat, is there not, Miss Fletcher?

"If that is a threat, Mr. Devos, there's no need for it. What you do with your own souvenirs is your business—although I'll admit I wondered why you would buy such a thing, only to throw it overboard just a few hours later. I bought one myself, so I know how much they cost."

"Buyer's remorse, Miss Fletcher, along with a, what would you say, a belated recollection of airline luggage limits. In fact, I realized it would be too large to take back home in my suitcase. I have many family members, you see—no, not children, for I am a bachelor. But many nieces and nephews to whom I bring back gifts when I travel. I thought my little niece Theodora would like the *caga tió*, but then I realized that if I put it in my suitcase, I would have no room left to bring gifts for her brothers and sisters. So I had to throw poor little Theodora's present overboard. Never fear, though, for she will not be forgotten. I shall buy her something else, something smaller and not so heavy."

"I see," I said, feeling a bit foolish for making a mystery where none existed. And yet it seemed a bit too convenient an explanation. If he had decided against taking the log home, why not offer it to a fellow passenger or, if he was determined to throw it away, why wait until the middle of the night to do so? He made it clear that he considered the matter closed, however, and I knew better than to question him further. And yet I couldn't quite let the matter drop. "It's a pity you didn't buy little—Theodora, didn't you say?—one of those Pinocchio marionettes in Florence. That would have been just the thing for a child and, unlike the *caga tió*, it could be played with all year long."

"I believe you are right," he said, apparently much struck. "What a pity you were not there in Florence to advise me. Would you perhaps accompany me the next time we dock?"

And *that*, I supposed, served me right for meddling in something that was none of my business. "I—er—I don't know what my aunt's plans are," I stammered.

"I understand," he assured me, and I had a feeling he understood a lot more than I wanted him to.

To my relief, the song wound to a close, and I stepped back out of his arms with perhaps a bit more haste than courtesy. "Thank you for asking me to dance, Mr. Devos, as well as satisfying my curiosity. Now, if you'll excuse me, I'd better see what Aunt Maggie is up to."

He didn't offer to escort me back to my table—or maybe I didn't linger long enough to give him the opportunity—so I threaded my way through the milling couples back to my table. I'd hardly sat down and fortified my shaken nerves with a sip of my piña colada when I was solicited once more for a dance.

"Miss Fletcher, will you do me the honor?"

I looked up and saw Markos, strikingly handsome in a white dinner jacket, black tie, and knife-creased black pants. "Off duty again?" I asked, forcing a smile I didn't quite feel. "Don't you ever work?"

As a joke, it went over like a lead balloon. "In fact, I *am* working. Since women always outnumber men onboard ship, all nonessential crewmembers—nonessential *male* crewmembers, that is—are expected to make themselves available as dance partners for the single female passengers."

"So you saw me sitting here and decided I was a wallflower in need of rescue." I don't know why I found the idea so galling, but I did.

"No, but it looks like your previous partner has deserted you, so . . ."

He shrugged, giving me to understand that he didn't care whether I danced with him or not. I stood up out of pure contrariness.

"All right, then, let's dance."

If dancing with Mr. Devos had felt awkward, dancing with Markos was uncomfortable in an entirely different way. I felt no urge to flinch when he drew me close (in fact, I was conscious of a little thrill I hadn't felt with Gene in quite some time) but I was still painfully aware of having made a fool of myself with my interrogation of Mr. Devos, while Markos—well, I didn't know what his problem was. Maybe he resented having to spend the evening dancing with wallflowers when there was so much work to be done; after all, I'd seen the line of passengers turning in film.

"I thought you'd be busy developing about seven hundred photos of the Leaning Tower and Michelangelo's *David*," I said, making an attempt at polite conversation.

"Some of them are drying, and the rest will have to wait their turn," he said, answering in kind. "I've seen your negatives, although I haven't yet printed them. It looks like you had a good time in Pisa."

"It's always interesting to see things in real life that you've only seen in pictures or read about in books," I said.

"Only wait until you see Rome," he predicted confidently. "Pisa will pale in comparison with the Eternal City."

I wondered if he would be sightseeing in Rome as well, but wouldn't let myself ask, for fear he might mistake idle curiosity for romantic interest. "What do you suggest I see?" I asked, although Maggie and I had already planned our itinerary with the aid of the guidebook.

Before he could answer, the song drew to a close, and we were obliged to join in the smattering of applause. Then the ship's activities director leaped up onto the dais with a microphone in his hand.

"All right, ladies and gentlemen, it's the moment you've all been waiting for: the dance-off! Grab your partners, and let's dance!"

Markos held out his hand to me. "Shall we?"

"Are you allowed?" I asked. "I mean, doesn't being part of the crew disqualify you?"

"Not at all. Oh, I'm not eligible to win a prize," he added hastily. "But when the women outnumber the men onboard nearly two to one, it would be a shame to exclude almost half the women on the ship."

"Well—" I hedged, then had a sudden and vivid recollection of college, when all the other girls were going to sorority dances while I spent the evening alone in the dorm, waiting for a fiancé who was away at sea. "Why not?" I declared recklessly, and we took our places among the dozen or so couples remaining on the floor for the competition. The newlywed Hollises, I noticed, were another. I looked around for Maggie and Paul, but they were nowhere in sight.

"In a minute, I'll tell you how the contest works," the activities director continued. "But first, let's have a big *Oceanus* welcome for our professional dancers, Marlene Williams and Roberto Ramón. Later in the cruise, they'll present a program you won't want to miss, as they demonstrate popular dances through history from the minuet to the twist. For tonight, though, *they'll* be watching *you!* As you dance to the sounds of our ship's band, Marlene or Roberto may tap you on the shoulder. If you or your partner are tapped, you are both out of the competition, although of course we hope you'll stick around to watch and cheer for the remaining couples. The last three couples standing will win valuable prizes! Are there any questions? No? Then all right everybody—let's dance!"

The band struck up the opening bars of "Night and Day," and the competition began. The Hollises, I noticed, were eliminated first, due in large part to Mr. Hollis's inability to keep up with the music, but they took their dismissal with a good grace and a cheerful demeanor that won them an enthusiastic round of applause from the people watching from the edges of the dance floor. An elderly couple who could barely shuffle their feet in time to the music was probably allowed to remain longer than they deserved out of respect for their age, followed by a crew member in dress whites partnering a sixty-something woman with improbably yellow hair. Eventually, I realized to my shock that there were only three couples remaining—and that Markos and I were one of them. It was hardly surprising that very shortly afterwards, I felt a light tap on my shoulder and turned to see Marlene smiling apologetically at me. We were out of the competition, but we—at least, *I*—had won third prize.

"We were at a disadvantage, really," Markos noted as we made our way back to my little table. "Some of these couples have been dancing together for years, and we've only just met."

I colored a bit at the unspoken suggestion that, given a little more time, we would be dancing as well together as the surprisingly spry white-haired gentleman spinning his partner under his arm and into a dip, to the loud applause of the spectators. No one was surprised when this couple was eventually crowned the champions, and when the winning couples were introduced and given their prizes, I realized I was now the proud owner of a tiny plastic trophy and five dollars' worth of credit at the ship's gift shop.

"Of course, it's good at the camera shop, too," Markos pointed out as I tucked my prize into my little silver bag.

"I'll bear it in mind in case I run low on film," I

promised. "But now I think I'd better turn in for the night. It's getting late and, well, Rome beckons."

"So it does," he agreed, offering his hand. I took it, and was thoroughly rattled when he bowed with exaggerated gallantry and kissed my fingers. "Until tomorrow, then."

I stammered something and made my escape, unsure whether to be annoyed with him for the gesture, or with myself for reacting to it just as the gauchest of my thirteen-year-old pupils might have done. Either way, I had no doubt I'd played right into his hands, so I held him entirely to blame for the fact that I failed to see Konstantin Devos lying in wait for me until it was too late to avoid him.

"Turning in early, Miss Fletcher?" he asked as he fell into step beside me, although in fact it was almost midnight. "A wise move. Tomorrow promises to be a full day."

"Yes," I said, determined not to give him anything that might be interpreted as encouragement. "Good night, Mr. Devos."

"Let me escort you back to your cabin," he urged. "It is not safe for a young woman to wander about alone so late at night."

Something about the gleam in his cold blue eyes made me wonder if he was thinking of the trek to my stateroom that lay ahead of me, or of the late-night ramble that had brought me above deck just as he'd disposed of Pedro's unfortunate cousin. The thought made me even less inclined to accept his offer of an escort.

"There are still plenty of people around, and the corridors are well-lit," I pointed out. "There's really no need for you to put yourself to any trouble."

I might as well have saved my breath. He made no attempt to take my arm, but made it clear he intended to accompany me whether I wanted his escort or not. There was no way to discourage him without making a scene, and what could I accuse him of, anyway? Other than the fact that I'd seen him throw a fairly expensive souvenir off the back of the ship, what reason did I have to distrust him? Maybe he was just one of those unfortunate, inept men who don't know how to express interest in a woman without coming across as a pervert. Resigning myself to his company, I started for the stairs, some sixth sense cautioning against the closed confines of the midships elevator.

To his credit, Mr. Devos was on his best behavior. Gesturing toward the small trophy, he congratulated me on my dancing prize, and spoke knowledgeably about what I might expect to see in Rome the next day. Even when we stood before my cabin door with the long, empty passageway curving gently away fore and aft, he made no attempt to take liberties, but wished me pleasant dreams and then retraced his steps back up the passageway. Having braced myself for fending off unwanted advances (or, in my more lurid imaginings, fighting for my life), I felt more than a little foolish as I watched him go. I shook off the feeling and unlocked my stateroom door.

I switched on the light and then closed and locked the door, shutting out all thoughts of Devos as I shot the bolt home.

"Pedro, you wouldn't believe what happened tonight," I told the painted log, setting the plastic trophy next to him.

Humming "Night and Day" under my breath, I regarded the distorted reflection of my engagement ring in the metallic gold paint for a long moment, then, obeying a sudden impulse, I tugged the ring off my finger and dropped it into the little plastic trophy, then tucked the whole thing into the top drawer of the nightstand.

"It's only for safekeeping," I told Pedro, "so you needn't look at me like that."

He grinned knowingly back at me.

With a little huff of annoyance, I got ready for bed and turned out the light.

The wind rose in the night, and the seas grew choppy. I woke to the sound of the waves slapping against the side of the ship and a not unpleasant sense of being rocked in a cradle as the *Oceanus* pitched in the rough water. And then, very faintly, came another sound.

Someone was in the cabin with me, fumbling among the clothes hanging in my tiny closet.

5

When Rome falls, so falls the world.
Attributed, THE VENERABLE BEDE

C autiously, lest I knock Pedro off the nightstand, I groped for the bedside lamp, located the switch, and pressed it, flooding the cabin with light. The closet door stood ajar, swinging gently to and fro with the motion of the ship. Inside, my tulle evening dress swayed on its hanger as if reliving the memory of dancing in Markos's arms. The unused hangers at one end of the closet collided together with faint click-clacking sounds; it was this noise that had awakened me.

"And what did you expect to find?" I scolded myself as I threw back the covers and padded across the room to close the closet door. "Mr. Devos ransacking your underwear? Face it, Fletcher, you're as jumpy as a—as a—"

But similes, which I spent one week of every school year pounding into the heads of reluctant eighth-graders, failed me. I gave a final tug to the closet door to make sure the latch was secure, then went back to bed and the gentle rocking of the waves.

The morning dawned bright and clear, perfect weather for exploring the Eternal City. I dressed quickly and joined Maggie for breakfast on the Firenze Deck, where Paul already sat nursing a cup of coffee. He rose as we approached, and pulled out a chair for Maggie.

"I hope the rough seas last night didn't disturb your sleep," he said after the requisite "good mornings" were exchanged.

"Not at all," Maggie assured him.

"In fact, it felt a bit like being rocked in a cradle," I agreed, saying nothing of the midnight scare that had, after all, proved to be nothing more than my own overactive imagination. I gazed out the big windows at the ship's stern at the port of Civitavecchia, bristling with cranes, crawling with trucks, and piled high with containers. "It seems a pity to me that the harbors of the most romantic cities in the world all manage to look exactly alike."

"Not really," Paul protested, chuckling. "You're just looking at the wrong things. See the big brick building? That's the Forte Michelangelo. It dates from the sixteenth century, and is built over the old Roman ruins. Civitavecchia has served as Rome's port for centuries, you know. In fact, if you look closely, you can see the base of one of the old Roman towers." He pointed toward a stout stone pillar, black with age, jutting up out of the water.

"I see it," I said, "but I'll admit I never would have noticed it if you hadn't pointed it out."

"Promise us you'll accompany us into Rome and point out the sights," Maggie urged him. "There's no telling what we might miss if we're allowed to wander on our own."

Seeing my duty clear, I swiped my guidebook off the table and shoved it to the bottom of my bag, professing my own ignorance as I added my entreaties to my aunt's. Paul protested that he didn't want to horn in on our plans, but eventually allowed himself (not too unwillingly, I thought) to be persuaded. After fortifying ourselves at the buffet, we followed the herd down the ship's gangplank and boarded one of the half-dozen buses bound for Rome. I hung back to allow Maggie and Paul to sit together, then took a seat immediately behind them—and was not at all pleased when Miss Duprée, casually elegant in close-fitting Capri pants, a striped boat-necked cotton sweater, and cat's-eye sunglasses, sat in the vacant seat beside me. Oh, well, I told myself as I murmured a greeting, I suppose it could have been worse. It could have been Mr. Devos.

"Good morning, Miss Duprée," Aunt Maggie said, turning in her seat. "Have you left Mr. Grimes on the ship today?"

"Yes, the poor lamb wasn't feeling well," she said, fishing a compact out of her large straw bag and reapplying carmine lipstick that had already looked flawless. "I think he got too much sun yesterday in Pisa."

We all made sympathetic noises, which were entirely sincere on my part; after all, if Mr. Grimes had been well, I would have been spared Miss Duprée's company on the long bus ride to Rome.

"I hope he'll feel better by dinnertime," Maggie said.

Miss Duprée lifted one tan shoulder. "I am sure he will."

Apparently she didn't mean to waste her day in Rome worrying about the health of the man who was no doubt funding the trip. But when the bus decanted us just outside St. Peter's Square two hours later, it became clear that she'd settled on other traveling companions to take his place.

"Where shall we begin?" she asked, slipping one hand through Maggie's arm and gesturing with the other in the direction of the curved colonnade surrounding the square—which, incidentally, wasn't square at all, but elliptical in shape.

We all looked askance at the long line of humanity snaking out from the Sistine Chapel, comprising mostly European or American tourists with cameras slung about their necks, liberally interspersed with groups of habited nuns or priests on a religious pilgrimage.

It was Paul who said what we were all thinking. "If we get in line now, we should be able to view the artwork in the

Chapel before boarding the bus back to the ship, but I'm not sure we would have time to see much of anything else." He looked down at Maggie. "What do you say we buy tickets for one of those tourist buses, and then we'll see what the line looks like when we get back?"

Maggie and I readily agreed to this plan; unfortunately, Miss Duprée made it very clear that she did not intend to be left behind. As we set out in search of a booth selling tickets for the tour buses, she fell into step beside my aunt. I hurried to catch up with her, determined not to let her monopolize Paul. It soon transpired, though, that she was less interested in stealing Paul away from Maggie than in stealing Maggie away from Paul. When the tour bus lurched to a stop with a hissing and squealing of brakes, she followed Maggie down the aisle of the crowded vehicle and plopped down onto the seat beside her, leaving Paul and me to sit in the only other vacant row, three rows behind them. Miss Duprée didn't strike me as the sort to bother cultivating friendships with other women when there was attractive male companionship to be had, so I couldn't help wondering what sort of game she was playing.

"Never mind," I told Paul, leaning close to be heard over the noise of the engine. "If I have to, I'll drag her off in search of the ladies' room or something."

He chuckled and gave my hand a squeeze. "I can see why your aunt is so fond of you."

"And I'm fond of her, as well," I said, prompting him to spend the next few minutes asking probing questions about my aunt, my late uncle, and, finally, the long illness that had taken Uncle Herman's life.

At last the bus set us down at the stop that served the Spanish Steps and the Trevi Fountain, and our attention turned to consulting maps and plotting the best route to see both sights with the least walking. We set out first for the Spanish Steps, the broad staircase named for the Spanish embassy to the Vatican located nearby. Built in the early eighteenth century, the one hundred and thirty-five steps served as a sort of pedestrian roadway up a steep slope, linking the Piazza di Spagna at the foot of the stairs with the Trinitá dei Monti church at the top—although it was a mystery to me how anyone could climb it without stepping on, or tripping over, the crowd of tourists posing for photographs or locals loitering on its treads.

No English teacher worth her salt could visit the Piazza de Spagna without paying special attention to the cream-colored building to the right of the Steps, where the poet John Keats had once lived. It was now a museum dedicated to the English Romantic poets, in particular Keats and Shelley. Recognizing that my interests were not necessarily shared by my traveling companions, I didn't push to spend our precious time in Rome touring the museum, but settled for fishing my camera from the depths of my bag and snapping a few shots of the exterior. Miss Duprée surprised me by offering to take one or two of me standing in front of the building, and I readily agreed, hoping that the sight of their teacher visiting the poet's house might make the subject more interesting to my students.

"What a fine camera," she purred as I pointed out which button to push. "Is it new?"

"Yes, I bought it just for the trip," I said proudly. It had been a major purchase on my part, and I was pleased that the Mistress approved; I suspected she wouldn't be impressed by cheap stuff. Yielding to a charitable impulse, I suggested, "Why don't I take one of you, so you can show Mr. Grimes what he missed?"

There followed a great deal of camera-swapping as the four of us took pictures of each other standing in front of the Fontana della Barcaccia, the fountain at the foot of the Spanish Steps, with the church of Trinitá dei Monti in the background at the top.

Having exhausted the glories of the Piazza de Spagna, we turned our steps southward toward the Trevi Fountain, the enormous and elaborate creation built right into the façade of the Palazzo Poli behind it. In its center, an arch supported by Corinthian columns framed a niche where a bearded male figure stood on what appeared to be a seashell, while winged horses cavorted at his feet. Below the horses, the detailed figures gave way to rough rocks over which the water cascaded.

"Poseidon?" I hazarded a guess as to the bearded man's identity. "Or, Neptune, maybe, since we're in Rome?"

"Oceanus," Paul corrected me.

"Just like our ship!" I exclaimed delightedly.

"Exactly. The ancient Greeks believed the ocean was a single enormous river circling the world. Oceanus was the god who ruled over it."

"I thought that was Poseidon," I said.

Paul shook his head dismissively. "Oh, Poseidon was only a local boy. He had charge of the Mediterranean. Oceanus was more exotic, and more powerful, having charge of the bigger and less familiar waters beyond Poseidon's territory. That's the theme of the fountain, you know, the taming of the waters. This fountain marks the location of one of the ancient Roman aquaducts. In fact, the water you see here still comes from the old aquaduct, although it's been rerouted since its source was first discovered in 19 B.C." He pointed to one of the bas reliefs forming the backdrop of the fountain. "If you'll look just to the right of our friend Oceanus, you'll see a representation of the young girl who, according to legend, led Roman soldiers to a source of pure water eight miles outside the city—no small thing for a city as large as Rome was, even in those days."

"All this Roman stuff is Greek to me," Maggie said, fishing in her purse. "I want to throw a coin into the fountain, like Dorothy McGuire in *Three Coins in the Fountain*."

I'll admit, I felt a bit like Maggie McNamara, the youngest of the three heroines of that film, as I turned my back to the fountain and—

And caught a glimpse of someone I was certain was Markos. But in the next instant, I lost sight of him among the crowd milling about the square, and I was left to wonder if I'd actually seen him at all.

"Robin, it's your turn, honey," Maggie said. "Sylvia and I have already thrown ours, and are guaranteed a return trip to Rome. We'd hate for you to be left behind."

Sylvia? Apparently my aunt and the Mistress were now on a first-name basis. I wasn't quite sure how I felt about that, but I hadn't time to consider the matter, not when everyone was waiting on me. Not wanting to waste any of my Italian coins—I had no very great faith that I would be returning to Rome, no matter how many wishes I made— I fished a good old American penny from the depths of my bag and, taking it in my right hand, tossed it over my left shoulder, just like they'd done in the movie.

"Perfect!" Maggie declared. "Make sure you keep your passport up to date, Robin."

After taking another round of photos, we began to walk back toward the bus stop. I kept my eyes peeled for another glimpse of Markos or his doppelgänger, but saw no sign of him.

"I'm parched," Maggie declared, pressing a hand to her throat. "Anyone else care for a drink?"

"That little place looks promising," Paul said, gesturing up the street a short distance toward an *osteria* with umbrella-covered tables set along the sidewalk. "What do you say we have a glass of wine while we watch the world go by?"

"It sounds heavenly," Maggie declared.

"Heavenly," agreed Miss Duprée. "But can we not go into that shoe shop first? I would like to buy a pair of flats. My feet, they are killing me."

Frankly, I thought anyone who chose to tiptoe about Rome in stiletto-heeled pumps was asking for pain, but seeing a chance to do Paul and Maggie a good turn, I spoke up quickly. "I'll go with you. I've always wanted a pair of Italian shoes."

Behind her back, Maggie gave me a grateful smile—apparently she wasn't any more thrilled with "Sylvia's" sudden chumminess than Paul was—and Paul puckered his lips at me in a silent approximation of a kiss. We agreed to meet in front of the *osteria* in an hour, and split into two pairs. I'd thought I was sacrificing myself for the sake of my aunt's romance, but I was pleasantly surprised. Miss Duprée was an enthusiastic shopper—no big surprise there—but an unexpectedly helpful companion as well. Maybe my own budget constraints gave her a chance to feel superior, or maybe I'd misjudged her in thinking she didn't care for female companionship. Whatever the case, she unerringly picked out the best deals and, when I found a pair of leather sandals that cost a bit more than I felt comfortable paying, she even persuaded the shopkeeper to offer a discount to "*la bella giovane americana.*" For herself, she more than made up for his loss, buying not only a pair of Porselli ballet flats handmade in Milan, but also a pair of genuine alligator pumps as well as a handbag to match, a purchase that probably cost more than I earned in a month.

"The Porsellis will be very useful tomorrow, when we visit Pompeii," she told my aunt after we'd rejoined Maggie and Paul an hour later outside the *osteria.* "The ruined streets there are very uneven. It would be easy to trip and fall."

"You've been there before?" Maggie asked.

"Once, but it was long ago." Realizing, no doubt, that she'd accidentally admitted to being older than she liked to pretend, she added hastily, "I was only a child at the time. I remember it particularly because I fell and scraped my knee."

Maggie and Paul exchanged knowing, secretive smiles that gave me the impression their little tête-à-tête had gone very well indeed. I made a mental note to demand the details from Maggie later, and resigned myself to spending my day in Rome squeezed onto the bus next to Sylvia Duprée and

SHERI COBB SOUTH

her cumbersome shopping bags.

We retraced our steps to the bus stop, and boarded the next tour bus for the Colosseum. I'd seen pictures, of course, but they didn't prepare me for the size of Rome's most famous ruin. The five-tiered oval structure was so enormous that I had trouble fitting the whole thing into my camera's viewfinder.

"Its name was originally the Flavian Amphitheatre," Paul said. He'd offered to hold my guidebook while I took photos, and apparently decided to make good use of it. "The name 'Colosseum' probably referred to a nearby statue of Nero, which was modeled after the Colossus of Rhodes, one of the Seven Wonders of the Ancient World. At some time, the Nero statue fell, or was pulled down so its bronze could be reused for some other building project, but by that time the name had come to stand for the amphitheatre itself."

"Two thousand years old, and yet in some ways it looks like any college football stadium," Maggie remarked.

"And is bigger than most," Paul said. "It could seat more than fifty thousand people." I'd finished taking photos by this time and we'd joined the line waiting to go inside, but he didn't seem in any hurry to return my guidebook.

"Forget college football," Maggie amended. "The Green Bay Packers would envy digs like this!"

"Oh, this isn't the half of it. According to Robin's book, it even had a retractable awning to protect spectators from sun and rain.”

As we drew nearer, we could see that the ground-level arches ringing the amphitheatre were numbered, just like a modern stadium—except that the numbers carved over each entrance were in Roman numerals.

“How would people know which section they were supposed to sit in?” Maggie asked. “Surely they didn’t have tickets!”

“Of course they did,” Paul said. “But instead of being printed on paper, they were scratched on pottery shards. Evidently pottery shards were the Roman equivalent of scrap paper.”

We passed beneath the arch designated XXVIII—twenty-eight—and found ourselves in a shady passageway with still more arched openings, beyond which were the areas that had once held seating.

“You ladies are going to love this bit,” predicted Paul, grinning broadly. “The amphitheatre was designed to be filled or evacuated quickly. The Latin word for the passageways that allowed for this rapid discharge of people is ‘vomitoria.’ Or, in the singular, ‘vomitorium.’ I’ll give you three guesses what English word is derived from it.”

Maggie and Sylvia grimaced, and my aunt spoke for all three of us when she said, “I think we only need one.”

“I’ll have to share that little tidbit with my class this fall,” I said drily. “There’s no better way to interest thirteen-year-old boys in language than to connect it to something vulgar."

Inside the Colosseum, still more surprises were in store. Most of the original floor was gone, exposing an elaborate system of underground tunnels. And over all, plants grew wherever they were able to put down roots in the crevices between the blocks of travertine stone.

"I didn't expect it to be so—so *green*," I said. Somehow the lush vegetation didn't seem to square with gory images of gladiators doing battle, or Christians being thrown to the lions.

"Apparently plants have grown inside the Colosseum for centuries," Paul said, referring once again to my guidebook. "Domenico Panaroli first catalogued them in 1643, and since then almost seven hundred different species have been identified."

"Seven hundred? But how did they all get here?" Maggie asked. Sylvia, I noticed, had apparently become bored with the discussion, for she had wandered off and was peering through each arched opening, almost as if she were looking for someone—more amusing company, I guessed. I hoped we hadn't been rude—I thought we'd been unusually gracious, under the circumstances—but I couldn't honestly say I would be sorry if she decided to abandon us in favor of someone else.

"Bird migration, changes in climate over the

centuries—one particularly romantic theory suggests that the seeds were caught in the fur of the animals brought in from all over the empire."

"Oh, I like that one," I said. "It would be nice to think they were responsible for bringing life to the Colosseum, rather than just death to all those poor Christians."

"There was something about that, now where did I see it?" Paul muttered, flipping back and forth a few pages. "Ah, here it is. Apparently there's a marked lack of historical records of Christians being martyred at the Colosseum, as it was used for executing common criminals—unless, of course, their 'crime' was failing to reverence the Roman gods, in which case it seems to be a matter of semantics. Most of the Christian persecutions were carried out at the Circus Maximus. But the animals weren't always the winners here, you know. The inaugural games lasted more than one hundred days, during which more than nine thousand animals—or possibly five thousand, depending on whose account you choose to believe—were slaughtered, either by fighting against each other or against a human opponent."

"That's horrible!" I exclaimed.

"To modern sensibilities, yes," Paul agreed. "But keep in mind, Titus had only just succeeded his father, Vespasian, as Emperor, and already he'd dealt with a fire that had burned in Rome for three days, an outbreak of plague in the city, and the eruption of Mount Vesuvius. The extravagant games were probably an attempt to appease his disgruntled subjects as much as placating the Roman gods."

Maggie peered down into the exposed tunnels. "I suppose the underground section is where they kept the animals."

"Part of it, yes," Paul said. "There was also an underground tunnel to the gladiators' barracks, as well as separate tunnels for the Emperor and the Vestal Virgins to enter and leave the Colosseum without having to mingle with the riff-raff."

"Can we go down there?" I asked. "I'd love to explore."

Paul shook his head. "The hypogeum—the underground part, that is—isn't open to the public, although it may be someday. It wasn't fully excavated until the 1930s, under Mussolini."

"It's nice to know he was good for something," Maggie muttered.

"Listen to this: the hypogeum wasn't part of the original structure. It was added later, when Titus's younger brother, Domitian, became Emperor. Before that, the entire arena could be flooded, and naval battles were re-enacted here, including a famous clash between the Greeks and the Corinthians."

"Now, *that* would've been something to see!" I said. "How much water do you suppose it must have taken to float a battleship?"

"Keep in mind, the ships of the time were quite small by today's standards," Paul pointed out. "Not nearly as large as our own *Oceanus*."

"Speaking of which," Maggie said, consulting her wristwatch, "we'd better hop back on the bus if we're going to see anything else before heading back to our ship."

Paul and I agreed, and so after reluctantly collecting Sylvia, we boarded the tour bus. I had assumed we were heading back to St. Peter's Square, but to my surprise, Paul stood up before we reached the familiar stop.

"Let's get off here," he said.

We did—there wasn't time to debate the matter—but when we got off the bus, Maggie voiced the question we were all thinking.

"What's here?"

"The church of Santa Maria in Cosmedin," he replied.

We all looked askance at the church we'd never even heard of before.

"I'm sure it's lovely, Paul, but if we stop to look at every historic church in Rome, we'll miss the 'all aboard,' " my aunt pointed out.

"This will only take a moment," he assured us. "We won't even go inside—just as far as the portico."

We followed Paul, obediently if not enthusiastically, to the portico, where he stopped before an enormous round marble representation of a human face, with crudely carved holes for its eyes, nostrils, and mouth.

"La Bocca della Verità," he said by way of explanation. "Or, in English, 'the Mouth of Truth.' It dates from the first century and was probably part of a fountain or, less romantically, a manhole cover. But since the Middle Ages it's served as a primitive sort of lie detector. If you tell a lie with your hand in its mouth, your hand will be bitten off. Anyone care to give it a try? What about you, Robin? Can you think of a good lie?"

I'm never going to marry Gene. It was the first thing that came into my head, and it was a lie—wasn't it? Of course it was! Still, I was strangely reluctant to stick my hand into the mouth and put it to the test. Because I didn't want Maggie to think I was having doubts, I told myself, not because I had any fear of losing my hand to a first-century Roman manhole cover.

"No?" Paul prompted. "Well then, I guess I'll have to do it myself."

He thought for a moment—thinking up a suitably convincing lie, no doubt—then stuck his hand into the stone mouth, turned to Sylvia, and announced, "My name is Graham Grimes."

"See," Maggie said, "nothing—"

"*Aauugghh!*" Paul let out a bloodcurdling scream, and withdrew his hand from the mouth. His arm ended abruptly at the sleeve of his sport coat. Maggie, Sylvia, and I stared stupefied at the hand that wasn't there for perhaps a fraction of a second and then, as if on cue, we all burst out laughing.

"Very funny," I chided him. "We've all seen *Roman Holiday*, you know. Gregory Peck played the same trick on Audrey Hepburn."

Paul shrugged with unimpaired good cheer. "Oh well, it was worth a try." He held his arm out straight, and his hand emerged, uninjured, from the end of his sleeve. "I knew I couldn't fool Maggie, but I thought maybe you would be too young to have seen that film." I noticed he wisely refrained from any speculations as to Sylvia's age.

"I never saw it in the theater, but they show it now and then on late-night television," I explained. "When your fiancé is off on a submarine somewhere, you spend a lot of nights at home watching TV," I added ruefully, just to remind myself of Gene, whom I fully intended to marry.

Having accomplished what he'd intended at the church of Santa Maria in Cosmedin, Paul shepherded us back to the bus stop, where we had to wait twenty minutes for the next bus to come along.

"You see what your little stunt has cost," Maggie scolded him playfully. "If we don't get to see the Sistine Chapel, we'll know who to blame."

But before we returned to St. Peter's Square, we had to find lunch somewhere. Maggie complained that the glass of

97

wine she'd had at the *osteria* near the Trevi Fountain had long since worn off, while Sylvia and I had had nothing to eat or drink since breakfast. Paul led us to a *ristorante* that had been highly recommended by a colleague of his. Here we made two discoveries: first, that the food was just as plentiful and delicious as Paul had been led to believe; and second, that the Italian idea of a meal was a leisurely event that stretched to two and a half hours. By the time we made our way back to St. Peter's Square, the line snaking out from the Sistine Chapel was even longer than it had been that morning.

"Now I see why we had to wish for a return trip to Rome back at the Trevi Fountain," I said. "It's impossible to see everything in one day."

"Sad, but true," Paul admitted. "A cruise is a great way to get an overview of several of the world's great cities all in one trip, but the tight schedule means you can only see the highlights of each port of call."

Resigning ourselves to the inevitable (and ignoring the many ticket hawkers who optimistically promised to get us inside the Chapel "*presto!*"), we contented ourselves with strolling about the plaza, enjoying the shade of the massive colonnades, cooling ourselves in the spray of the twin Bernini fountains, and taking photos of the Egyptian obelisk marking the center, whose shadow—according to the guidebook I'd finally reclaimed from Paul—marked the time like a giant sundial. Then, too, there was the ever-popular pastime of people-watching. A cardinal, dignified in flowing scarlet robes, frowned at a gaggle of brown-skinned young novices, all giggling amongst themselves like any American teenyboppers. I did wonder, though, what sort of lurid secrets might be shared between young women sworn to a life of celibacy. The thought of romantic secrets reminded me of Maggie and her tête-à-tête with Paul, and I resolved to demand a full accounting once we were back in the privacy of our own staterooms.

Back at the ship, however, it became clear that any confidences would have to wait. As we reached our cabin doors, Maggie, fumbling in her purse, grumbled, "I can't find my key!"

"Are you sure you had it this morning?" Even as I asked the question, I already knew the answer. A woman suddenly living alone again after decades of marriage would be unlikely to forget to lock her door, and the stateroom doors couldn't be locked from the outside without the key, making it impossible for Maggie to have accidentally locked herself out.

"It isn't here!" she exclaimed in growing impatience, having by this time dropped to her knees and dumped the contents of her purse out into the passageway, the better to sift through the odds and ends it contained. "Did I give it to you, Robin?"

"No." I smiled slyly at her. "Did you give it to Paul, by any chance?"

She paused in her search long enough to look up at me with a stern look belied by the twinkle in her eye. "Why, Robin, I'm surprised at you! What would your mother say?"

"Probably that you're a bad influence on me—or maybe that I'm a bad influence on you. I don't remember your giving me your key, but I'll check." Following my aunt's example, I dumped out my purse and sorted through its contents. Just as I'd expected, the only key I found was my own. "So what happens now?"

Maggie sighed. "I suppose I'd better go down to the purser's desk and see if anyone has found it and turned it in there. If not, I'll ask if they have a spare. There must be extras, else how would the cabin steward get in?"

"I'll go with you."

By the time we'd collected a replacement key from the purser and returned to our cabins, we barely had time to dress for dinner. After a full meal, all I wanted to do was put up my aching feet and rest in preparation for the next day's excursion to Pompeii. The juicy details of Maggie's date, I decided, would just have to wait.

6

I stood among them, but not of them.
GEORGE NOEL GORDON, LORD BYRON,
Childe Harold's Pilgrimage

I awoke the next morning just as the ship was docking in Naples. Recalling Miss Duprée's warnings about the uneven streets of Pompeii, I resisted the urge to try out my new Italian sandals and settled instead on a pair of less stylish but more practical Keds, along with a sleeveless shirtwaist dress of plaid seersucker. Once dressed, I knocked on Maggie's door, but she didn't answer. I knocked again, with no more response, and was debating the wisdom of going down to breakfast alone when I heard the distant swish of the midships elevator sliding to a stop, and a moment later Maggie came hurrying down the passageway.

"I'm so sorry, Robin," she said, fumbling in her bag for her replacement key. "I awoke an hour ago, so I went down for an early breakfast. I thought I would be back before you were up and about."

"It's all right," I assured her. Driven by some demon of

mischief, I asked, "And how is Paul this morning?"

"He's fine. He—" Realizing she'd stepped very neatly into the trap I'd set for her, she gave me a rather sheepish smile. "He's fine. Will you mind very much if he accompanies us to Pompeii?"

"Of course not! I'd much rather have Paul's company than Sylvia Duprée's. I hope Mr. Grimes is recovered. I'm not sure I can take her for two days in a row."

But as we boarded the bus, there was no sign of either the Mistress or her Sugar Daddy. He'd come down to dinner last night, but had not been the charming dinner companion of the previous evening; he hadn't taken part in the conversation at all, and had only picked at the lavish meal set before him. I wondered if Miss Duprée had decided to stay on the ship and play the devoted nurse. Somehow I couldn't quite picture her in the role.

In any case, I had a row all to myself this time, since no one came to claim the seat beside me. I slid over to the window, and prepared to enjoy the view. And what a view it was! The Bay of Naples spread out before us, and in the distance a gently curved mountain appeared hazy against the blue sky.

"It looks harmless enough, doesn't it?" asked Paul, turning around in his seat to address me. "Hard to believe it was responsible for the destruction of two cities."

"That's Mount Vesuvius?" I exclaimed, regarding the

deceptively peaceful-looking slope with new eyes.

Paul was right: It was strange to think that this was the same volcano whose eruption in 79 A.D. had buried Pompeii and Herculaneum under more than twenty feet of volcanic ash. We would explore Pompeii later in the day, but first our bus driver treated us to a drive along the dramatic Amalfi Coast. Since I was seated on the right-hand side of the bus, I had an unobstructed view of the five-hundred-foot drop to the sea; better that, I supposed, than that of the passengers seated on the left, whose view included the oncoming traffic swerving toward us around hairpin bends so sharp that it seemed as if the passengers seated in the front of the bus must be able to see the ones in the rear through the window as we rounded the curve.

We spent the morning in Sorrento, where lemon trees grew within scaffolds of wood and wire, an ingenious arrangement that allowed orchards to thrive on the almost vertical cliffs that surrounded the town. We strolled down the narrow streets of the old medieval city toward the bay for photographs, and as we retraced our steps up the slope toward the town center, I bought a couple of pieces of fruit at an outdoor market and tucked them into my bag for a snack later, having been warned that there would be nowhere to eat amongst the Pompeiian ruins. By now the sun was high enough to penetrate the dark canyonlike streets, and we stopped at a tiny *osteria* whose outdoor tables took advantage of the shade cast by the surrounding buildings.

"We can't leave for Pompeii without first trying the *limoncello*," Maggie declared. "After all, Sorrento is famous for it."

"So *that's* what all the lemon trees are for!" I exclaimed. "I'll admit, I wondered. I'd never thought of Italians as being all that fond of lemonade."

"Oh, you can probably get lemonade if you want it," Paul said. "Still, as long as we're here, I figure 'when in Rome,' and all that."

"Rome was yesterday," I pointed out. "You're getting your days mixed up, Paul."

He made a face at me. "No one likes a smart-aleck, Robin."

"It serves you right for that stunt with the Mouth of Truth," I retorted, still conscious of having betrayed more than I'd intended there. Or was it that I was uncomfortable with confronting the truth about myself and Gene?

"Children, children, don't fight," Maggie scolded, as our waiter arrived with a tray containing three small glasses, each filled with a bright neon yellow liquid. He set one glass before each of us, and my aunt lifted hers in a toast. "Cheers!"

"Lemonade never looked like this," I said, and followed my aunt's example. "Lemonade never tasted like this, either."

"Too much of this, and I won't be able to walk by the time we reach Pompeii," Maggie said, signaling to the waiter for a refill nevertheless. "No, Paul," she intervened as he reached for his wallet. "You paid for mine in Rome, so I insist on returning the favor."

Paul allowed her to override his objections, and soon we returned to the city center for the bus to Pompeii. All three of us were in a mellow mood, no doubt the effect of good company, romantic surroundings, and a beverage the same color as the Italian sun.

There was still no sign of Sylvia Duprée or Mr. Grimes, but I did recognize several of our other shipmates on the bus, including the couple who had won the dance competition as well as the newlywed Hollises, who waved enthusiastically when they saw us, but made no attempt to join our party.

After we disembarked outside the ruins, I smiled at the sight of Mrs. Hollis buying a cheap plastic fan from a vendor's booth. But by the time we'd spent half an hour among the ruins with the sun beating down on our heads, I decided Mrs. Hollis was the smartest one of the lot of us. Many of the buildings still stood, but they had long since lost their roofs—I supposed they had either been set afire by live embers landing on the tiles or, perhaps more likely, had collapsed under the weight of the ash that had buried the city—and therefore offered no shade to speak of.

When our tour guide led us to the House of the Vetti—a

once-luxurious residence, or *domus*, that had been reconstructed, complete with red tile roof—we eagerly went inside, if only to escape from the sun a little while. We stepped inside and found ourselves in a small vestibule, an enclosed space so dim that it took our eyes a few seconds to adjust. The vestibule led into a larger atrium with a square opening in the middle of its reconstructed roof that corresponded with a sunken area, called an *impluvium*, directly beneath. This was not for decorative purposes, as I'd first thought, but served to collect rainwater, which drained into a cistern—an ingenious bit of Roman civil engineering that ensured the family would always have a supply of cool water available for their private use. Beyond the atrium, a peristyle—a wraparound porch with a roof upheld by rows of Doric columns—surrounded a courtyard fully open to the sky and, according to our guide, planted with flowers and shrubs that might have been found in Pompeii at the time of Vesuvius's eruption. The formal rooms opened onto the peristyle, and featured exquisitely detailed frescoes in vivid shades of red, yellow, and black. I found it charming, this glimpse into the lives of first-century Romans, until a room in the back corner jerked me back to reality. There, under a protective layer of plexiglass, lay some half a dozen human skulls.

"I guess they gathered together in the part of the house where they thought they would be safe," Maggie said in a subdued voice, putting my own thoughts into words. "It's so very sad, isn't it? Even after almost two thousand years."

"At least they were together when they died, whoever they were," I said. "I hope they found some comfort in that."

She put her hand on my shoulder and gave it a squeeze. "Yes, there are certainly worse ways to go than being surrounded by loved ones," she agreed, and I knew she was thinking of Uncle Herman.

Out in the street once more, we picked our way up the stone-paved street past the remains of more modest homes featuring storefronts along the street, complete with counters inset with earthenware jars from which the family could dish out the first-century equivalent of fast food to paying customers during the day.

"I see what Sylvia meant about the streets," Maggie grumbled, stepping cautiously to avoid one of three large stones jutting up much higher than the street in which they were embedded. "I'm sure the ancient Pompeiians had an excellent reason for putting big rocks in the middle of the road, but I can't imagine what it might have been."

"Can you not?" Paul asked, chuckling. "I can tell you that, and I don't even need Robin's guidebook. They're stepping-stones. Pedestrians could use them to cross the street without having to walk through sewage or other effluvia that would have been tossed into the street. The gaps between the stones would allow for vehicles to pass."

Maggie regarded the narrow spaces between the stones. "The gaps aren't all that wide, are they? That would take a pretty skilled driver."

I laughed, remembering my not-so-long-ago driver's ed class. "I can just imagine some Roman teenager moaning, 'I failed the stepping-stone portion of my driver's license exam! I hit a rock and almost ejected the examiner from Dad's chariot!' "

"It's a shame you teach English, Robin," Paul said. "You'd have made a hell of a history teacher."

I shook my head. "Oh, I like history, but not necessarily the famous people and important dates that are taught in class. I'm much more interested in what life would have been like for ordinary people."

It was true. The forum, amphitheatre, and baths were impressive, and the plaster casts on display near the forum were heart-wrenching, showing how the volcano's victims— men, women, and children of all ages, even a dog struggling to escape from its chain—would have appeared at the time of their deaths. Still, I preferred the *domūs* of prosperous Roman families, with their hints of how these people would have lived before their world came to such an abrupt and terrifying end. And it wasn't all tragic; the Pompeiians had not been without a sense of humor. The floor of one merchant's house bore the inscription "*Salve, lucru,*" or, in English, "Welcome, profit," while the vestibule of another house featured an elaborate mosaic on its floor with a detailed image of a black and white dog, along with the words "*cave canum*"—a warning to visitors to "Beware of the dog."

As it turned out, it wasn't a dog that posed the danger. We followed our tour guide past a remarkably well-preserved building with an upper floor jutting over the lower, casting the street into welcome shade. A number of tourists—curiously, they were all men—were lined up at the door awaiting admittance, while a trickle of grinning sightseers, also all men, squeezed past them as they exited the building. It seemed to me that our tour guide was trying to hustle us past with undue haste.

"What's that?" I asked. "It seems to be awfully popular. Why aren't we stopping, do you suppose?"

To my surprise, the usually unflappable Paul looked uncomfortable. "That building, er, it's called the lupanar."

"What he means, Robin, is that it was a brothel," my aunt said, not mincing words. "It's closed to the public, except to men willing to pay an additional fee to, er, admire the paintings on the walls."

"Oh," I said, feeling my face grow warm.

"Being a Mere Woman, I've never seen them, of course, but one assumes they served to advertise the services available. Paul, if you'd like to investigate—purely in the name of historical research, of course—we understand."

SHERI COBB SOUTH

Paul shook his head. "That's very big of you, Maggie, but I think I'll pass. I'm in no hurry to exchange the charms of my present company for those of some long-dead ladies of the evening."

"And they say chivalry is dead!" exclaimed Maggie, rolling her eyes. "Robin, I'm not sure whether we should take that as a compliment or an insult."

"I meant it as a compliment, however clumsily expressed," Paul said a bit sheepishly. "But if I remember my college Latin correctly, 'lupanar' means 'wolf's den.' I wonder what that says about the women who worked here."

"Probably that they—*oh!*"

Maggie broke off abruptly as she tripped over one of the stepping-stones. It all happened so quickly that neither Paul nor I could grab her in time to stop her as she fell sprawling in the street.

"*Maggie!*" we exclaimed as one. "Are you all right?"

"Oh, I'm just dandy," she muttered, sitting up with some assistance from Paul. "Just me and the rest of the effluvia." She lifted her skirt to expose her scraped and bloodied knee. "These stockings were brand new, and now look at them!"

"It isn't your stockings that I'm worried about," Paul said, kneeling beside her in the street. "Where does it hurt?"

"Other than my pride, you mean? My ankle, mostly. I think I may have sprained it."

"It doesn't seem to be broken," Paul said, probing her ankle gingerly.

Our tour guide, no doubt realizing she'd lost some of her group, came hurrying forward, pushing her way through the crowd of well-intentioned tourists offering unsolicited medical advice in a babble of languages.

"I have to keep the group on schedule," she said apologetically, after seeing for herself that Maggie's injuries were not serious. "If you wish to return to the ship, here is a card with a number you can call for a taxi. Otherwise, just meet the group back at the entrance at four o'clock for the bus back to Naples."

Paul thanked her and took the business card she offered. After she had led the tour group off, he looked up at me. "Robin, get rid of them, will you?"

He jerked his chin to indicate the tourists who showed no inclination to leave and miss all the excitement.

I turned and thanked them for their concern, explaining that my aunt was quite all right. "He is a doctor," I assured them. For the sake of those who didn't understand English, I gestured toward Paul and then pretended to listen to an invisible patient's heartbeat through a stethoscope. The crowd reluctantly dispersed, and once my aunt could be assured of relative privacy, Paul draped her arm over his own shoulders and stood up, raising her to her rather shaky feet.

"I can walk," Maggie assured him.

Unfortunately, it soon became obvious that the injured ankle would not bear her weight.

"It's back to the ship for you, my girl," Paul told her.

"But—"

"No buts," he said in a voice that brooked no argument. "You need to elevate that foot and ice that ankle down. If you can make it as far as the entrance, I'll get us a taxi back to Naples."

"I'm coming, too," I said, taking up a position at Maggie's other side.

"Oh Robin, if I make you miss your day in Pompeii, it'll make me feel that much worse," she protested. "Stay here, take lots of pictures, and then you can show me what I missed."

I reluctantly agreed, but insisted on accompanying them as far as the entrance to the ruins.

"All right, you can carry my purse," Maggie said, surrendering her handbag.

We slowly retraced our steps, Maggie hopping on one foot while Paul supported her with his arm around her waist. After what seemed an eternity, we reached the entrance, where Maggie sank gratefully onto a stone bench while Paul communicated our need for a taxi. Feeling helpless—and more than a little bit guilty for remaining in Pompeii while my aunt's holiday was so rudely cut short—I gave her a piece of slightly bruised fruit from my bag and once again offered to return to the *Oceanus* with her.

"Not on your life!" she declared. "I'll be just fine, and I'll expect to hear all about your adventures this evening. Oh, and Robin—"

"Yes, Maggie?" I prompted eagerly. "What is it?"

"If you tell anyone back home that I was injured outside a Roman brothel, I'll cut you out of my will!"

"I promise," I conceded, laughing.

I waited with Maggie and Paul until the taxi arrived, and then, after seeing Paul settle Maggie tenderly on the back seat and climb in beside her on the other side of the vehicle, waved them on their way before returning to my interrupted tour of the famous ruins. The tour group, unsurprisingly, was nowhere to be seen, and so I decided to explore on my own rather than spend the rest of the afternoon chasing up and down the ancient streets in search of them. Strange as it seemed, I almost envied my aunt, her injury notwithstanding. True, her day in Pompeii had been cut short, but the chance to be cosseted by a handsome and charming man of her own generation was surely nothing to sneeze at. I found myself wishing I had someone close to my age with whom to explore the ruins, and my thoughts turned, not to my fiancé, as might be expected, but to Markos. I wondered if he had stayed on the ship today, and decided probably not; after all, he seemed to do hardly any work on board that I could tell. He was probably somewhere in Naples at this very minute, sketching statues, or else he was one of the "art connoisseurs" leering at the frescoes in the lupanar. *The snake,* I thought. *I'm better off without him.*

Dismissing him from my thoughts, I consulted the crude mimeographed map we'd all been given at the beginning of the tour, and found my way back to one of the streets where several of the better-preserved *domūs* had been. They were not so crowded now, and I was able to explore at my leisure, taking note of some of the details I had missed the first time. I was especially drawn to one dwelling place that had been given the romantic designation of House of the Tragic Poet. Along its façade, two storefronts flanked the entrance— poetry, after all, was not the steadiest way to make a living, even in ancient Rome—and between them the familiar vestibule led to another atrium, with its open roof and ingenious water collection system, as well as the frescoes featuring the almost life-sized figures from Roman myth- ology for which this particular house was famous.

I passed through the atrium on my way to the sunlit courtyard where, according to my guidebook, the shell of a tortoise had been found when the house was excavated— perhaps the remains of a family pet that had been kept there. Just before I emerged onto the peristyle, I realized I was not alone in the house. Apparently a couple of tourists, a man and a woman, had reached the courtyard before me, and had taken advantage of the relative privacy to indulge in a heated argument. They were speaking in a foreign language—I thought perhaps it was French, although my one year of studying that language in college was insufficient to follow a rapid and vehement exchange between speakers far more fluent than I. Which was probably a good thing, now that I thought of it. I stood there in the dimly lit atrium, debating whether to make my presence known or make a discreet exit, when the matter was settled by two little words, the only part of the conversation that I had understood.

The words were "*Mademoiselle* Fletcher."

I froze, afraid to move, afraid to breathe for fear that even so small a sound should betray my presence. Remaining where I stood, however, was not an option. The House of the Tragic Poet was not so well-preserved as the House of the Vetti had been—or, rather, had not undergone a similar reconstruction—and within its broken walls and gaping doorways, I felt almost nakedly exposed. More to the point, if the other ruined *domūs* I'd seen were anything to judge by, any rear exit from the courtyard would be chained off, closed to the public. The quarreling pair, whoever they were, would have only one way to leave the house: through the atrium, where they would have to walk right past me. Choosing my steps with care lest I kick some loose stone or flaking bit of floor, I stepped slowly away from the opening onto the courtyard. Still, I could not quite bring myself to abandon the house altogether—not without at least trying to catch a glimpse of the couple who had spoken my name in an obviously hostile context. I looked about for a likely hiding place, and noticed a dark doorway in one corner of the room. I ducked inside and waited. In the atrium just beyond my hiding place, the painted figures on the walls seemed to gaze down at me with the wisdom of the ages in their faded eyes.

At last the sounds from the courtyard indicated the pair was ready to leave, although to judge by their clipped voices and short, snappish speech, their disagreement was by no means settled. I waited in my hidey-hole, and soon was rewarded with a look at their retreating forms. I couldn't see their faces, but then, I didn't have to.

I would have recognized Sylvia Duprée and Konstantin Devos from any angle.

7

Beware of entrance to a quarrel.
WILLIAM SHAKESPEARE, *Hamlet*

I'd thought Sylvia and Devos were merely chance-met acquaintances, like the rest of us assigned to that particular dining room table. I couldn't imagine what they might be arguing about, much less what their disagreement might have to do with me, any more than I could guess why Devos insisted on once again wearing long sleeves in spite of the sweltering heat. Was it possible Sylvia was jealous because he'd danced with me? Granted, I couldn't imagine myself as much of a threat to a woman like her, but Sylvia Duprée struck me as the sort of female who would expect masculine admiration to be focused exclusively on herself, whether she was interested in the man or not. Only witness the way she'd shoehorned herself into our day in Rome: Once she'd established herself as one of our party, she'd shown very little interest in attracting Paul's attention, just so long as she kept Maggie from having a monopoly on him.

I don't remember anything about the next few hours. I suppose I must have stumbled up and down the ruined streets until time to meet the bus for the trip back to the ship. Eventually, I climbed the steps onto the vehicle and sank onto a seat against the window. The Hollises claimed the seat behind me, and the need to be friendly to my shipmates forced me to thrust the strange quarrel to the back of my mind, at least for a while.

"That was fascinating!" declared Mrs. Hollis, wafting her fan to and fro. "I used up a whole roll of film—I can't wait to show the pictures to my friends at church."

I closed my eyes, enjoying the breeze she created. "Mrs. Hollis, you're a genius! I wish I'd been smart enough to buy a fan."

"I wouldn't call myself a genius," she protested modestly. "I expect I paid too much for it—I don't know how liras compare to dollars—but I figure when we get back home, I can send it to Henry's little granddaughter. She's almost six."

"She'll love it," I predicted warmly. "I know I would have when I was little."

Henry and Martha Hollis seemed so nice and so, well, *normal* that it seemed impossible to believe I had really heard what I thought I'd heard. Was it possible I had misunderstood? Sometimes words in a foreign language could sound strangely like English words to which they had absolutely no relation: I still remembered the hilarity that had ensued in my college French class when the professor pointed to a poster on the wall and announced, *"C'est une affiche,"* to which the entire class responded, "Tuna fish." Was it possible they hadn't said my name at all, but some other French word or words that to my untrained ear had sounded like it? Surely that must be it; no other explanation made sense.

I made up my mind to dismiss the argument from my thoughts and focus instead on my aunt. She would want to hear all about the rest of my day in Pompeii, and I had no intention of worrying her with groundless suspicions. I realized to my surprise that I, like Mrs. Hollis, had finished a roll of film, and resolved to drop it off for developing; I would be as curious as Maggie to see what I'd taken pictures of, for I couldn't remember anything that happened after that strange encounter in the House of the Tragic Poet.

Once back on ship, I headed straight for the photo counter, and was unaccountably relieved to find Markos there in his crisp white uniform; evidently he hadn't been ashore in Pompeii "admiring the artwork" in the lupanar, after all.

"Good evening, Miss Fletcher," he said with a smile, white teeth gleaming against his tan. "Did you enjoy your day ashore?"

I nodded. "The first half of it, anyway. But Maggie—

my aunt, Mrs. Watson, that is—had to return to the ship early, and I'll admit I missed having her company."

"So you were left on your own for the rest of the excursion?"

The question seemed innocent enough, but there was something—an intensity about his eyes, perhaps—that suggested some hidden meaning, although I couldn't imagine what it might be. One thing was certain, however: my charming dance partner of two nights ago was gone, and this suspicious and faintly accusing stranger had taken his place.

"Yes," I retorted defensively, although exactly what I was defending myself against, I couldn't have said. "I promised Maggie I would take plenty of pictures so she could see what she missed. So if you could put a rush on these, I would appreciate it. I don't suppose my photos from Pisa are ready yet?"

"Unfortunately, Miss Fletcher, there are six hundred passengers and two hundred crew members on board the *Oceanus*, and every one of them believes his—or her—photos are more important than anyone else's."

If he'd hoped to put me in my place, he was going to be doomed to disappointment. "Maybe if you'd been working yesterday instead of gallivanting about Rome, you would be caught up by now." I grimaced inwardly at my own choice of words. Gallivanting? I sounded like my own grandmother. Fortunately, the English term seemed to escape Markos.

"I don't know what you mean," he said woodenly.

"I saw you yesterday, near the Trevi Fountain."

He shook his head. "I'm afraid you must have mistaken me for someone else, Miss Fletcher."

If I had been uncertain before, I was dead sure now, although what Markos had been doing in Rome—and why he was lying about it—I couldn't even begin to guess. I was given no chance to challenge his assertion, for he had already turned to assist the next passenger. The message was clear: He had nothing more to say to me. With a little huff of annoyance, I turned on my heel and made straight for Maggie's stateroom. I tapped on the door, and a muffled voice invited me to come in.

I found my aunt sitting on her bed reading, leaning back against the headboard with her injured foot propped up on a pillow. When she saw me, she closed her book and laid it aside.

"I noticed the passageway was suddenly noisier, and hoped it meant the tour buses were returning," she said, tilting her head so I could kiss her on the cheek. "How was the rest of Pompeii?"

"Beautiful and sad," I said. "I dropped my film off as I came up. When I get my photos back, we'll look at them together. But did you see the ship's doctor? What did he say about your ankle?"

"Paul was right: It isn't broken, but you couldn't prove

it by me. The doctor gave me something for pain and told me to keep it elevated. So I'm afraid I won't be going to dinner with you," she added apologetically.

"Never mind that," I said impatiently, wondering at the same time how I was ever going to look Sylvia and Devos in the face. "How are you going to eat?"

"The cabin steward is going to bring me something on a tray. Make my excuses to everyone at dinner, will you?"

I promised her I would, and returned to my stateroom to shower and dress for dinner, grateful in a way that my aunt's injury would give me something to talk about without blurting out my suspicions regarding Sylvia and Devos.

As it turned out, I needn't have worried. Graham Grimes had come down to dinner, apparently recovered at last, and everyone was eager to express their pleasure at his return to our little group. Sylvia was as devoted to him as anyone might have wished. She and Devos, on the other hand, addressed one another—when they addressed one another at all—with the sort of impersonal courtesy of chance-met strangers. I became more convinced than ever that I had misunderstood the words I'd heard in the House of the Tragic Poet.

Still, I reminded myself, they *had* been together, and they *had* been arguing; of that much I was certain. And so, when the subject turned from Mr. Grimes to the missing members of our party—Paul as well as my aunt—I seized my opportunity. "My aunt is stuck in her stateroom tonight with her foot up on a pillow," I explained when Mr. Grimes asked. "She took a tumble in Pompeii this afternoon and sprained her ankle. I imagine Paul is with her, keeping her company."

"I expect he's giving her mouth-to-mouth resuscitation," Henry Hollis said with a twinkle in his eye.

"Henry!" cried Mrs. Hollis, shocked.

"After all, Martha, he *is* a doctor," pointed out Mr. Hollis, the very picture of wounded innocence.

"I suspect you're probably right," I said, grinning at him. "It's so important for foot injuries, you know."

"And you've been on your own all afternoon?" Mrs. Hollis asked, embarrassment on her husband's behalf giving way to concern for mine. "You poor dear! You should have joined us—Henry and me, I mean."

"That's very kind of you, Mrs. Hollis," I said, and meant it. "I would have, if I'd seen you. It would have been more fun than wandering about on my own." I turned to address Sylvia and Devos, both of whom had remained silent throughout the exchange. "What about you, Sylvia? Mr. Devos? Did either of you visit Pompeii today?"

They exchanged a quick look—a look so subtle that I wouldn't have noticed, had I not seen and heard what I had that afternoon—and Sylvia spoke first.

"We did. In fact, my experience was much like yours,

except that I became separated from my tour group. I wandered about by myself until I came upon Mr. Devos, who was sightseeing on his own."

"Then it *was* you I saw!" I exclaimed brightly. "I thought I recognized the two of you coming out of a *domus*. The House of the Tragic Poet, I believe. What a romantic name, don't you think?"

"Oh, but you should have joined us, Miss Fletcher," Devos chided me with an air of exaggerated gallantry.

"I thought about it," I lied blithely, "but you seemed so deep in conversation that I didn't want to interrupt."

Devos regarded me with narrowed eyes, and I met his suspicious gaze with a look of wide-eyed innocence.

Sylvia gave a laugh that was just a bit too hearty to be real. "What she means is that she heard us quarreling. And so we were, for this—this philistine—" She waved one manicured hand toward Devos—"insisted that the frescoes on the walls of the atrium are examples of the Pompeiian Second Style, when any fool can see they represent the later Fourth Style."

"I guess I'm one of the fools, then," Mr. Hollis confessed cheerfully, shrugging his stooped shoulders. "I wouldn't know one style from another—or either one of them from a hole in the wall."

I found the Midwestern farmer's self-deprecating humor rather charming, but Mr. Grimes came gallantly to his defense. "I'm sure you do yourself less than justice, Mr. Hollis. I suspect you would not only recognize a hole in the wall, but you'd know just how to repair that hole, too." He turned to Sylvia and beamed at her, obviously proud of her knowledge of art history. "I'm afraid you have the advantage of the rest of us, my dear."

The rest of us all murmured our agreement, but behind my smile, my head was spinning. I knew that experts, whatever their field, could get into vehement debates over details that would seem minor to anyone else—I remembered two professors in my college's English department who had been quarreling bitterly for more than a decade over the identity of Shakespeare's Dark Lady—but I didn't believe for one minute that Sylvia and Devos had been arguing over the art in the atrium. For one thing, they had been standing in the peristyle when I'd overheard them. If Sylvia had really wanted to prove a point about Pompeiian art, she surely would have dragged him back into the atrium to point out the differences in the respective styles. For another, I couldn't quite picture Sylvia as an art historian. Sylvia had brains, all right, but it seemed to me that her kind of intelligence tilted more toward the cunning than the scholarly. Clearly, she had some knowledge, but where she might have gained it, and why, I couldn't imagine.

All in all, it was a relief when I could excuse myself, claiming the need to check on my aunt—or chaperone her, as

I laughingly confided to Henry Hollis—and make my escape from the dinner table. But my ordeal was not yet ended. As I reached the dining room doors, I all but ran into Markos, camera in hand. I stammered an apology, which he accepted with a terse nod, and hurried past. At the foot of the staircase I turned back, and saw him still standing just outside the double doors leading into the dining room, regarding me with suspicion in his dark eyes.

The next day was spent at sea as our ship plowed its way eastward toward the Greek island of Mykonos. Maggie was thankful for a day to spend relaxing on deck, as it gave her some time to recuperate before our next port of call. Although my need wasn't quite so urgent, three days of sightseeing had left me glad of a day to revel in slothfulness and, judging from the number of sunbathing bodies lounging about the swimming pool, it appeared that most of our shipmates felt the same.

We staked our claim on two deck chairs, spreading beach towels over them to pad the wooden slats. Maggie picked up her thick paperback copy of James Michener's *Hawaii*, and I slipped out of my short terry cloth cover-up, prepared to christen my navy-and-white nautically-inspired one-piece with a dip in the pool.

"Oh, drat!" Maggie grumbled.

I folded my cover-up in half and draped it over the back

of the deck chair. "What's the matter?"

She squinted at the bricklike book in her hand. "I forgot to bring my reading glasses. I left them on the nightstand beside the bed—and a fat lot of good they'll do me there."

"Give me your key." I picked up the terry robe I'd just shed and shrugged my arms into its sleeves. "I'll go get them for you."

"Would you?" Maggie surrendered her stateroom key gratefully. "You're a doll, Robin."

"I know," I said with a grin, then retraced my steps back to our staterooms on Capri Deck, my open robe flapping about my legs. I fitted Maggie's key in the lock, gave it a twist, and pushed the door open.

The curtains covering the porthole were still tightly drawn—it was funny, in a way, how we still closed the curtains when we dressed even though there was nothing beyond the porthole but miles of open sea—but in the dim light I could see Maggie's closet door standing ajar, swinging back and forth with the pitch and roll of the ship. It reminded me of my self-inflicted midnight scare two nights earlier, and I turned away, shuddering. One of the dresser drawers gaped open, and a cut-glass bottle of Shalimar perfume lay on its side. I felt a pang of guilt at seeing such signs of neglect on the part of my usually tidy aunt; apparently Maggie had had a difficult time of it, hobbling about on one ankle. Although the cabin steward would soon set things to rights, that didn't excuse my failure to at least offer to help her. I picked up the bottle of perfume, sniffed for any sign of leakage, and tightened the gold cap before setting the rather top-heavy bottle upright. I slid the gaping drawer shut, then crossed the tiny cabin to the closet and pushed the door closed until I heard the latch click.

I found the reading glasses on the nightstand, exactly where my aunt had said they would be. I picked them up and tucked them into the pocket of my robe, then exited the cabin and locked the door behind me.

As I turned away, something—I didn't know exactly what—froze me in my tracks. I stood there in the passageway, trying to determine what was wrong, when I noticed a sliver of sunlight shining on the floor from beneath my own stateroom door; unlike Maggie, I had thrown open the curtains after dressing, flooding the tiny cabin with sunlight. But even as I watched, a shadow moved across the wedge of bright light, blotting it out. Something—or someone—had moved between the porthole of my stateroom and the door to the passageway. Even as my brain struggled to make sense of this discovery, I became aware of a tremor, a series of rhythmic vibrations unconnected with the deeper throbbing of the ship's engines or its bobbing motion through the waves. No, this movement was not mechanical, but human.

Someone was in my cabin. The footsteps were

approaching the door, and in a matter of seconds, the door would open, bringing me face to face with the intruder.

8

The passengers are just that distance from death.
ANACHARSIS, *Diogenes Laertius*

I glanced wildly about me, searching desperately for somewhere to hide. My aunt's stateroom was the obvious place, but my hands were shaking so badly I doubted my ability to unlock the door and shut myself inside before the door to my own cabin was opened. I was too far from the midships staircase for it to be of any use, and waiting for the elevator was obviously out of the question. Although the passageway curved slightly, echoing the line of the ship's hull, the trajectory of the curve was so slight that I would have to run almost the entire length of the ship before I would be hidden from sight. There was nowhere to hide in the passageway itself, nothing but blank doors at intervals down its long length—doors of staterooms like my own and my aunt's, along with one door marked "CREW ONLY."

I didn't hesitate. I ran to the forbidden door, threw my weight against it, and ducked inside. I found myself in a corridor that ran parallel to the one I'd just left, only here there were none of the luxuries provided for the passengers. The floor beneath my feet was not carpet but linoleum tile, and the walls were painted a utilitarian white. Only a few feet away, a narrow staircase of perforated metal treads led down into the bowels of the ship. Driven by sheer terror and a mindless need to escape whoever was about to emerge from my stateroom, I plunged headlong down the stairs, silently cursing the loud ringing of my sandals against metal. I reached the landing and took the lower corridor at a dead run, then turned a corner—and ran full tilt into a crew member. I looked up and found myself face to face with Markos, who regarded me with puzzled concern.

"I'm afraid this area is for crew only, Miss Fletcher," he said.

"S-s-someone in m-my cabin—" I stammered incoherently. "There's someone in my cabin."

He put his hands on my shoulders and gave them a reassuring squeeze. "I'm sure it's nothing to worry about. It's probably the cabin steward."

"No," I insisted, shaking my head so emphatically that my hair swung back and forth. "It isn't the steward. Maggie's bed isn't made yet."

"Maggie's bed?" echoed Markos, all at sea in more ways than one.

"I'd gone to Aunt Maggie's stateroom to fetch her

reading glasses," I said, annoyed at the necessity of wasting time making explanations. "Her bed wasn't made, and her cabin obviously hadn't been straightened."

"There you are, then," Markos said in the same tone he might have used to soothe a frightened child. "The cabin steward is probably working in your stateroom, and he'll move on to your aunt's when he's finished."

"I'm telling you, it *can't* be!" I insisted. "The steward always leaves the door open while he's cleaning, and my door was—is—closed."

"If the door was closed, how do you know someone was inside?" His dark eyes narrowed as concern gradually gave way to suspicion, and suddenly I remembered that I was dressed in nothing more than a bathing suit and robe—and realized that I was clinging to the front of his shirt as if he were my last hope of heaven.

I released my death grip on his formerly crisp uniform shirt and took a step backwards, grabbing the dangling belt of my robe and cinching it tightly about my waist. "I saw his shadow in the crack beneath the door. And I heard—or felt, rather—the vibration of footsteps."

"And do you know of any reason why someone would want to break into your stateroom?"

"I wasn't aware that thieves had to have a reason," I retorted, goaded by his obvious skepticism.

"All right, then, let's go have a look," he said.

Without waiting for an answer, he grabbed my hand and led me back up the corridor to the stairs. I wasn't sure if I had convinced him, or if he had just decided it was the only way of getting me out of the forbidden "crew only" area; I suspected it would not reflect well on him if we were discovered together there, especially given my current state of undress.

Soon we were standing outside the door from which I'd fled in such haste only moments earlier. Markos dropped my hand and put his ear to the door.

"I don't hear anything."

"Maybe he's gone by now," I suggested. "After all, I was right next door in Maggie's stateroom, and I wasn't making any effort to be quiet. He had to know someone was nearby."

Markos grinned at me. "In other words, you gave him just as much of a scare as he gave you."

Somehow I doubted it. I had never thought of myself as particularly terrifying, but the absurd picture Markos proposed—a hardened criminal fleeing in terror from a young woman in a bathing suit—was enough to drag a shaky smile from me.

"Let's take a look inside, shall we?" he suggested.

I fished my key out of the pocket of my robe and opened the door. The sun reflecting off the waves beyond the porthole cast dancing patterns of light onto the ceiling, giving the cabin such a bright and cheerful look that it was hard to believe anything frightening could have taken place here. Granted, it was a bit messy; the cabin steward hadn't yet been in, just as I'd told Markos, so the bed was still unmade—a circumstance that I should have found highly gratifying, since it proved that my intruder could not have been the steward, as Markos suggested. Instead, something about being in such close quarters with him made my cheeks burn. I suppose it had something to do with my skimpy outfit, combined with the fact that we were of necessity only a few feet from my bed, complete with rumpled sheets and a filmy nightgown thrown across the mattress.

"I'll check the bathroom," Markos said, and it seemed to me that he carefully avoided looking at the bed as he slid past me toward the tiny bath.

"Nothing there, nor in the closet," he said a moment later, returning to where I stood before the nightstand, looking inside my tiny plastic dancing trophy. "Miss Fletcher? Are you all right?"

"Yes," I said distractedly, noting that Gene's ring was still right there where I had left it. Whatever someone had been doing in my stateroom, it was clear that ordinary garden-variety theft was not the motive.

Markos glanced up at the bobbing reflections of sunlight on the ceiling. "Is it possible that this is what you saw beneath the door?"

"No," I insisted. "Someone was in this room, someone who moved between the door and the light coming in from the porthole."

"Very well, then, is anything missing?"

"No—at least, I don't think so. Still, something is different, something I can't quite put my finger—"

But even as I said the words, I realized what had changed. I'd set Pedro on the nightstand facing the door to greet me whenever I returned to the room. But now he sat staring straight ahead at the blank wall directly opposite him.

"That's it!" I exclaimed. "It's Pedro!"

"Pedro?" Markos echoed, frowning.

"I'm sorry—it's the *caga tió* I bought in Barcelona. I named him Pedro—Pooping Pedro, actually—and I had put him here, facing the door. He's been moved."

"Why would anyone break into your stateroom only to rearrange your souvenirs?" Markos asked skeptically.

"How should I know? Maybe someone was poking about looking for something worth stealing." I pulled open the top drawer of the nightstand and looked inside. There was the little trophy, with my ring inside. "But the only thing of value in the room is my ring, and it's still here."

Markos frowned down at it, a sparkling circle of gold lying in a gilt-painted plastic cup. I fully expected him to say something hateful about my being unhappily engaged, but here I misjudged him. "Perhaps it's as I said, and you frightened him away before he could do any damage. Still, I'd find a safer place to keep this if I were you. The purser can lock it up for you, if you'd like."

I agreed, and he led me, pale and subdued, to the purser's desk on Europa Deck, where I filled out a few forms and surrendered my ring. By the time I returned to Maggie, twenty minutes had past since I'd set out in search of her reading glasses.

"*There* you are!" she exclaimed, setting aside the book she'd been squinting at. "I was beginning to wonder if I should send out a search party. Were they not on my nightstand?"

So much had happened since I'd left her that it took me a moment to remember what "they" were. "Oh, your reading glasses!" I exclaimed, digging them out of my pocket. "Yes, they were just where you said they'd be. I'm sorry it took me so long. I, er, I ran into Markos," I said with perfect truth. Somehow I couldn't quite bring myself to burden my aunt by telling her about my scare. I had absolutely no proof, beyond Pedro's apparently moving about on his stubby wooden legs (which in retrospect I was forced to admit *might* have been my own unconscious doing), and it seemed to me that between an ankle injury and a budding romance, Maggie had quite enough to worry about. I removed my robe for the second time and finally took my long-delayed dip in the pool—from which I quickly emerged, shivering and with chattering teeth.

"Brrr!" I exclaimed, snatching up my towel. "It's c-c-cold!"

"It's the movement of the ship," Maggie said without looking up from her book. I'd noticed she had shown no interest in taking to the water, and now I knew why. "The ship is moving at thirty knots, so it's like swimming in a thirty-five-mile-per-hour wind."

"*Now* you tell me," I grumbled, blotting myself dry before stretching out on my deck chair and picking up the book I'd bought for the trip. I'd paid almost five dollars for the new hardcover release by Georgette Heyer, but I couldn't honestly say I was enjoying *A Civil Contract*. I had no patience with the heroine, who was so desperately in love with the hero that she was willing to marry him knowing quite well that he had no real interest in her apart from her dowry. Where was her pride? And if a little voice whispered, "Where is yours?"—well, it was nothing a piña colada or two wouldn't drown out.

The rest of the day passed uneventfully, which made a welcome change after the hectic pace of the last few days, to say nothing of the scare of that morning. The feeling of pleasant slothfulness continued into dinner, where even Sylvia Duprée yielded to the general lassitude by appearing at the table in a relatively casual halter dress of gaily striped cotton that left her tanned shoulders bare. After dinner, I tactfully left Maggie and Paul alone at a piano bar, listening to love songs from the war years and furtively holding hands beneath the table—as if I didn't know, I thought, smiling. I wandered up to the Promenade Deck and leaned against the rail, savoring the feel of the breeze on the back of my neck, tugging my hair loose from its chignon and pressing the full skirts of my pink satin dress against my legs. The sun had set, turning the sky from purple to black, and somewhere in the distance a light blinked—on and off, on and off.

"It's a beautiful night, isn't it, Miss Fletcher?"

Recognizing the slightly accented English, I turned and saw Markos in his dress uniform, the pristine white fabric a stark contrast to the velvety black of the night sky beyond his shoulder. "Yes, it is," I agreed.

"I trust you've had no more disturbances?"

"No." I stared fixedly down at my hands on the deck rail, reluctant to revisit the terror of that morning. I still wasn't sure he believed me—and who could blame him for doubting? There had been no physical proof of an intruder, unless one counted a slight change in the position of a painted log. On the contrary, the fact that my engagement ring had been undisturbed would tend to prove the opposite. Desperate to change the subject, I gestured toward the blinking light in the distance. "What is it? The light, I mean."

"It's a lighthouse. Although I, being Greek, prefer to call it a *pharos*," he added with a flash of white teeth. "The Greek islands are dotted with them."

Sure enough, as our ship left the blinking light in its wake, another one became just visible far ahead.

"How many are there?" I asked.

"Islands, or lighthouses?"

I shrugged. "Either one."

"How many lighthouses, I couldn't begin to guess. Greek islands, somewhere between twelve hundred and six thousand, depending on how large you require a pile of volcanic rock to be before you consider it worthy of the name."

"*Twelve hundred?*" I echoed. "Even the smallest figure staggers the imagination."

"But only about two hundred are inhabited," he amended quickly, almost apologetically, as if he were personally responsible for the lack of population distribution.

"Only two hundred?" I scoffed playfully. "Is *that* all?"

He grinned, but any retort he might have made was suspended when a scream sounded from somewhere aft. Markos and I exchanged bewildered looks for a fraction of a second, then he grabbed me by the wrist and took the Promenade Deck at a run. By the time we reached the stern, a crowd had gathered, many of them leaning over the rail to look down into the dark sea below. The great engines juddered to a stop, and phosphorescent bubbles rose to the surface from the propellers beneath the waves as we lolled aimlessly on top of the water. In the sudden stillness, I could hear murmurs of "man overboard" from my fellow passengers.

Markos tapped the shoulder of a man standing nearby. "What happened?"

"I don't know," he said, glancing away from the railing just long enough to answer. "They say someone fell overboard from one of the decks above."

"Who could fall over these?" I asked, slapping the deck railing with the flat of my hand. "Surely they're high enough to prevent such a thing."

"You would think so," Markos said thoughtfully. "But you'd be surprised how many people have too much to drink and decide it would be fun to climb over the railing."

By this time a life preserver had been thrown from a deck somewhere far below us and now bobbed crazily on the surface of the water, a pale ring of white against the black of the sea. I couldn't help noticing that no desperate hands reached up from the depths to grab it. Apparently the would-be rescuers reached the same conclusion, for within minutes a door was opened far below. Bright lights spilled from the hatchway, turning the black water to an eerie green. Unseen hands reeled in the useless life preserver, and a few minutes later two men in scuba gear entered the water with a splash.

Even though they must have had a very good idea where to look, fully half an hour passed before they returned to the ship, bearing between them what appeared at first glance to be a collection of sodden rags. But I was not deceived. I recognized the gaily striped fabric at once, as well as the long dark hair that streamed with water.

It was Sylvia Duprée, and even from this distance I could tell she was dead.

9

Things are not always what they seem.
PHAEDRUS, *Fables*

A s the body that had once been Sylvia Duprée was brought back on board along with her rescuers—her recoverers, rather, since no hope of rescue appeared possible—the crowd began to disperse, all murmuring speculations as to what had happened and how. Markos grabbed me by the arm and dragged me backwards, away from the railing and the gruesome sight below. "It's time you and I had a little talk, Miss Fletcher."

Mutely, I allowed him to lead me to the nightclub aft, where the lively music of a jazz combo made a bizarre contrast to the somber scene a few decks below. Markos steered me to a small table in a dark corner, plopped me down somewhat roughly onto a spindle-legged chair with a padded seat, and sat down opposite me.

"Well, Miss Fletcher?" he prompted, when I seemed disinclined to talk.

" 'Well,' what, Markos?"

He leaned across the table, and although his voice was pitched softly enough to prevent its being heard over the music, I wasn't fool enough to mistake his lack of volume for absence of intensity. "Don't play games with me! You know something you're not telling. You look like you've just seen a ghost."

I turned to look at my reflection in the big picture window stretching across the stern of the ship. In the daytime, it would give a lovely view over the water, but now the darkness beyond turned the glass into an enormous mirror, a mirror that reflected a terrified girl with eyes too big for her white, strained face.

"Isn't it time to admit that you're in over your head?" he asked a bit more gently.

"I don't know what you're talking about!" My voice rose, and Markos put his hand over mine and gave it a warning squeeze.

"It's all right, Miss Fletcher—"

"How can it be all right?" I interrupted, lowering my voice nonetheless. "A woman is dead! Two days ago I was wishing she would go away and leave us alone, and now—" I broke off, pressing a hand to my eyes as if I could somehow erase the sight of Sylvia Duprée's drowned body.

"I'll do my best to see you safe if you'll tell me everything you know about Konstantin Devos."

143

"Devos? How can I tell you anything? I never saw the man until that first night out of Barcelona, when I saw him throwing his Pedro overboard." I considered what I'd just said, and choked back a giggle. "Throwing his Pedro overboard. That sounds a little bit dirty, doesn't it?"

It was no use. I began to giggle uncontrollably. Markos gave me an exasperated look and flagged down a waiter. "Bring me an ouzo." He glanced at me again. "On second thought, better make it a double."

He was silent until the waiter returned, apparently giving up as a lost cause any thought of getting coherent speech out of me without alcoholic stimulant. After the glass was set down before him and the waiter took himself off, Markos pushed it across the table to me. "Drink," he ordered, "but go slowly. It's stronger than it seems."

I took a gulp, and choked. The ouzo was cold—*very* cold—and yet it burned as it went down. It had none of the fruity flavors of this morning's piña colada or yesterday's limoncello, but the taste was not unpleasant. In fact, it reminded me of something—something I hadn't tasted in a long time.

"Jelly beans," I announced, holding the glass up to the light and peering into the clear liquid. "It tastes like black jelly beans. Or it would, if black jelly beans scorched your throat on their way down."

"It's the anise flavoring," Markos said, taking the glass

from my shaky hand and returning it to the table before I could spill it. "Now, back to the subject at hand. Who is, or was, Pedro?"

"Not a who, but a what." I said, resisting the urge to start giggling again. "Don't you remember? I told you." I reminded him of the *caga tió* I'd bought in Barcelona, and then described to him the strange fate of Mr. Devos's identical souvenir.

"Interesting," he said when I'd finished. "What else do you know about Konstantin Devos?"

I frowned at him. "Shouldn't you be asking me what I know about Sylvia Duprée? After all, she's the one who's dead."

"Very well, then," he said with exaggerated patience, "what *do* you know about Sylvia Duprée?"

" 'Very well, then,' " I mimicked. "I didn't know anyone talked like that outside of novels. Where did you learn your English?"

"Miss Fletcher—" he said, sounding considerably less patient this time.

"All right, all right! I know Sylvia—Miss Duprée, that is—made a pest of herself in Rome, sticking to Aunt Maggie like glue. I thought she was making a play for Paul, but apparently I was wrong. Do you suppose she was just lonely, what with Mr. Grimes being ill and unable to accompany her?"

"I haven't the faintest idea. Anything else?"

"Only that she was rude to the Hollises that first night at dinner, which I find very hard to forgive, because they're such sweet people! And that at Pompeii, she got into a rather heated argument with—oh!"

"With Konstantin Devos," Markos finished my sentence. There was also the fact that my name had come up in that conversation, but Markos seemed to be unaware of this circumstance, and some instinct told me not to divulge the information.

"Do you think—" I glanced around to make sure no one was listening, then lowered my voice to a conspiratorial whisper. "Do you think Mr. Devos pushed her overboard?"

"I couldn't begin to guess," Markos said tonelessly. "What do you think?"

"How should I know?" I asked rather wildly. "I know nothing about the man! I never laid eyes on him until four days ago."

"And yet you were sitting next to him at dinner and dancing with him less than twenty-four hours later," he pointed out.

"That doesn't prove anything!" I said, insulted by the suggestion that I had something to hide. "He was assigned to the same table, and there happened to be an empty seat next to me. Besides, I was dancing with you, too, if you'll recall. That doesn't mean there's any deep, dark history between the two of us."

"Point taken," he conceded. "Still, the two of you were pretty chummy in Pisa, if your photographs are anything to judge by."

The ouzo must have gone some way toward settling my frayed nerves, for I instantly recognized the contradiction in this statement. "I thought you said my photos hadn't yet been developed."

"I never said any such thing. You said you supposed they weren't yet ready, and I said nothing to contradict you."

"If they've been developed, then I want them back," I demanded. "What possible reason do you have for keeping them from me?"

"I've fallen desperately in love with you, and can't bear to part with them," Markos said, and although he spoke sarcastically, it seemed to me that he flushed slightly beneath his tan.

"Why, sir, this is so sudden!" I exclaimed, no doubt influenced by the Regency novel I'd been reading that afternoon. I felt another fit of giggles welling up, so I picked up my glass and took another sip. "But really, Markos, I don't know what you're talking about. I spent the whole day with Maggie and Paul. I never saw Mr. Devos at all."

Markos regarded me skeptically. "I'm sorry to disagree, but if, as your English saying goes, a picture is worth a million words—"

"A thousand."

"Very well, a thousand—then nine hundred and ninety-nine of them say you are lying."

"Prove it," I said, setting my glass down with a *clink*.

"I beg your pardon?"

"You say my pictures show me with Mr. Devos; I say I'll have to see it to believe it. So show me."

Markos hesitated only a moment. "All right. Let's go." He pushed back his chair and stood up, then fumbled in his wallet for the money to cover my drink.

"Never mind," I said. "I can have it charged to my stateroom."

"No, I insist." He'd found what he needed, and tossed a few coins onto the table, then took me by the elbow and practically frog-marched me to the photography shop on Europa Deck. Ignoring the "closed" sign, he opened the door, switched on the light, and pushed me inside, then closed the door behind us. I looked around, and found myself in a tiny stock room with a metal desk bolted to the floor in one rear corner. Shelves held cameras and supplies—film, flashbulbs, and batteries—while open bins were stuffed with fat envelopes of developed photos waiting to be picked up by passengers. A door emblazoned with signs reading "DO NOT OPEN" in several languages obviously led to the darkroom. Markos pulled open one of the desk drawers and removed an envelope of photos, one that had clearly been set apart from the others. He pulled the photographs from the envelope and began flipping through them. I recognized my photos at once: the massive cathedral of Florence, the Ponte Vecchio, Michelangelo's *David*, Pisa's Field of Miracles with its Leaning Tower—

The Leaning Tower. Markos slapped one of the photos down on the desk, but I knew even without looking what I would see. Still, I was taken aback by the scene captured in that glossy three-and-a-half-inch square. There I stood in front of the famous bell tower, turned slightly to my right with the toes of my left foot pointed toward the camera just as I'd been taught as a twelve-year-old at charm school, smiling at Maggie in eager anticipation of mailing the photo to Gene. And there beside me was Konstantin Devos, scowling slightly at the camera as if he resented my turning away from him even for the short time it took for my aunt to take the photo.

"I remember now," I said slowly. "He walked past just as Maggie snapped the photo. She was rather annoyed about it, and insisted on taking another shot. See? There it is—the very next picture. In fact, if you'll notice, Mr. Devos isn't in any of the others, which ought to be proof enough that he and I weren't—"

Suddenly I remembered something Markos had said earlier, something that hadn't made sense at the time. "What did you mean, up there on the Promenade Deck?" I asked, my eyes narrowing in suspicion. "Something about trying to see me safe?"

"Nothing, really," Markos said in an off-hand manner that didn't fool me for a moment. "The shock of Miss Duprée's death, you know—I was just, what do you say, running off at the mouth. Saying whatever came into my head."

Somehow I doubted Markos had ever said a thoughtless word in his life. "You're not really a ship's photographer, are you?"

"Of course I am!" exclaimed Markos, the picture of maligned innocence. He waved one hand in a gesture that took in all the minutiae of photography that surrounded us. "What else would I be doing here?"

"Oh, I know you've been making a nuisance of yourself snapping photos of unsuspecting passengers every time we turn around. But that's not really who you are, is it?"

"Isn't it?" he challenged. "Who do you think I am, then?"

"I don't know," I confessed, regarding him speculatively. "Are you a policeman? A detective, I mean?"

"No!" he said so indignantly that I was forced to concede the point.

"Interpol, maybe?"

"Good God, no! Where do you get these ideas?"

"Whoever you are," I continued doggedly, "you think

something fishy is going on—something illegal, I mean," I amended quickly, lest he claim ignorance of American colloquialisms in order to avoid questions he didn't care to answer, "—and you think I'm involved in it."

"On the contrary, Miss Fletcher," he said, flipping idly through the photos, "I *know* you are involved in it, intentionally or not."

"But how can I be, when I don't even know—" I broke off as the significance of his words dawned. "You *did* believe there was someone in my cabin earlier today, after all!"

Markos nodded. "I thought it quite possible."

Any gratification I might have felt was short-lived. "You might have told me so, instead of treating me like a hysterical ninny who was scared of her own shadow!"

"If I did that, Miss Fletcher, I am extremely sorry. I did not want to give you more of a fright than you had already had," he said, gazing at me with such a mournful expression in his dark eyes that I felt *I* ought to be begging *his* pardon, instead of the other way around.

I ruthlessly squashed the feeling. "If I'm in some kind of danger, don't you think I have a right to know?"

Markos hesitated, obviously choosing his next words with care. "I don't know that you are in any sort of personal danger, Miss Fletcher."

"Of course not," I said sweetly. "And Sylvia Duprée

just decided to practice her high-dive off the end of the ship."

"We don't know that Miss Duprée's death has anything to do with—with this other thing."

"We don't know that it doesn't, either. Anyway, 'knowledge is power,' isn't it?"

He sighed. "In this case, Miss Fletcher, knowledge might well be fatal. In other words, the less you know about this business, the better." I was still struggling to grasp this observation when he shocked me with another, less frightening, perhaps, but no less disturbing, albeit on a personal level. "Tomorrow morning we will dock at Mykonos. I would be very honored if you will allow me to show you something of my homeland."

I looked up at him, and studied his face. There was no hint of suspicion or mockery, just the admiring gaze of a man interested in a woman, which looks the same all over the world. I realized I was holding my breath, and forced myself to exhale slowly and evenly.

"All right," I said. "I would like that very much."

It was with a somewhat lighter heart that I returned to my stateroom. Sylvia Duprée was still dead, it was true, but her death might well have been an accident that had nothing to do with Devos at all; certainly it had nothing to do with me, although I did feel sorry for her, and for Mr. Grimes, left all alone in his luxurious suite. Surely if there were anything suspicious about it, Markos (who, I was firmly convinced, was more than a ship's photographer, however much he might try to deny it) wouldn't choose such a time to go haring off to a romantic Greek island with a girl. And if some instinct suggested that that was exactly why he'd wanted to keep a close eye on me, well, he was the one who would have egg on his face when he realized I proved to be nothing but an innocent bystander, just as I'd insisted all along.

After exchanging my pink dress for my nightgown, I crawled into bed, sat up against the pillows, and looked through the photos I'd taken in Florence. Markos had surrendered them to me as proof that I was no longer under suspicion, and had even insisted on paying for their development himself by way of apology. I smiled as I came to a photo Paul had taken of Maggie and me standing in front of the Leaning Tower. In the background over my aunt's shoulder, a young man, probably a college student on spring break, stretched out his hands while a companion took his picture; the end result, I deduced, would make it appear that he was trying to push the tower back to an upright position. Meanwhile, over my own shoulder—

I stretched out a hand to switch on the nightstand lamp for a closer look. Yes, in the left middle ground behind me was Konstantin Devos. He was turned slightly away from the camera, but I recognized him by the same shirt he'd been wearing in the other photo, the one he'd walked into. In this shot, he appeared to be shaking hands with another man. No, on closer inspection he wasn't shaking the man's hand, but giving him—or perhaps receiving from him—a rectangular box slightly larger than the shoe boxes Sylvia and I had brought back from Rome.

Markos might claim that I was better off remaining in ignorance, but I suspected he would not believe the same rule applied to himself. Resolving to show him the photo in the morning during our outing on Mykonos, I tucked it into my bag and turned off the lights.

The events of what was supposed to have been a relaxing day at sea had taken their toll, and I collapsed onto the pillow, exhausted and ready to allow sleep to claim me. But as darkness enveloped the cabin, all the horror of Sylvia Duprée's death came rushing back to my mind, and it was a long time before I finally fell into a restless sleep, to dream of tanned masculine hands shoving me over the ship's railing into Homer's wine-dark sea.

10

Kiss me, and be quiet.
LADY MARY WORTLEY MONTAGU,
A Summary of Lord Lyttelton's Advice

I woke abruptly to find myself safe in my own stateroom, with brilliant sunlight spilling through the small gap between the curtains. The ship's engines were silent, and I realized we were no longer moving. The nightmares of the previous night had all been banished by the brilliant light of day, and we had arrived at the Greek island of Mykonos. I threw back the covers, hurried to the porthole, and flung back the curtain. The water was as blue as ever, while on land, a cluster of whitewashed buildings hugged the shoreline, blinding in the sun. To their right, half a dozen stout thatch-roofed windmills stretched bare spokes against the sky—the famous windmills of Mykonos. Farther inland, a few widely spaced buildings straggled up the hill, their square shapes and whitewashed walls giving them the appearance of a handful of dice rolled by a giant hand.

"Zeus's, I suppose," I told Pedro as I turned back into

the room and pulled a blue and white seersucker sundress from its hanger in the closet. "After all, this is his territory."

Fraternization between crew and passengers, although not expressly forbidden, was not encouraged—at least not beyond the crewmen's availability as extra dance partners— so Markos and I had agreed not to meet on the ship; instead, he had promised to wait for me ashore. He proved to be as good as his word, standing at the foot of the gangplank casually dressed in dun-colored trousers and a white cotton sport shirt that made the most of his bronzed skin and dark hair.

"Good morning," he called cheerfully. "I hope you slept well."

I shuddered at the wisps of nightmare that lingered in my mind. "About as well as can be expected." I glanced back at the ship, which rivaled the white buildings in its brilliance. It was hard to believe that somewhere in a cool, dark hold deep within the ship, lay Sylvia's body. Mykonos was too small to boast an airport, so the body would remain aboard until we reached Istanbul. Or so the rumors at breakfast had said. It was amazing how quickly word got around in the close confines of the ship.

"Don't think about it," Markos said, reading my thoughts with very little difficulty. "There's nothing you can do, so at least for today, put it out of your mind and enjoy your visit to Mykonos."

I gave him a feeble smile. "Words to live by," I said, although privately I thought they were probably easier to say than to do.

"I suppose you want to see the windmills first," he said. "Everyone does."

I agreed to this plan, and allowed him to lead the way. We passed along the town's waterfront, and then through a maze of narrow flagstone-paved streets flanked with whitewashed walls that blocked any hint of a breeze. I took off my wide-brimmed hat and fanned my face with it for a moment before plunking it back on my head.

"Someone could get lost here and never be seen again," I said, puffing slightly from the climb as we moved inland.

"That was the idea, at least so I have been told," Markos said. He took my hand to steer me through a bottleneck formed by a narrow staircase taking up one side of the street and a host of tourists heading downhill toward the sea from the other direction. Once the obstacle was cleared, he made no move to release my hand, and I didn't push the issue.

"I suppose the residents want tourists to get lost here until they've spent all their money," I remarked, pausing to glance through a wide storefront window at the offerings within. The shop signs were literally Greek to me; although I recognized certain letters from the fraternity houses at my alma mater, connecting them into recognizable words was beyond me.

"Very likely," Markos agreed. "But these buildings are much older than the tourist trade. It is said they are built that way to discourage invaders. Not that it has always been successful," he added.

At last the maze decanted us onto the western side of the island and the hillside where the windmills stood sentry. Now that we were no longer surrounded by the suffocating walls, the stiff sea breeze tugged at my hat, making it easy to see why this particular location had been chosen for harnessing the power of the wind.

"Lovely!" I fished my camera from my straw bag and trained its viewfinder on the scene. "What do they do, exactly?"

"These days, they pose for tourists' photos," Markos said, grinning broadly. "Before that, they ground wheat and barley. There were once many more of them on the island, but only about a dozen remain—half of them here on this one spot."

"I've never thought of Greece having windmills," I confessed. "I'd always thought they were a Dutch thing."

"These happen to be Venetian."

"Okay, now I'm *really* confused," I said. "I thought Venice was all about canals."

"Oh, they are, as you will see at the end of the cruise, but Mykonos was conquered by the Venetians in the Middle Ages. Venice was the gateway between Europe and Asia in those days, and Mykonos was a great trade center. The Venetians set up windmills in the sixteenth century to use the sea wind in order to keep their ships supplied with—" Here his excellent English failed him. "What do you call it, the dry bread sailors used to eat?"

What a naval boyfriend hadn't taught me about sailing, *The Rime of the Ancient Mariner* had. "Hardtack," I said.

"Yes, that is it. Hardtack," he echoed, as if committing the term to memory. He might have saved himself the trouble, as it was unlikely to come up in conversation again.

As we turned away from the windmills, Markos pointed toward a small spit of land just north of where we stood. Here the ubiquitous whitewashed shops were built right up against the sea, with their gaily colored balconies hanging out over the water.

"This section is called Little Venice," he said.

I cocked a speculative eyebrow at him. "The conquering Venetians again?"

He shook his head. "No, these are newer—built in the eighteenth century, when Mykonos was part of the Ottoman Empire. Most are restaurants or nightclubs now, but they were originally fisherman's cottages—although the fact that they have cellar doors opening directly over the sea suggests that fish were not the only thing being caught."

"Pirates, you mean?" I exclaimed delightedly.

"Oh, yes. The Greeks invented piracy thousands of

years before Long John Silver ever stumped about the deck on his peg leg."

"*Where* did you learn your English?" I demanded, not for the first time.

He merely laughed. "Come, there is something I wish to show you."

He led the way to a paved square dominated by the bust of a woman at its center.

"Robin Fletcher, I should like you to meet *Kyria* Manto Mavrogenous." He gave the statue an exaggerated bow, and I followed suit with my best charm school curtsey. "*Kyria* Mavrogenous is a great heroine in Greece. She was a wealthy heiress who spent her entire fortune to free her country—and mine—from the Turks, even selling her jewelry to outfit a fleet of battleships. Sadly, she died in poverty, but she is much revered today, as you can see. The English poet, Lord Byron, is also highly esteemed as a hero of the Greek cause."

Lord Byron was an old acquaintance from my college days. "He was highly esteemed by all the English ladies of his day, too," I told him. "Especially Lady Caroline Lamb, who called him 'mad, bad, and dangerous to know.' Of course, that didn't stop her from having a passionate affair with him, or being obsessed with him for the rest of her life, so that criticism should be taken with a very large grain of salt."

"Unless she found dangerous men attractive," Markos pointed out, giving me a speculative look. "I understand some women do."

My hackles rose. "If you still think there's something going on between me and Devos—"

"No, no," he assured me hastily. "I was quite wrong in that regard, I freely admit it. No, you seem to be the type who would prefer a safe man to a dangerous one."

I nodded emphatically. "Exactly!"

"But this, too, may not be a good thing. Sometimes what appears to be safety is actually stagnation."

My eyes narrowed in suspicion. "Have you been talking to my aunt?"

"No," he said, laughing. "Should I?"

"No." Impatient to change a subject that had become uncomfortably personal, I asked a bit too eagerly, "What should we see next?"

"Not what; who. There is someone I want you to meet."

We plunged back into the labyrinthine white-walled streets—whether they were the same ones we'd passed through before, or entirely different ones, I couldn't tell—and at last Markos stopped to open a tiny gate at the foot of a narrow whitewashed stone staircase climbing up the outside of the building.

"Up here," he said, pressing himself against the wall in order to let me pass. "But watch your step; the stairs are a bit uneven. We've tried to persuade her to move to a ground-level flat, but she won't be budged."

This rather cryptic observation was explained a short time later, when we reached the top of the stairs. Markos knocked on the brightly painted blue door, which was opened by an elderly woman in a long and rather shapeless black dress. Upon recognizing her visitor, she launched into a flood of impassioned Greek. I would have thought she was angry with him, had it not been for the fact that her wiry arms circled his neck with the strength of a vise, and she interrupted herself several times to plant a loud, smacking kiss on his tan cheek.

He finally extricated himself, saying in English, "But you must not ignore your other guest, *YiaYia*. I have brought someone to meet you. This is *Despoinis* Robin Fletcher. Robin, *Kyria* Odessa Rondo—my grandmother."

Did they shake hands in Greece? I wasn't sure, but I decided it was better to make the gesture rather than insulting her through ignorance. "How do you do?"

She took my hand in her own gnarled one, and regarded me with black shoe-button eyes. "You are English?"

She was not nearly as fluent as her grandson, but her English probably compared favorably to my own schoolgirl French, to say nothing of my nonexistent Greek. "I'm an American."

She gave a little grunt that might have indicated

anything from grudging acceptance to outright scorn, but at least she didn't shut the door in my face. "Come, sit!" she urged, flapping her hands in the direction of the small, dimly lit parlor.

I followed Markos's example, and sat down beside him on a worn sofa. "Robin is a passenger on the cruise ship *Oceanus*," he explained.

"She is not traveling alone!" The elderly woman clearly had no opinion of the sort of female who would undertake such a journey on her own, so I was glad to be able to reassure her on this point.

"No, I'm accompanying my aunt. She is a widow," I added by way of explanation.

She bent her sharp black gaze upon me once again, and nodded in approval. "This is good. You are a good niece."

"Thank you. I hope I am a good niece, for she is a very good aunt."

This comment delighted her, and her laughter was far out of proportion to what the remark warranted; apparently my lack of Greekness was forgiven. "You did well to bring her to me, Markias. It is past time you find a good girl and settle down to a life of—a life of—" Her broken English failed her.

"Safety," I said demurely.

"I think 'domesticity' is the word you want, *YiaYia*," Markos said, flushing. "But it isn't like that. I am merely showing Robin the sights of Mykonos. She already has a boyfriend."

My face flushed. Markos had made no mention of the fact that I was no longer wearing my ring, other than suggesting I leave it with the purser for safekeeping. And yet, he'd said I had a boyfriend, not a fiancé. Did he think I'd broken my engagement? Should I correct that assumption? In any case, *Kyria* Rondo gave me little time to ponder the question.

"Boyfriend!" She gave a snort of derision. "A girl may have a hundred boyfriends, but these are nothing to one husband." She bent that sharp black gaze upon me again. "So, you are seeing the sights? You have seen the windmills, yes?"

"Oh yes," I said, welcoming the change of subject. Alas, *Kyria* Rondo wasn't finished with us yet.

"When I was a girl, I would take the barley from my father's farm to be ground. My father, he would send me to the mill because I could get a good price. I was very beautiful in those days, and the men at the mill liked to look at me."

I could readily believe it. Her face might be lined with wrinkles, but she possessed the kind of bone structure that, combined with those dark eyes, must have made her a stunning beauty in her youth.

"Markias, now, he is the one to show you all the sights.

He has always liked the, what do you call it, the old things?"

"Antiquities?" I suggested.

"Yes, the antiquities." She gave me an approving look. "It is good to know that he can appreciate young things, too."

Markos leaped up from the sofa, looking more flustered than I'd ever seen him. If I hadn't liked his grandmother already, that fact alone would have won me over. "I think we'd better be going, *YiaYia*," he said. "We have other things to see before Robin must return to the ship."

I said goodbye to *Kyria* Rondo, politely deflecting her invitation to come see her again, but all the while my brain was spinning. Markos had said I must return to the ship, but he'd made no mention of the fact that he worked on board the *Oceanus*. Clearly, his grandmother didn't know—and he didn't mean for her to know. Why not? Granted, "my grandson, the ship's photographer" didn't have quite the same cachet as "my grandson, the doctor" or "my grandson, the lawyer," but surely it was nothing to be ashamed of.

"Are you hungry?" Markos asked, once we had descended the stairs into the street. "I know a little place where we can get a good lunch without having to fight the tourists for a table."

I agreed to this, and after we were served platters of moussaka and a green salad with Kalamata olives and feta cheese, I remarked on the puzzle. "Your grandmother doesn't know you're working on the *Oceanus*."

"No. It's not that I'm ashamed of my job onboard the ship," he added hastily, "but *YiaYia* would not understand."

"Why not? She seemed pretty sharp to me."

He grinned at that. "Oh, she is—sometimes terrifyingly so. But I studied something else, and she wouldn't understand why I'm not doing that."

"The 'old things,' " I said, hazarding a guess.

He surprised me by admitting to it. "Yes. When I was about ten years old, a well was being dug on my family's farm—"

"Would this be the same farm where the barley was grown that your beautiful young grandmother once took to be milled?"

"The very same," he said, smiling. "They turned up archaeological remains from the period of Roman occupation—nothing of great value in itself, but taken all together, of sufficient importance for the state to take an interest. In Greece, you see, antiquities discovered on private property belong to the nation, as they are part of our shared history."

"Bad luck for you and your family," I remarked, not without sympathy.

"Oh, but those who own the land on which they were found are compensated by the state. Whether that compensation truly represents what the discovery might be worth—

at auction, for instance, or on the black market—is a matter of debate, of course, but in my family's case it was enough to fund my education in a manner my parents could not have provided on their own."

"I should think a ten-year-old boy would be over the moon," I said. "Like discovering buried treasure practically in his own back yard."

"Exactly! I am told I made a nuisance of myself while the dig was in progress, but I also found my calling. When I went off to university—"

" 'Off' where?" I interrupted.

His eyes slid away from mine. "I went to study in England. So many of the finest Greek antiquities have ended up in the British Museum that it seemed only natural—"

"In England," I echoed, my eyes narrowing in suspicion. "Did you by any chance attend Oxford?"

"Oxford is not the only university in England," he pointed out.

I was not so easily put off. "Oxford. Yes or no?"

"Well—yes."

"Do you mean to tell me you have a degree in archaeology from Oxford," I demanded, "and yet you spend your days taking photos of tourists on a cruise ship?"

"Not *all* my days," he pointed out defensively. "Today I'm showing you about Mykonos."

"No wonder you don't want your grandmother to know

how you're making a living. It would break her heart, seeing that expensive education going to waste."

"Jobs in archaeology are hard to come by," he protested feebly.

"Still, you could try. Maybe you should start with the British Museum. If they have as many Greek artifacts as you say, they might be able to use a native—"

"So I should go to work for the country who stole my own country's heritage?" he scoffed. "I think not."

"Well, it's good to know you're not bitter."

He was silent for a long moment before answering. "It is true that Greece did not always recognize the value of her own cultural heritage," he said at last. "I suppose we must be grateful, in a way, that the British have preserved what might otherwise have been destroyed. But now that Greece— indeed, the whole world—knows the importance of preserving one's cultural heritage, I think the artifacts should be returned to their rightful place, and their rightful owners."

"And you'll never bring that change about by spending your days snapping photos of happy people in Hawaiian shirts," I said bluntly.

"Shall we reach an agreement, Miss Fletcher?" he suggested, stretching his hand across the table toward me. "If you'll refrain from telling me how to live my life, I'll resist the temptation to tell you how to live yours."

I thought of my engagement ring lying in my stateroom

all but forgotten, and decided I wasn't the best person to be giving anyone else advice. "I suppose I'd better accept, if I'm to avoid becoming 'Miss Fletcher' again," I conceded, and took his proffered hand.

We shook on the matter, and left the restaurant in a state of rather cautious détente.

The rest of the afternoon passed in a pleasant blur of sightseeing. We toured the Archaeological Museum of Mykonos, where I was no longer surprised at the depth of Markos's knowledge, and he no longer felt the need to conceal it. We strolled along the waterfront, eventually taking off our shoes and wading along the pebble-strewn beach. Somehow it seemed only natural that sunset should find us at Little Venice, where we leaned against the railing of one of the balconies overhanging the water and watched the sun turning the whitewashed buildings to gold as it slipped below the horizon.

"There is an old tradition here on Mykonos," he remarked. "They say it is good luck to kiss just as the sun disappears into the waves."

I was suddenly breathless, and my heart pounded in a way that had nothing to do with the fact that I'd been hiking all over a hilly island. "I would be a fool to turn down any good luck on offer," I said, my voice hardly above a whisper.

"Very wise," murmured Markos, lowering his head to

mine. "I believe one should not ignore whatever opportunities Fate offers."

I would have agreed with this very admirable sentiment, but then his lips met mine, and I ceased to think at all.

At last we drew apart, and I looked up at him, trying to read his expression in the rapidly darkening dusk. "That's not really an 'old tradition,' is it?"

"No. Do you mind?"

"No," I said, and we kissed again.

11

Cock a doodle doo!
My dame has lost her shoe;
My master's lost his fiddle stick
And knows not what to do.
ANONYMOUS, *Cock a Doodle Doo*

It's a funny thing about kissing. Some girls hear bells ring; others recall choirs of angels singing. I gradually became aware of a long, low blast like the distant sound of—

"The ship's horn!" Markos tore his lips from mine. "They're sounding the 'all aboard'!"

He grabbed my hand and we ran out of the restaurant, dodging tables and lovestruck couples, then sprinted up the road that led along the waterfront, darting in and out between tourists, fishermen, and small Greek children.

All to no avail. By the time we reached the berth where the ship had docked, the gangway had been withdrawn, and a stout little tugboat was pushing our own much larger vessel out to sea.

"What do we do now?" I puffed, out of breath from our futile race.

He grinned at me. "Are you up for an adventure?"

"That all depends," I said, but he had already turned away, calling in Greek to a man working aboard a small motorboat, and motioning toward the departing *Oceanus*.

"*Kalá!*" Markos pronounced at the end of their brief exchange. "Climb aboard, Robin."

He took my elbow to help me down into the boat, but I wasn't at all sure I wanted to go. "Surely we're not following the ship all the way to Istanbul in that!"

"Of course not!"

"Then what—?"

"Will you please get in? We haven't time to waste."

I did as I was told, but no sooner had I settled myself on a cracked vinyl seat covered with a ratty-looking towel than I returned to my questioning. "What, exactly, are we going to do?"

"We're going to catch the ship."

"Oh, and I suppose the captain will be delighted to stop for us."

"No. We'll have to climb up the side."

"*What?*" I spun toward him so fast I almost fell off my seat.

"They won't stop, but they'll throw down a ladder for us."

"Markos, I—I can't!"

"Of course you can," he said bracingly. "Only think

172

what a tale you'll have to tell when you get back home."

Strangely enough, it was the prospect of recounting the adventure to Gene that gave me courage. Granted, Gene wasn't at home waiting to hear about my adventures; no, he was somewhere underwater on a submarine, maybe even— jarring thought!—beneath this same sea, where I'd just been gazing out over the water and kissing another man. In its own way, climbing up the side of a moving ship was less daunting than the prospect of explaining my lapse, either to Gene or to myself.

The tugboat had finished its task by this time and was returning to port, but the *Oceanus* had not yet reached her top speed. As we approached, Markos stood up in the boat, cupped his hands around his mouth and bellowed at the top of his voice, "Ahoy! Ahoy there, *Oceanus*!"

Apparently someone on the bridge heard, or saw, for within minutes two uniformed officers appeared at the deck railing, one of them motioning for us to draw carefully up alongside. The captain of our own little craft did as he was bid, slowing his speed to match that of the ship and maneuvering into position alongside her. A moment later a collapsible ladder was fastened to the deck railing and released, rattling down the side of the ship as it descended.

"Ready for that adventure, Robin?" Markos asked, holding out his hand to me. "I'll be right behind you."

For the first time it occurred to me that I was wearing a

dress, and that Markos, or the sailor whose boat he had commandeered, would be able to see straight up my skirts. I supposed there was nothing I could do about the man in the boat, but Markos was another matter.

"No, you go first," I said. "My dress—"

He grinned at me. "If your only concern is modesty, I am convinced you will do very well. I will be watching my step on the ladder, while as for our friend here—" He gestured toward the man at the wheel of the boat, and said something to him in Greek. "He will close his eyes."

I thought that rather unlikely, as he would have to maintain the boat's position alongside the ship. Still, I would have to trust that the task would keep him too busy to steal glimpses up my skirt. Markos, however—

"After you," I insisted.

He agreed to this (with a certain reluctance, I thought), then grasped the ladder and began to climb. I would have followed him, but our Good Samaritan stopped me with a few unintelligible Greek words and a restraining hand on my arm, giving me to understand that I was to wait until Markos had reached the top before beginning my own climb. As soon as Markos was beyond hailing distance I began, perversely, to wish I'd let him follow me up the ladder after all. Without him behind me, there would be no one to steady me if I lost my grip, no one to catch me if I fell—nothing at all between me and the cold embrace of the sea.

At a word from the man at the wheel and a waving motion from the officers at the railing above, I took a deep breath and wiped my clammy hands on my damp skirt, then grasped the rung at about the level of my head and stepped over the side of the boat. The ladder lurched crazily beneath my feet, and the wind yanked the hat from my head and flung it into the sea. "Better it than me," I muttered, and started to climb. I was determined not to look down, so I fixed my gaze instead on Markos, standing at the deck railing beside the two officers. By this time everyone on board knew what was going on, and passengers lined the railing, many calling down encouraging words that were snatched away by the wind long before they ever reached me.

With each step I left the safety of the motorboat farther behind, and at some point I began to think of Sylvia Duprée. Had she still been conscious at this distance from the water? Had she known what was happening to her? After what seemed an eternity, I finally reached the top, and a pair of hands stretched out to help me over the railing. I knew a moment's panic as the memory of last night's dream came back to me, a memory of strong bronzed hands pushing me over the deck railing and into the thrashing sea below. But these hands belonged to Markos, and although there were many things I didn't understand about him, I knew I would be safe with him. I released my white-knuckled grip on the ladder and fell into his waiting arms.

"You scared us all to death!" Aunt Maggie chided some time later. I had showered the salt spray from my skin and hair, and was now sitting on Maggie's bed with my feet curled up under me. Maggie, following doctor's orders, was propped up against the headboard with her injured foot elevated. "I hope your day on Mykonos was worth it."

I thought of that balcony in Little Venice, where Markos and I had kissed as the sun sank into the sea. Oh yes, it was worth it. "Maggie," I said thoughtfully, inspecting a fingernail I'd snagged at some point during my climb, "did you ever regret marrying Uncle Herman? Marrying so young, I mean?"

She regarded me keenly. "Does this question have anything to do with the fact that you're no longer wearing your engagement ring?"

I should have known my sharp-eyed aunt wouldn't miss a detail like that. "Maybe," I said, shrugging my shoulders in an attempt at nonchalance that probably didn't fool her any more than my ringless finger had.

"I don't want you to misunderstand me, Robin, or think I dislike Gene on principle." She reached across the mattress to give my hand a squeeze. "Your Uncle Herman was my high school sweetheart, just as Gene was yours. Early marriages can work—my own certainly did—but both parties have to go into it with the understanding that they won't be the same person in twenty or thirty years that they were in high school. You have to give one another permission to grow and change—and you each have to commit to loving the person the other becomes, as well as the one who said 'I do.' The Herman Watson who returned from the war was not the one who'd left with flags waving and bands playing. It changed him."

"I knew he'd been awarded a Purple Heart, but I didn't realize his injuries had been so serious."

"Oh, they healed very well," she assured me. "But I'm not talking about injuries, or at least, not *only* about injuries. He'd had experiences, he'd seen things, that were beyond my imagination. There were things he never told me about his war—probably because I could never have understood, even if he had. Mind you, I'd changed, too. I'd worked at a munitions plant during the war, and for the first time in my life I'd had money of my own, and no obligation to account to anyone as to how I spent it. I learned how to balance a checkbook, and how to manage ration coupons without using them all up in the first week of every month, and how to run the household on a budget. When Herman came home, I resented the idea that I should meekly surrender the household accounts and let him handle everything." She smiled at the memory. "You may find it hard to imagine me fighting with your uncle, but I can promise you we had our share of battles on the subject before we reached a compromise."

"I should think so!" I said, roused to her defense. "The idea that women can't manage money—why, it's absolutely Victorian!"

"Yes, and if you marry a man who's off on a submarine for months at a time, you'll have plenty of opportunity for handling the family finances. Still, there will always be new challenges. Times may change, but human nature doesn't."

"Gene would want me to be able to cope during his absences," I insisted, but even as I said the words, I wondered if they were true. To be sure, Gene had been proud when I'd been named salutatorian of our senior class, and he'd been pleased as punch when I'd received a modest scholarship to the state university. "It'll be something to keep you busy while I'm at sea," he'd said at the time, and I hadn't argued, because I'd seen it in much the same way. But as Maggie suggested, the Robin he'd be coming home to would not be the Robin he'd left. What would Gene think of this new Robin, the one who'd climbed up the side of a moving ship, and who seemed to have become embroiled in some sort of skullduggery at sea—and who had kissed a handsome foreigner on a sun-drenched Greek island without a second thought?

Before I could begin to form an answer, a knock sounded on Maggie's stateroom door.

"Drat! Can you see who that is, honey?" she asked.

"Sure," I said, grateful for the interruption. I unfolded my legs and crossed the tiny cabin to open the door. The cabin steward stood there holding an alligator handbag.

"Good evening, Miss Fletcher. Is Mrs. Watson in?"

"Yes, but she's indisposed at present." I gestured inside the cabin to where Maggie sat propped up against the headboard with a pillow beneath her foot. She wiggled her fingers at the steward, giving him to understand that I could act on her behalf.

"Miss Fletcher, I am pleased to report that your aunt's handbag has been found."

I couldn't remember Maggie ever having an alligator handbag, much less losing one. Still, it did look vaguely familiar. "My aunt's—?"

His smile faded. "I apologize for the delay. It was found up on the Promenade Deck late last night, and with all the activity following the disturbance—" His suddenly sober expression gave me to understand that he was talking about Sylvia Duprée's death.

"Of course. But are you certain this belongs to my aunt?"

If he was certain before, he didn't look quite so sure now. "You must ask her, of course, but the key to this stateroom was found inside, and since the ship's manifest shows this cabin registered to Mrs. Watson, we naturally assumed it must be hers."

"Of course," I said again. My brain was spinning, for I had just recognized where I'd seen this particular handbag before. I thanked the cabin steward and shut the door.

"Maggie," I said unsteadily, turning back into the room, "is this your purse?"

"No, but I'll take it if no one else wants it." She eyed the bag appreciatively. "I'd be willing to bet that's genuine alligator."

"You'd win that bet. It belonged to Sylvia Duprée. She bought it when we were in Rome."

"So why did the steward bring it here?"

"It was found on the Promenade Deck last night. Your stateroom key was inside."

"So *that's* what happened to it! I suppose I must have lost it on the bus that day, and Sylvia found it." Her expression grew sober. "Poor Sylvia! I never even had a chance to thank her."

I made no comment. I didn't think Sylvia deserved thanks. In fact, I thought I had discovered the reason she had clung so tightly to my aunt during our excursion to Rome. I recalled the signs of untidiness in Maggie's stateroom, and wondered for the first time if the intruder in my cabin yesterday had broken into my room only after unsuccessfully searching my aunt's. But surely those footfalls I'd been conscious of inside my own stateroom must have been made by someone heavier than the slender Frenchwoman. Did she have an accomplice—Mr. Devos, perhaps? And if so, what had they been looking for? I couldn't begin to guess. I only hoped the trouble, whatever it might have been, had died with her.

"I suppose we'd better make sure the bag is returned to Mr. Grimes," Maggie continued. "He'll be leaving the ship tomorrow when we dock in Istanbul, accompanying Sylvia's body back to France, or wherever it is she'll be buried. Would you mind taking it back down to the purser's desk? I would, but—" She gestured toward her injured foot.

"Of course." Actually, I had no intention of taking it down to the purser's desk. I was going up to Aegea Deck, where the luxury suites were, and I was going to put it in Mr. Grimes's hands myself. And while I was at it, I was going to see what I could learn about Sylvia Duprée. "I'll be right back."

Upstairs on Aegea Deck, I discovered eight identical doors arranged in paired groups of four, all spaced more widely apart than the cabins on the lower decks. Clearly, these were the larger suites—and outside each door, just as outside our own, a small nameplate held a card containing the last name and first initial of the passengers staying in it; the only difference was that these nameplates were made of polished brass, while our own was a far more mundane aluminum. Two of the plates were empty—apparently not all the suites were occupied—and a third bore an unfamiliar name that looked Oriental. I was just about to move farther down to inspect the next group when one of the doors opened and a uniformed crew member backed into the passageway, still talking to someone inside.

"—when we dock in Istanbul. Someone will come to fetch you, and transport to the airport has been arranged. Let me say again on behalf of the captain and crew of the *Oceanus* how very sorry we are for your loss. We take the safety of our passengers very seriously, and will continue to look into the cause of this tragic incident."

"Thank you, and please express my gratitude to the captain and crew for all you have done." The cultured voice belonged to Mr. Grimes, but he sounded weary and—and *old* in a way he had not before.

As the door closed behind him, the crewman gave a brief nod in my direction and took himself off, no doubt relieved to have his unpleasant duty done, at least until the ship docked in the morning. I waited until I could no longer hear his footsteps on the midships staircase, then stepped up to Mr. Grimes's door and rapped gently.

It swung open at once. "Yes, what else—? Oh, forgive me, Miss Fletcher. What may I do for you?"

"I wanted to return this to you." I handed over the alligator bag, feeling vaguely ratlike for harboring ulterior motives. "It was Miss Duprée's. She'd bought it when we were in Rome. My aunt lost her cabin key that day, and apparently Miss Duprée found it, because it was in her bag. The purser's mate returned the bag to my aunt by mistake."

"Thank you." He took the bag and turned it over in his hands as if he didn't know quite what to do with it. Mr. Grimes had always struck me as a man who would never be at a loss, whatever the situation, and I found his changed demeanor pathetic.

"Mr. Grimes," I said impulsively, "will there be someone to go to the airport with you tomorrow? I mean, if not, I would be happy to—" Maybe "happy" was the wrong word, but I couldn't leave this man to face such a task alone, no matter my opinion of the woman he mourned.

"You are a very sweet young lady," he told me with a sad smile, "but you need not worry about me. My children have flown to Constantinople"—he used the old name for the city—"and will be waiting at the dock when I disembark. One of the ship's crew has been assigned to accompany me down the ramp as well, so I won't be alone."

"I'm glad of that, anyway."

He regarded me speculatively. "Tell me, Miss Fletcher, what is your shoe size?"

"I beg your pardon?"

"My daughter never liked Sylvia," he said, and somehow I wasn't surprised; as a prospective stepmother, she would be the kind of woman who inspired a hundred fairy tales. "I doubt my Marla would have any interest in owning any of Sylvia's possessions. But poor Sylvia had enjoyed that day in Rome with you and your aunt, and hers was a life that had known its share of tragedy. I think she would have wanted you to have these—this handbag and the shoes that match it, if you can wear them."

To my shame, I knew a moment of pure, unadulterated greed. "I—I would be honored," I said, trying not to betray any unseemly eagerness.

"If you'll come inside, then, I'll fetch them for you."

He stood aside to let me pass, and I stifled a gasp. This, I decided at once, was the way to travel. Where my stateroom was only slightly larger than the average walk-in closet, this one had a separate living room with wood-paneled walls. There was no sign of a bed—a fact that spared me, at least, any of the details regarding Mr. Grimes's and Miss Duprée's sleeping arrangements—so I could only assume the suite contained a separate bedroom. One corner of the living room was taken up with what appeared to be a compact yet fully stocked bar, and on the outer wall, sliding doors opened onto a small balcony. Which raised yet another question regarding Sylvia Duprée's death: with her own private balcony to enjoy, what had she been doing on one of the public decks?

"Here they are." Mr. Grimes emerged from the bedroom area bearing a red and white cardboard box I recognized at once from my shopping trip with Sylvia Duprée. "The box says they're size thirty-eight, but that will be a European size. How it translates into American sizing, I have no idea."

"Neither do I," I confessed. Although I'd bought a pair of leather sandals at the same shop, I didn't remember what size they were, if I had ever noticed it at all. I'd just tried on pairs until I'd found one that fit. I took the box Mr. Grimes offered, removed the lid, and carefully lifted one of the high-heeled shoes from its tissue paper nest. I felt a bit like Cinderella as I slid my foot inside—and doubly so when I discovered it fit.

"Perfect!" I pronounced, rolling my ankle back and forth to admire the effect. I was sorely tempted to put the other shoe on and strut back and forth across the cabin like a model on the catwalk, but managed to restrain my eagerness when I considered how these shoes had come into my possession.

Mr. Grimes's thoughts must have been running along similar lines. "I would be honored if you would take these, Miss Fletcher, and wear them in memory of poor Sylvia. She did so enjoy shopping with you that day in Rome."

"Thank you, Mr. Grimes, I will. She was a wonderful shopping companion. Her tastes were exquisite, but she had an eye for a bargain, as well." I meant the compliment just as sincerely as I'd ever meant anything—but that didn't mean I wasn't going to get what information I could before basic courtesy demanded that I leave the chief mourner in peace. "But you said her life had been tragic. In what way? If you don't mind my asking," I added quickly.

"I don't see how it can hurt; nothing can hurt her anymore," he said with a sigh. "Sylvia was a widow. She'd made a hasty marriage during the war—so many young women did, you understand, not knowing if their sweethearts would be alive to marry them afterwards—and her husband was a hero of the Resistance. He managed to come through relatively unscathed, but jobs were scarce, and the country could, or would, do nothing to help. The economy was wrecked after the Nazi occupation, and the nation had no money to spare, not even for her heroes."

"I'm sorry," I said, not knowing what else to say. It didn't shed any light on her death, much less her quarrel with Devos, but it explained, at least to some extent, why she'd latched onto a wealthy man decades older than herself.

"I may be old, Miss Fletcher, but I'm not stupid," the wealthy man in question said with a twinkle in his faded blue eyes. "I knew exactly what appeal I held for Sylvia, and I could not fault her for it. She'd been poor and hungry. Who can blame her for wanting to enjoy a taste of luxury before her youth slipped away?"

I glanced from the alligator shoes in my lap to the luxurious cabin in which I sat, and thought he'd given Sylvia more than just a taste.

"My children didn't understand," he continued. "They thought she was taking advantage of me, or maybe they feared I was frittering away on Sylvia the money they hoped would someday be their inheritance. But I had needs of my own, too. I needed companionship—beauty—youth—"

It was hard for me, at twenty-three, to think of Sylvia's forty as being young, but I supposed to Mr. Grimes it was.

"I was tired of being alone," he said with a shrug. "My wife had died years ago, and my children were busy with their own lives, which is as it should be. As long as we weren't hurting anyone else, what did it matter?"

Clearly, something about Sylvia had "mattered" to someone. Mr. Grimes picked up a long-necked square bottle from a small table next to the sofa and poured two fingers of amber liquid into a glass. His hand shook slightly—no surprise there, given what he'd been through—and when he picked up the glass, I noticed for the first time the numerous residual rings on the tabletop. How many times, I wondered, had that glass been refilled in the last twenty-four hours? His manner toward me had been so urbane, so charming, that I hadn't noticed he'd been drinking. And apparently drinking a lot, for the bottle was almost empty. Drowning his grief— or, perhaps, anesthetizing a guilty conscience? Was it possible Devos was not the villain of the piece after all, but one-third of a love triangle? I'd never even thought of that possibility, but wasn't the spouse or lover the first person the police looked at in the case of murder, or possible murder? True, there had been no hint of anything between Sylvia and Devos at the dinner table, but she struck me as too smart, or at least too cunning, to tip her hand. If that was the case, then their quarrel in Pompeii may have been about nothing more sinister than a frustrated lover's demand that his mistress make up her mind and choose between him and another. And if *that* was the case, then my own name might have meant nothing more than Devos venting his frustration at the dining room seating arrangements that placed him between me and Mrs. Hollis, as far as possible from Sylvia.

Was the whole thing really that simple? Had I created a mystery where none existed, all because I'd seen Devos up on deck in the middle of the night? Granted, there was something about that scenario that didn't quite add up, something that concerned Markos and the photos I'd taken in Pisa, but my adventure at sea was beginning to catch up with me, and I was too tired to think any more. Perhaps my head would be clearer in the morning, but in the meantime, I felt as if a great weight had been lifted from my shoulders. For if Sylvia's death had been what the mystery novels called a crime of passion, then my own personal nightmare—most of which would have turned out to be all in my head after all—should end with Mr. Grimes's departure from the ship in less than eight hours.

Still, if Mr. Grimes had shoved Sylvia overboard in a fit of jealousy, then I was at that moment alone in the suite with a murderer. Discretion being the better part of valor, I rose to my feet, thanking him for the shoes and bag and expressing my condolences once again (with mixed emotions this time) before returning to my cabin, where I soon slept the sleep of the just.

12

Beware of desp'rate steps!
WILLIAM COWPER, *The Needless Alarm*

T he next morning, I rose and dressed for the day in Istanbul, then took a circuitous route to the dining room that would take me past the ship's camera shop. I hadn't seen Markos since I'd climbed up the side of the ship and into his arms, and I wasn't quite sure what I would say to him when I did. Had our little escapade on Mykonos gotten him a dressing down from the captain for missing the "all aboard"? If so, I owed him an apology. As for me, I had a fiancé, for heaven's sake! What had I been thinking, kissing a handsome Greek while the boy I'd loved since high school was somewhere at sea serving his country? To my shame, I felt far worse about the possibility of causing trouble for Markos than I did the fact that I'd betrayed my fiancé. When I reached the camera shop and found it closed, I hardly knew what to think. I was spared, at least for a while, the necessity of seeing Markos again and explaining why the most glorious experience of my life had been a terrible mistake—the kiss, that is, not the nerve-racking climb up the side of a moving ship; on the other hand, I couldn't help wondering if his absence from the shop meant that our indiscretion had cost him his job.

The dining room was far less formal in the mornings than it was at dinner, and tables were not assigned. I found Maggie and Paul seated near a window and greeted them cheerfully, resolutely thrusting both Markos and Gene to the back of my mind. I gave the waiter my order, then turned toward the window to watch the bustle of activity below. Dock workers swarmed about the ship, securing her in her berth with thick ropes. Beyond them, wooden pallets were stacked high with sacks of onions and potatoes; apparently the galley stores would be replenished while we were docked here at a major port.

"So this is Istanbul, the gateway to Asia," I remarked. "And yet potatoes and onions look the same all over the world."

"Actually, this is Europe," Paul corrected me. "Asia is over there." He gestured with his fork across the water to the opposite bank. "Istanbul is the only city in the world that straddles two continents."

"Isn't that the spot Lord Byron swam across, Robin?" Maggie asked, hunching down for a better look. "It's awfully wide, isn't it?"

I shook my head. "Actually, Byron swam across the Dardanelles—although it was called Hellespont at the time—which we would have passed at some point in the early hours of the morning. I believe it's even wider than this."

"Three-quarters of a mile, while this is less than half," Paul concurred. "All the more remarkable when one considers he did it in spite of a club foot."

"Or maybe *because* of a club foot," I suggested. "Or maybe he was just trying to get away from Lady Caroline Lamb."

"Either way, he has my sympathy," Maggie said, glaring at her own bad foot. "At least I know mine will heal—although not in time to salvage my trip."

"What are your plans for the day?" I asked. "Will you get to see any of Istanbul?"

"I contacted the purser's desk, and they were able to make a reservation for Paul and me on a Bosporus cruise," she said, brightening. "The price includes a full Turkish meal on board the boat, so I'll get a taste of the city in more ways than one, all without too much walking. I would have included you in the reservation, Robin, but I thought you would prefer a more in-depth exploration on foot."

"I would, but I hope you have a wonderful time all the same," I assured her.

"Oh, look," Maggie said, unexpectedly sober.

I turned back to the window and saw a crewman in starched white solemnly pushing a stretcher bearing an elongated bundle wrapped in what appeared to be oilcloth. A tall, silver-haired man kept pace beside him, occasionally reaching out to lay a gentle hand on the oilcloth. I didn't have to see his face to recognize Graham Grimes, escorting Sylvia for the last time. Even from this distance his grief was obvious. The sorrow of loss, I wondered, or remorse at the impulsive act of violence that had deprived him of feminine companionship? There was something wrong with that theory, something missing, but before I could put my finger on it Maggie spoke again, and I lost my train of thought.

"It's a shame he's all alone. If we'd known, we could have stayed with him," she added to Paul. "After all, we've been through it ourselves."

"He told me his children would be here to meet him." Even as I said the words, a trio of well-dressed, middle-aged adults—two men and a woman—stepped out from between the vegetable-laden pallets. The woman broke into a run, and threw her arms around her father's neck. Clearly, whatever her opinion of Sylvia (and I wasn't at all certain I wouldn't have felt the same way, if it had been my own father who had taken up with Sylvia or someone like her), she loved her father. I was relieved to see he was in good hands, whatever he might have done.

"I'm glad of that, anyway—although it does make for a

solemn beginning to our day in Istanbul," Maggie said. "Oh, speaking of solemnity, that reminds me! Robin, if you're planning to visit the Blue Mosque, you'll need a head covering. Do you have a scarf? You can borrow my green one, if you need it. You'll also have to take off your shoes, so you might want to be sure and wear a pair that slips on and off with no buckles or laces to deal with."

I assured her I already had it taken care of, even offering proof by directing her attention to my espadrille-clad feet and digging my blue chiffon scarf out from under the camera that took up most of the room in my straw bag. Having finished our breakfast, we left the restaurant and headed down to the lowest of the public decks, which offered access to the gangway. Once on the dock we parted ways. Maggie and Paul took a taxi to the much smaller pier from which the dinner cruises departed, while I boarded a bus for the historic city center. From there, the man at the purser's desk had assured me, I could board a tour bus much like the ones we'd taken in Rome.

As the bus set out from the dock, I stared out the window, practically pressing my nose against the glass in my eagerness to learn as much as I could about this exotic and mysterious port of call in one day. The skyscrapers in the near distance would have looked right at home in New York or Chicago, but the needlelike minarets puncturing the skyline at intervals made it clear that this was no Western city, at least not entirely. Likewise, the people milling up and down the crowded sidewalks ranged from bearded and turbaned men in the flowing robes of the Middle East to well-tailored Dapper Dans in business suits that might have come straight from Savile Row. Women in the latest from Paris or Milan mingled with others covered from head to toe in long black garments with veils over their heads and faces, covering them entirely but for an occasional glimpse of liquid dark eyes. No, whatever its influence over Western civilization over the centuries, this was no Western city.

At last the bus lurched to a stop with a hiss of brakes. I disembarked with the other passengers and got in line at a kiosk where I parted with several of my Turkish lira and received in exchange a ticket for one of the tour buses that crisscrossed the city, stopping at all the most popular sites. Our first stop was the Topkapi Palace, royal residence of the Ottoman sultans for almost four hundred years. The imposing crenellated structure flanked by coned towers, which I assumed was the palace, was actually the enormous Gate of Salutation, the entrance to the second courtyard. Beyond this gate, a series of paved paths radiated outward like the spokes of a wheel. I chose one at random, and began my exploration. I turned to the right, where the extensive kitchens were recognizable by the double row of round chimneys rising from the roofs, resembling the smokestacks of a ship. Inside, the sultans' extensive collection of blue and white Chinese porcelain held pride of place, each piece having been transported by camel caravan over the old Silk Road. I couldn't help wondering how many additional pieces had broken along the way.

After leaving the kitchens, I passed through yet another gate into the third courtyard. Here was the aptly named Conqueror's Pavilion, which held the imperial treasury. The sultan's gold and jewel-encrusted armor was on display here, along with his sword, shield, and golden stirrups. I had to wonder how practical such showy pieces would actually be in battle, but given the wealth of riches that surrounded me, I certainly couldn't argue with the results. A second room housed the gold- and emerald-adorned Topkapi Dagger in a glass case in the center of the room, but I was more impressed with the cases lining its perimeter, in which were displayed the elaborate crown jewels, either gifts from foreign powers hoping to curry favor or spoils taken by force from conquered enemies. This observation, along with the armor displayed in yet another room, served as a stark reminder of how much violence this city had seen in its long history.

From the treasury, I wandered to the seraglio where the women of the harem would have been kept secluded from prying eyes. Here were no sunny courtyards, but a series of bewildering corridors and a rabbit warren of rooms opening from one into the next. Which was not to say they weren't beautiful; the walls were decorated with blue and white Iznik tiles, the windows made of stained glass or covered with lattice screens that filtered the bright sunlight and cast geometric patterns onto the floor, giving the women of the harem distant glimpses of the water that was the city's lifeblood, yet preventing them being seen by the outside world. Still, I wondered what it must have been like for the young women who lived here in these opulent surroundings day after day and year after year, awaiting the sultan's pleasure. A gilded cage, perhaps, but a cage all the same. If any one of them had been discovered betraying the sultan as I had betrayed Gene, she would have been stuffed into a sack and thrown into the Bosporus. Would she have considered it worth the risk? Did I? Not that anyone would throw me into the Bosporus, of course, but what would Gene do if he found out about me and Markos—for instance, if Maggie let something slip? Would he break the engagement? Did I want him to?

Did I want him to? That was the question, and I wasn't sure I wanted to know the answer. I hurried away from the claustrophobic surroundings of the seraglio and returned to the bus stop. I didn't have to wait long for the next bus, and soon my fellow passengers and I were set down at the edge of a busy square flanked on each side by enormous domed buildings bristling with minarets—the red and gray Hagia Sophia on our left, and the aptly named Blue Mosque on our right. Most of the crowd drifted to the right—a lifelong habit of following traffic laws, I supposed—so I went against the flow and turned left, toward the Hagia Sophia.

The massive structure—not named for Saint Sophia, as I'd assumed, but for Holy Wisdom—had stood for more than fourteen hundred years, and had changed hands several times. First built as a Christian Orthodox church in the sixth century, it had briefly become Roman Catholic after falling to the Crusaders in the thirteenth. The biggest change had come two hundred years later, when Constantinople was conquered by the Ottomans and the church was converted into a mosque. The building, already almost a thousand years old, had fallen into disrepair by that time, and it was quite possible that the Muslim invasion saved it from collapse— which was probably small comfort for the many defenseless Christians who had fled to the church for sanctuary during the siege only to find themselves part of the spoils of war when the city fell and the invaders sacked and pillaged the building.

Only twenty-five years ago, in 1935, the Hagia Sophia had been converted into a museum, and now, looking about me, I could see signs of its mixed heritage. The four minarets outside, of course, were the most obvious sign of its Muslim years, but inside were more: the raised lectern where the imam would have preached, as well as large round disks bearing calligraphic writing, the meaning of which I couldn't begin to guess. On the Christian side, the mosaics had not been destroyed, but only covered in plaster, and now the tranquil gazes of Jesus and the Virgin Mary, along with various saints and angels, gazed serenely down from ceilings and walls, and the carpets had been removed to expose the marble decorations inlaid into the floor, including the Omphalion, the circular marble slab where the Byzantine emperors had once been crowned.

Having looked my fill at the Hagia Sophia, I exited through the massive doors and crossed the square to the Blue Mosque. At "only" three hundred years old, this was practically new compared to its neighbor, and had been built as a deliberate attempt at one-upmanship. As Maggie had predicted, I had to take off my shoes and leave them with an attendant, who thanked me in broken English and offered me a piece of plain cotton cloth to use as a head covering. I declined with a smile and withdrew the chiffon scarf from my handbag, then draped it loosely over my head and passed through the open door.

I'd assumed the Blue Mosque was named for its bluish-gray exterior, but once inside I realized my error. Here were no mosaics as in the Hagia Sophia, as the Muslim religion prohibited the representation of living beings; instead, the interior of the mosque was decorated with twenty thousand blue and white Iznik tiles and more than two hundred blue stained glass windows. Where the Hagia Sophia spoke of power, antiquity, and a turbulent past, the Blue Mosque whispered of beauty and elegance on a grand scale. I padded about on the thick red carpet, snapping photos to show my aunt.

Eventually I retraced my steps back to the bus stop, where I boarded the bus to the Grand Bazaar, a sort of fifteenth-century shopping mall encompassing sixty-one streets and over four thousand shops, all under one roof. Somewhere in my bag, among the sunglasses, scarf, camera, passport, and all the other accoutrements of travel, I had Turkish lira, and I was ready to spend them. I passed through the gate into the covered pedestrian thoroughfare with its arched ceiling, blinking as my eyes adjusted to the dimmer light within. I groped in my bag for my camera and stopped just inside to take a photo. The place was packed with tourists as well as locals, and merchandise spilled out of the cramped little shops and into the passageway where it impeded the shoppers' progress, forcing them to slow down for a better look whether they wanted one or not. Young Turkish men, no doubt the shopkeepers' assistants, worked the crowds, their voices echoing in the enclosed space as they called out to potential customers in fractured English to come and inspect their wares.

"Beautiful English lady!" one called, obviously speaking to me even though I wasn't English and had never thought of myself as beautiful. "Beautiful English lady want good Turkish rug? Only forty lira!"

Even *I* knew forty lira was far too little to pay for a "good Turkish rug," but I had to give him credit for trying. I smiled at him and shook my head, and soon discovered my mistake. He took my smile for encouragement and stepped up his efforts, joined by his counterparts from several other stores.

"Come look at rugs and buy!"

"Pretty lady want gold? I give good price!"

"Buy leather jacket for boyfriend!"

And would that be Gene or Markos? a mocking little voice in my head asked as I hurried on, escaping one aggressive salesman only to find myself confronted with another—or two or three.

"Come and look! Come and buy!"

"Bracelets to protect pretty lady from Evil Eye!"

What I needed was something to protect me from importunate salesmen, I thought desperately, as I squeezed past a stout German couple debating the virtues of a "real Turkish rug" with a shopkeeper. I came suddenly upon a corner, and turned into another covered street. This one was a bit less crowded, and I stopped to catch my breath. Remembering Paul's warning about pickpockets in Rome, I felt for my bag, and was relieved to find that it was still there. A trio of women in head-to-toe black robes and face veils turned the corner, and I looked up to smile

SHERI COBB SOUTH

sympathetically in the general direction of their hidden faces. If Muslim men were always this persistent, I understood why the women felt the need to conceal themselves.

They were on me before I could react, one locking surprisingly strong arms around me while the other two grabbed for my camera. In retrospect, I suppose I should have given it up without a fight; after all, I had no way of knowing what kind of weapons might have been secreted away beneath those all-encompassing black robes. But I didn't have time to think. I clutched the camera to my chest and began swinging my elbows back and forth wildly. The woman who held me struggled to maintain her grip, and in the struggle her long sleeve fell back, revealing a muscular forearm liberally sprinkled with dark hair and bearing a tattoo reading "ELAS."

This was no woman.

Remembering the self-defense class that had been required of all freshman girls at my university, I twisted in her—his—grasp and jerked my knee up. His hold on me loosened at once, and I heard a very satisfying groan of pain. I wrenched myself free and began to run, back toward the busy main shopping street. Footsteps ringing on the pavement told me at least two of the three were in hot pursuit, and although their long black robes might hinder them to some extent, it was unlikely I would be able to outrun two men for very long. I reached the intersection and

202

plunged back into the crowd, ignoring the calls of the salesmen as I dodged in and out among the shoppers. Suddenly a couple of tourists came to a dead halt right in front of me. I couldn't stop in time. I plowed right into them, all but knocking the woman off her feet.

"I'm so sorry," I panted, taking her by the arm to steady her. "I didn't mean—"

"Why, Miss Fletcher!" she exclaimed, and relief flooded through me at the sight of Mrs. Hollis's pleasant, homely face. "Look, Henry, it's Miss Fletcher!"

"Are you okay?" Mr. Hollis asked, subjecting me to an intense gaze.

"You look a bit pale," his wife agreed.

"I'm all right," I said breathlessly, "although I was never so glad to see anyone in my life! Someone—someone tried to steal my camera." I looked behind me, but saw no sign of my assailants among the crowd.

"They were probably wanting to sell it on the black market," Mr. Hollis said grimly. "They saw a pretty young girl traveling alone, and thought you were an easy mark."

"It's a good thing it was no worse," Mrs. Hollis concurred. "Maybe you'd better stay with us until we return to the ship."

Suddenly I'd lost all interest in souvenir shopping. "Thank you, but I think I'm ready to go back to the ship now," I said.

"If you can wait a minute longer, we're just about to go catch the bus ourselves," Mr. Hollis assured me. "Martha wanted to buy a little something she could show all her friends back home."

At that moment I wanted nothing so much as to hole up in my stateroom and not come out until we reached Venice, or at least until Maggie and Paul returned. Still, shopping with the Hollises seemed less traumatic than running the gauntlet of shoppers and salesmen back through the Grand Bazaar to the entrance gate. "All right, but only for a minute," I agreed halfheartedly.

"I won't be long, I promise. I'm not superstitious, but I do like those little blue Evil Eyes," she said, turning back to gaze at the cluttered display in a shop window, which featured a number of glass disks and teardrop shapes featuring concentric circles of blue, black, and white. "Look, that one is set in the middle of a little yellow cross. Does that make it look a bit less heathen, do you think? I'd hate for us to be kicked out of church, what with Henry being an elder."

"Maybe you'd better buy one too, Miss Fletcher," Mr. Hollis suggested with a reassuring twinkle in his eye. "After all, a little extra protection never hurt anybody."

I wasn't sure how much the salesman hovering near the door had understood of this exchange, but seeing us heading in his direction, he perked up at once, inviting us inside with elaborate gestures and pressing on us tiny cups of apple tea. I took a sip, and found it sweet and strangely soothing. As I paid for my purchases—one of Mrs. Hollis's Evil Eyes as well as a couple of large colorful towels of striped Turkish cotton, a guilt-inspired addition to my neglected hope chest—it occurred to me to wonder if the attack had actually been an orchestrated plot to make tourists feel more vulnerable, and therefore more likely to buy Evil Eyes for protection. No, surely not. Given the sheer number of shoppers in the Grand Bazaar, and the popularity of the symbol as one of the more affordable souvenirs to be had, so elaborate a scheme would be unnecessary.

Still, I felt a little better as I walked to the bus stop, although I couldn't have said whether my relief was due to the solid, dependable couple at my side, or the little circle of blue glass tucked away into the bottom of my bag.

13

One may smile, and smile, and be a villain.
WILLIAM SHAKESPEARE, *Hamlet*

I wasn't quite sure how much, if anything, I should tell my aunt about the incident in the Grand Bazaar. I should have known the Hollises would take the matter out of my hands. We had scarcely sat down to dinner when Mrs. Hollis turned to Maggie and said, "I suppose your niece told you she had quite a fright today."

"No, she didn't." My aunt didn't show any signs of panic or hysterics, and although Maggie wasn't the hysterical type, I wasn't sure if she was really that poised, or merely suspected Mrs. Hollis of exaggerating. "What happened, Robin?"

"It was nothing, really," I protested feebly, aware that every eye at the table, and a few at the surrounding tables, had turned in my direction. "Someone tried to steal my camera, but I got away. Mr. Hollis thinks it was someone hoping to sell it on the black market."

"Robin!" Maggie exclaimed. "Are you all right? Granted, I don't *see* any injuries, but still—"

"I'm fine," I assured her.

"Did you report it to the police?" Leave it to Paul to get to the heart of the matter.

"There's nothing to report," I insisted. "I managed to hang onto my camera, so there was no theft, not really. Besides, they were so heavily veiled, I would never be able to pick them out of a police lineup—assuming they have such things in Turkey. They may not, for all I know."

"Veiled?" Mr. Hollis echoed. "You didn't mention that. Do you mean it was a woman who attacked you?"

"They?" Maggie said at the same time. "There was more than one of them?"

"There were three." I thought of that muscular forearm, and shuddered. Still, my aunt would surely find the thought of three female assailants less threatening than the reality. "And yes, they were women—or men dressed as women, in black from head to toe, and with their faces veiled."

"Then they had to be women," Paul put in. "No Muslim man would wear a woman's clothes. He would be insulted at the very idea."

"But not every man in Istanbul is a Muslim," Maggie pointed out. "There are Christians here too, you know—even a sizeable Jewish community."

Mr. Hollis frowned. "I don't think any very religious

people would go around assaulting young women, regardless of what faith they practice."

"Very true." I couldn't help smiling at his Midwestern common sense.

"Speaking of faith," Mrs. Hollis put in, glancing at the two empty places before the window where Mr. Grimes and Sylvia had sat, "I can't help thinking we ought to say a prayer or have a moment of silence or something for Miss Duprée. Henry and I watched from our window as poor Mr. Grimes left the ship with her body this morning. It was one of the saddest things I've ever seen."

Everyone agreed, and I silently blessed her for changing the subject. Alas, not for long. Our moment of silence had hardly ended when Maggie said, "Still, I can't feel right about Robin wandering about Ephesus on her own tomorrow."

"Oh, will you not be exploring the ruins?" Mrs. Hollis asked. "I have to say, that's one of the stops I've been looking forward to the most. I want to take pictures to show my friends at church. Paul's letter to the Ephesians, you know."

"The book of Revelations mentions the church at Ephesus, too," her husband put in.

Maggie nodded. "Yes, and I hate having to miss out. But the ship's doctor warned me that the roads there are very rough—apparently it's still the original pavement from

Roman times—and he advised me not to risk it." Everyone at the table made suitably sympathetic noises, and Maggie turned abruptly to Mr. Devos, who had been mostly silent so far. "Mr. Devos, may I ask you as a personal favor to go with Robin tomorrow? After what happened to her today in Istanbul, I'll feel better knowing she has someone with her."

"Maggie!" I exclaimed, mortified.

Devos bared his teeth at her in a wolfish smile. "I regret that I cannot oblige you, Mrs. Watson, but I fear I will not be touring the ruins myself."

"Oh," said my aunt, rather daunted. "I'm sorry."

"So am I sorry, that I must decline the offer of such charming companionship," Devos assured her, giving what I supposed was meant to be a courteous nod in my direction.

"We'd be glad to have you come with us," Mrs. Hollis told me.

"But you're on your honeymoon," I protested.

"Never you mind that," Mr. Hollis said, then smiled rather sheepishly at his wife. "After all, Martha and I will have the rest of our lives together."

"Just so," Mrs. Hollis agreed, nodding. "I'll admit I wouldn't feel right leaving you on your own, not after what happened at the Grand Bazaar."

I was glad they made the offer directly to me, instead of talking to my aunt as if I weren't there, an inconvenient burden to be disposed of. Still, I wished people would stop trying to pair me off with Devos: first my aunt, and then Markos, and then my aunt again—

Markos. Markos had thought I was involved with Devos when he'd seen my photos from Pisa. That was what I'd forgotten when trying to picture Mr. Grimes in the role of jealous lover. I'd been physically and emotionally exhausted after my climb up the side of a moving ship, and I hadn't been thinking clearly. So many strange things had happened on this voyage that they were beginning to run together, and I couldn't discern a pattern. But surely it was no coincidence that my photography—this time not the photographs, but the camera itself—was at the center of the confrontation in the Grand Bazaar. I wished I could put this theory to Markos, and see what he thought of it. But Markos had been making himself scarce ever since Mykonos, and I wasn't quite sure what to think of his absence. Was it possible that he'd been confined to quarters, or whatever they did to crew members who broke the rules? Or was he deliberately trying to avoid me? Was I reading too much into a kiss that Markos had already forgotten, like Lady Caroline Lamb chasing after Lord Byron long after he had lost interest in her? It was a lowering thought. Suddenly I wanted desperately to see Markos again, just for the sake of ignoring him. Failing that, there was only one thing I could do.

"I would be delighted to tour Ephesus with you," I told Mrs. Hollis with more warmth than I felt.

Having settled the next day's plans to our satisfaction, we all tucked into the excellent dinner that was set before us, Turkish fare in honor of our day in Istanbul: pieces of succulent lamb grilled on skewers, along with rice pilaf, vegetables, and flatbread. For dessert there was baklava, paper-thin sheets of phyllo layered with nuts and drizzled with honey. It wasn't until the party broke up and we'd left the dining room that I thought to ask my aunt what she intended to do the next morning, since the ruins of Ephesus were off-limits.

"Paul suggested we organize an impromptu shuffle-board competition for the passengers who are remaining on board. Most of them are older than I am, so I can't be the only one who's not up to the rough walking." She stopped in the middle of the atrium, snapping her fingers as a sudden thought occurred to her. "We should have asked Mr. Devos to play, since he won't be leaving the ship tomorrow! Robin, could you stop by his stateroom and ask him? I would do it myself, but my ankle is telling me I've done enough walking for one day."

I couldn't think of anything I wanted to do less. "I—I don't know which cabin is his," I protested.

"No, but we'll be walking right by the purser's desk, and I'm sure they can tell us." Seeing my lack of enthusiasm, she added with some asperity, "I know you don't like the man, Robin, but surely there's no harm in stopping by just long enough to deliver a message."

And that was how I found myself standing outside Devos's stateroom on Barcelona Deck, knocking at the door and hoping he was off enjoying an after-dinner drink at one of the ship's bars, so I could honestly report back to Maggie that he hadn't been in his cabin.

But no, I felt the faint vibrations of his heavy tread, and a moment later the door swung open a scant twelve inches to reveal Devos framed in the opening. He had already begun to change out of the tuxedo he'd worn at dinner, and was now clad in only the dress trousers and the white cotton T-shirt he'd worn beneath his pleated formal shirt—and he did not look pleased to see me.

"Good evening, Miss Fletcher," he said with barely concealed impatience. "I am sorry to disappoint you, but it is as I told your charming aunt: I cannot escort you to Ephesus tomorrow."

I didn't want his company any more than he wanted mine; still, his attitude was hardly flattering, besides being a far cry from the gallant if heavy-handed Devos who had not only asked me to dance, but even insisted on escorting me back to my stateroom afterward.

"I know you can't, and I'm sorry she put you on the spot that way," I replied with equal candor. "Actually, it's on her account that I'm here. She and Paul are putting together a shuffleboard tournament for passengers who are going to be on the ship tomorrow, and she wanted to invite you to join them."

"I see. But I fear I must decline once again, for I will not be on the ship tomorrow."

"Oh," I said, rather taken aback. "You said you weren't going to Ephesus, so I—that is, my aunt—assumed you meant to spend the day onboard the ship."

"I said I will not be touring the ruins. As it happens, I have other plans. I will be meeting a friend in Kusadasi, where the ship will dock."

He darted a quick, almost surreptitious glance over his shoulder, and I wondered if there was a woman in the room with him. I couldn't see into his cabin—his bulk, and the door itself, prevented that—but there was a mirror on the adjacent wall that I could just glimpse over his shoulder. It reflected a partial view of the bed, which was not occupied by a scantily clad female, but covered with a collection of small figurines, vases, and pottery. There were about a dozen or so, and even from this poor vantage point I could tell they were a cut above the usual souvenir fare.

"As you see, I have been shopping again," he said, grinning at me with that feral smile. "My little nieces and nephews, their Uncle Konstantin must keep them happy, yes?"

"Oh, I hope you won't give those things to very young children! They must be very fragile. The pieces, that is, not the children," I added quickly. "May I—do you mind letting me have a closer look at the figurine of the lady?"

He seemed to struggle with himself for a moment; I wasn't sure if he didn't trust me not to break it, or simply wanted me to go away. I hadn't wanted to knock on his door in the first place but, perversely, the more he wanted to get rid of me, the more determined I was to stay. Apparently he recognized this, for at last he shrugged his shoulders in resignation. "But of course."

He closed the door practically in my face, and when he opened it a few seconds later, he held the figurine cradled in one arm. She was a thing of beauty, about as tall as Pooping Pedro was long, with her draped robe hanging from one shoulder in a way that left her right breast bare. One elegantly shaped hand was raised as if to rectify this situation—or call attention to it—and her face was turned slightly away, smiling coyly as if in invitation to a lover. I hadn't seen anything like this in any of the souvenir shops; if I had, I would have bought her, even if it cost me my last drachma.

"Do you mind if I ask where you bought her?"

He lifted his broad shoulders in a shrug. "Where else but at the Grand Bazaar? It is often said that if it cannot be found at the Grand Bazaar, it is not worth having."

"Oh," I said in some surprise. "I thought she looked more Greek than Turkish. Don't the Muslims object to artwork depicting human figures?" Much less a female figure exposing even half so much skin, but I kept this observation to myself.

"Indeed they do, but convictions tend to fall by the wayside where there is money to be had. In the Grand Bazaar, one may buy objects from all over the world."

I didn't remember seeing a shop offering such things, but then, I'd had very little opportunity to look. I felt a wholly illogical resentment at the trio of attackers who had deprived me of the chance to buy such a figurine for myself.

"Will you sell her to me?" I asked on sudden impulse. "I'll gladly pay you something for your trouble in addition to whatever you paid for her."

He shook his head. "I am sorry, Miss Fletcher, but I cannot. My little niece Sophia would be, what do you say, devastated."

"I thought you said her name was Theodora."

"That is my other niece. Sophia is her older sister."

He hadn't missed a beat, but he was lying; I knew it beyond a shadow of a doubt. I wasn't quite sure why he would feel the need to lie about such a thing, but it was clear he had no intention of letting me buy the figurine from him. "Anyway, the offer stands," I said, conceding defeat. "If you change your mind between now and the time we disembark in Venice, I hope you'll let me know."

"I will bear it in mind, Miss Fletcher, but I would not

like to raise false hopes. And now I must bid you goodnight. Please thank your aunt for her kind invitation, and give her my regrets."

And with that, I was firmly dismissed. He closed the door so swiftly that I was obliged to take a step backwards to prevent its hitting me in the nose. But as it swung shut, I caught a quick glimpse of the inside of his bare forearm, and the tattoo that read "ELAS."

14

Fair Greece! sad relic of departed worth!
Immortal, though no more; though fallen, great!
GEORGE NOEL GORDON, LORD BYRON,
Childe Harold's Pilgrimage

E phesus had been a bustling port city in the apostle Paul's day, but when the Goths started harassing the Roman Empire in the third century, Rome could no longer spare the manpower to dredge the river Cayster, which emptied into the city's harbor. In the ensuing years, silt from the river had filled in the harbor, eventually eliminating the source of the city's wealth. What the siltation of its harbor had begun, an earthquake in the seventh century had finished, and the people who could afford to do so had abandoned the city altogether. The end result was that Ephesus—or what remained of it—was now more than three miles from the sea, and the colonnaded marble road that had once led to the docks now ended abruptly in a swampy tangle of scrubby bushes and marsh grass.

The ruins of the city, however, were well worth a day

spent exploring them. The amphitheatre where Paul had preached was a popular sight, as was the much larger coliseum that stood at the landward end of the marble road. For my part, aside from the pleasure of escaping, at least for a while, the creepy Devos and the memory of Sylvia—God rest her soul—I admired the pretty little Temple of Hadrian with its graceful arch. The doctor had been quite right in advising Maggie not to attempt the trip, however; the large slabs of marble that served to pave the street had shifted over the centuries, leaving an uneven surface for walking on, and yet many of the individual stones were as slick as glass. I had trouble at times maintaining my balance on the downward slope toward where the sea had once been, meaning poor Mr. Hollis had to navigate the slippery road while supporting his wife with one arm and me with the other.

Eventually, we made our way back up the jagged pavement to where the bus waited to take us back to Kusadasi and the ship. Once back on board the *Oceanus*, I stopped by the little camera shop to drop off my film, and found Markos working the counter.

"Miss Fletcher!" he seemed pleased to see me, although I noticed I was back to being "Miss Fletcher" rather than "Robin." I wasn't sure if this was because he had to maintain a professional demeanor while on the ship, or if he was trying to distance himself from me for more personal reasons.

"Mr. Rondo," I said coolly.

"I hope you have suffered no ill effects from our adventure," he said, and I was glad he brought it up first.

"No, none. What about you? You weren't at the counter this morning, so I couldn't help wondering—" I broke off, unsure how to finish.

He grinned broadly, his teeth white against his bronzed face. "You couldn't help wondering if I'd been thrown into the brig, or forced to walk the plank?"

"I knew you hadn't walked the plank!" I said, feeling more than a little foolish for worrying about him. If anyone could take care of himself, surely Markos was the man.

"But the brig you weren't so sure about?" He snatched an envelope from beneath the counter and shoved it toward me. "You know the drill: name, address, and cabin number, please."

I quickly filled in the information, then dropped my film into the envelope and handed it back to him, but made no move to leave.

"Yes, Miss Fletcher?" he asked. "Do you have any questions?"

"Only one," I said. "What does 'ELAS' mean?"

"Where did you hear that?" Markos grabbed a rag from underneath the counter and began wiping down the already spotless surface; I suspected it was more to avoid looking me in the eye than out of any concern for cleanliness.

"I didn't hear it; I saw it," I said. "Twice, in fact." I darted a quick glance around to make sure no other passengers were within earshot, then explained quickly about the tattoo on Devos's arm and the circumstances that had led to my seeing it.

Markos seemed to consider for a long moment before explaining. "ELAS—it is an acronym in Greek, although it doesn't translate into English—stands for the Greek People's Liberation Army. It was a resistance movement during World War II."

"Really?" That was the last thing I'd expected to hear. "I knew the French had an organized resistance movement, but I didn't know the Greeks had one."

"Actually, we had several, but the main two were ELAS and EDES. Probably both would have done better if they hadn't spent almost as much time and energy fighting each other as they did the Nazi occupation. ELAS did have some success, though; they even managed to liberate part of the mainland from the Nazis."

"But—but that would mean Devos is a hero, not a villain!"

Markos frowned. "It's a strange sort of hero who attacks young women in Istanbul's Grand Bazaar."

"Yes, but you know what I mean."

"Let me finish before you go all gushy—that is correct?

Gushy?" He must have read the indignation on my face as affirmation, for he continued with no change in adjective. "Before you go all gushy over Devos's wartime heroics. As I was saying, ELAS had some success against the Germans, and in a rare cooperative effort, they and EDES blew up a bridge that prevented Italian reinforcements from arriving. They won a lot of popular support as a result. The only trouble was that they were a bit too chummy with the Communists. Before the war was even over, my country was embroiled in a civil war of its own."

"I'm assuming ELAS must have lost that one, since Greece isn't a communist country today."

"Yes, but there's still a lot of bitterness from those former freedom fighters who were defeated by their own countrymen—with support from the British, I might add. Be very careful around Devos, Robin. Avoid him altogether, if you can. There are few things more dangerous than a revolutionary with a grudge. Now, Miss Fletcher," he added brightly, "what are your plans for seeing Athens tomorrow?"

I blinked at his sudden change of tone, until I saw out of the corner of my eye two more passengers approaching the photo counter. "I—I expect I'll be taking a bus tour with my aunt," I stammered. "And you?" He'd once offered to show me the city, but there was nothing in his manner now to indicate that he even remembered, much less intended to make good on his offer.

"I'll probably spend the day running errands, but I hope you'll enjoy your visit to Athens," he said noncommittally. "Yes, sir, how can I help you?"

"Do you have flashbulbs to fit a Kodak camera?" the man asked.

"Yes, sir. How many do you need?" Markos turned away to fetch them, and I was gently but firmly dismissed.

Maggie, Paul, and I reached Athens after a short bus ride from the port city of Piraeus, and bought tickets for a bus tour just as we had in Rome—minus, of course, the company of Sylvia Duprée, but I wasn't going to think about that, not now, anyway. Our first stop was at the Panathenaic Stadium, built for the 1896 Olympic Games—the first modern Olympics—on the site of the original stadium, which dated to around 330 B.C. To my delight, we could turn our backs to the stadium and see the Parthenon in the distance, looking down over the city from the Acropolis. I hadn't realized how huge, or how high, it was, and was ashamed to feel a pang of something like resentment that Maggie's foot injury prevented me from getting a closer look.

We finally ended up at the National Archaeological Museum, a massive neo-classical building that housed one of the most extensive collections of antiquities in the world. As I wandered from room to room admiring the statues and peering into the glass cases, I remembered the story Markos had told me of artifacts being found on his family's property on Mykonos, and wondered if any of them were on display here. In fact, I thought, strolling past a door that led not to further exhibits but to what appeared to be a corridor of offices, it was almost as if I could hear Markos's voice—

Suddenly one of the office doors opened, and the sound came to me more clearly. He was speaking in Greek, so I didn't understand a word, but I would have recognized the voice anywhere. Sure enough, there was Markos, not dressed in his starched white uniform, or even in the casual clothes he had worn on Mykonos and in Florence, but in a dark blue suit and striped tie. He shook hands with a second, older man, also dressed in business clothes, then turned away as the other man closed the door behind him, effectively ending the interview.

The interview. It occurred to me that Markos looked like—like—

Like a job applicant. Apparently our little escapade on Mykonos had cost him more than he'd let on.

"Markos?"

He flinched at the sight of me, and I had the distinct impression that if he could have escaped without speaking to me, he would've done it in a heartbeat.

"Miss Fletcher—Robin!" he exclaimed with a bright smile that didn't fool me for a minute. "What a pleasant surprise!"

"Don't give me that! You're applying for a job here, aren't you?" It was an accusation, not a question. "Did the captain fire you, or just make you miserable enough that you were forced to quit?"

His dark eyes opened wide. "But I thought you would be pleased! You said I was wasting my education on the *Oceanus*!"

"Yes, but there's a difference between choosing to find a new job and being forced to. And the fact that it's my fault—"

"Your fault? How do you figure that?"

"You were with me on Mykonos, and I—" I was already speaking softly, but I lowered my voice still further, and glanced around to make sure no one, least of all my aunt, could hear what I had to say. "I led you on. I let you— let you take certain liberties—" There I was again, talking like a Jane Austen heroine.

"Yes, it was very wrong of you to pin me down and force yourself on me that way," he said with mock severity. "Robin, don't be ridiculous! I was an equal participant, you know. In fact, you could argue that I started the whole thing. After all, I'd wanted to kiss you ever since you boarded the ship in Barcelona."

"Oh," I said in a very small voice. There was no reason, no reason at all, for that revelation to warm my heart so. I was probably the only person on the ship under the age of forty, not counting the crew, so if it was a shipboard romance Markos was looking for, it wasn't as if he had a vast selection of women to choose from. Still, there was something wrong with this assertion—and suddenly I knew what it was. "You had not! Until the night Sylvia—fell—you thought I was involved with Devos!"

"Well, yes, but one does not preclude the other, you know."

I regarded him quizzically. "What would you have done if I was?"

He shook his head, suddenly and unexpectedly serious. "Don't ask me that, Robin. I've asked myself a thousand times, and never have found an answer."

All at once the air in the corridor seemed very thick and still, as if the air conditioning had gone out, although I was vaguely aware of it humming somewhere in the background. Before I could form an intelligent reply, I heard the click-click-click of footsteps on the hardwood floors, and Maggie burst through the doorway with Paul in her wake.

"*There* you are, Robin! We've been looking everywhere!" Recognizing my companion, she exclaimed, "Why, Markos! Don't you look handsome!"

"Mrs. Watson." He nodded in greeting, and offered his hand to Paul. "Dr. Hurley."

"So you have a day off from the ship?" my aunt

continued. "But you don't look like you're dressed for sightseeing."

"No, I'm in Athens today on business," Markos told her.

"Markos is applying for a job here at the museum," I explained.

"Really?" Maggie turned to Markos for confirmation, and he gave her a pleasant smile. "Well, I'm sure the *Oceanus*'s loss will be the museum's gain."

"It's very kind of you to say so, Mrs. Watson, but I'm sure you'll understand when I say I don't want word to get around the ship just yet."

"Wise man," Paul said.

"Your secret is safe with me, cross my heart," Maggie declared, sketching a big "X" across her chest with one hand. "Are you finished here? Can you join us for lunch? We'll even let you choose the place, if you know of a good one nearby."

"Thank you, Mrs. Watson, I would be glad to. As for a restaurant, I think I can suggest one. It is unknown to most tourists, so the food is more authentic. Cheaper, too."

"You're singing my song," Maggie declared, looping her arm through his. "Lead the way!"

Paul and I fell in behind them, but by the time we exited the museum, we had somehow switched partners. Markos hailed a taxi and we all piled in, Markos sitting in front to give the driver directions in his native tongue while Maggie, Paul and I squeezed into the back. Markos was as good as his word, and soon we were deposited in front of a small restaurant, where we were shown to a table in the window and served a plate piled high with fresh pita bread, which we tore into pieces and dipped into a communal bowl of hummus.

"I have to hand it to you, Markos, I never would have found this place on my own," Paul said, leaning forward slightly to scoop a blob of hummus onto the soft pita bread. "Are you very familiar with Athens?"

He nodded. "I have a small flat in the city."

"Do you?" Paul's salt-and-pepper eyebrows rose in mild surprise. "I should have thought it would be more convenient to stay in Barcelona or Venice."

To my amazement, this simple observation rendered Markos more flustered than our adventure on Mykonos or even Sylvia's death had done.

"Yes, well, there's—there's something about one's own country, you know," he stammered, adding, "Besides, I don't live here year 'round, only during the off-season. Tell me, Mrs. Watson, have you ever tried moussaka?"

And if that isn't an attempt to change the subject, I don't know what is, I thought, wondering why Markos's living arrangements should be such a mystery. Still, it served its purpose, for Maggie denied any knowledge of moussaka and began plying him with questions regarding the various items on the menu.

"Everything seems to be lamb," she remarked. "Why no beef, or even mutton? Couldn't you at least let those poor little lambs grow up before you slaughter them?"

"Some must be allowed to grow up, in order to replenish the flocks," Markos assured her. "But on the whole, the ground is too stony to support grazing for large animals—certainly not cattle, and few fully grown sheep. So you have lamb. If you don't like it, there is always chicken, or seafood," he added apologetically, as if he were personally responsible for the lack of red meat on offer.

"No, no, it all sounds delicious," Maggie assured him. "What would you suggest?"

Since we would be eating a large meal on the ship that night, Markos suggested gyros (which he pronounced "YEE-rohs," in spite of its spelling), a sort of Greek sandwich of pita bread stuffed with lettuce, cucumber, tomato, and the ubiquitous lamb, all topped with tzatziki sauce, a creamy white mixture of yogurt and cucumber seasoned with garlic.

"Delicious!" Paul declared after the food was served and he'd taken a big bite.

"It is," Maggie agreed, dabbing a bit of tzatziki sauce from the corner of her mouth. "It was lucky for us that we ran across you in the museum, Markos. It's just a pity we couldn't have found you first thing this morning. We'd have had our very own Greek tour guide."

"And I would have been happy to oblige," Markos said. "Tell me, have you visited the Parthenon yet?"

"Only from a distance," my aunt said. "This damned foot won't let me make the climb."

He turned to me. "What about you, Robin?"

I shook my head. "I'm spending the day with Maggie and Paul, and since she can't—"

"Don't miss it on my account," Maggie protested. "After all, when are you going to have another chance? Markos, if you would take Robin to see the Parthenon, I would consider it a personal favor."

"Maggie!" I wished my aunt would stop throwing me at men—although I was forced to admit that, given a choice, I would rather be thrown at Markos than at Devos any day.

"I would be glad to, but as a favor to Paul," Markos told Maggie's beau, grinning. "Robin is an enchanting young lady, but don't tell me she hasn't been just the least bit superfluous. I am familiar with the English proverb that says 'two is company, but three is too crowded.' "

"That's 'two's company, *three's a crowd,*' so maybe you're not quite as familiar with it as you think," I retorted, only slightly mollified by that "enchanting" remark.

"There's another proverb that says 'a friend in need is a friend indeed,' " Paul told him. "If you ever need a favor, Markos, I owe you one."

Maggie beamed at both of them, and I gave in gracefully for her sake. I couldn't help wondering what would happen when we reached Venice, and she and Paul parted ways. I would hate to see her come to terms with Uncle Herman's death only to be left heartbroken a second time. For that matter, I wondered what would happen to me. Could Gene and I ever go back to the way we were before? Did I even want us to?

But there would be time to think of that later. For now, I was going to climb the path up the Acropolis to see the Parthenon. While Maggie and Paul hailed a taxi to take them back to the ship, Markos and I scrambled into a second cab and were soon set down near the foot of a broad paved path lined with olive trees. Markos purchased our tickets from a nearby booth, and we started to climb. It was easy going at first, gently sloping ramps interspersed with wide, shallow steps. As we climbed, however, the slope became steeper and the path narrower and more rugged. It was also crowded, and at one point I was jostled by a large school group on their way down. I pitched heavily into Markos, and he caught me against his chest, glaring at the noisy ten-year-olds barreling down the path oblivious to the havoc they'd caused. When we resumed our climb, he insisted on holding me firmly by the arm—not that I fought him very hard on the issue.

"I would put you on the inside, but the view is better

from the outside," he explained.

"Just promise me you won't let me go over the edge," I said, glancing warily down at the steep drop.

"An onerous assignment, but I think I can manage," he said, and pulled me a bit closer to his side. "See the rock there, to the northwest?"

I hadn't any idea which way was northwest, but I looked down and to the left in the direction he indicated, and saw a dome of bare rock jutting up over the tops of the surrounding cypress trees. A dozen or so people milled about on its bald surface, and from this angle it was impossible to tell how they'd gotten up there. "The one with all the people on it?"

"Yes, that's the one. That is the Aeropagus, where murderers were tried in ancient times. The first part of the name is said to be derived from Ares, who according to myth was tried there by the gods for the murder of Poseidon's son."

"And the second part of the name?"

He grinned broadly. " 'Pagos' is Greek for 'big piece of rock.' "

"A practical lot, those Greeks."

"We can be. But the Romans had another name for the Aeropagus. They called it Mars Hill."

I gasped, thinking of the Hollises. "*The* Mars Hill? The one where Paul preached?"

He nodded. "The very same."

I stopped climbing and stepped back out of the way to dig in my bag without blocking the tourists coming up behind us. "Oh, I hope the Hollises are able to see it! But I'll take a couple of photos just in case, and if they missed it, I'll send them one."

I snapped three shots, just to be sure of getting a good one, then I put away my camera and we resumed our climb. At last we reached the Beulé Gate—a curiously French name for a Greek structure, I thought, but Markos told me it was named for the French archaeologist who had identified it in the middle of the nineteenth century.

"It's newer than the rest of the ruins here," he added, puffing slightly from the climb, "if something dating from the third century can be called new."

"Architectural styles must have changed, and not for the better," I said, eyeing the gate with disfavor. "It isn't nearly as beautiful as the pictures I've seen of the Parthenon."

"Being Greek myself, I will take that as a compliment, for the Beulé Gate was not built by the Greeks, but by the Romans. We may have been conquered by Rome in the second century before Christ, but the Romans tried to emulate our culture in some ways." He grinned. "The playground bully may beat up the class egghead and take his lunch money, but he secretly envies the boy he knows is smarter than himself."

This sounded so much like the junior high dynamics I saw every day that I had to smile. But life had a way of evening things out, and I'd also seen the other side of the equation: college athletes begging for tutoring from the same young men they had tormented only a few years earlier.

"As for the gate's lack of beauty," Markos continued, "there is a reason for that. Unlike the temples on the Acropolis that were built to please the gods, this gate was built purely for defensive purposes, using fragments of earlier buildings destroyed by the Goths. If you know where to look, you can even see some of the carved inscriptions from the original structures."

We passed through the Beulé Gate and began climbing the stairs to the massive Propylaia, the original (and much more impressive) entrance to the Acropolis. If I hadn't known better from the guidebooks, I might have mistaken this for the Parthenon, for it had huge Doric columns that would once have supported a roof, just like the more famous structure. But once I saw the Parthenon, there was no confusing it with anything else. The pictures I'd seen didn't do justice to its size. Each of its forty-six columns was thirty-four feet high, and wider in diameter than I was tall— and each, when seen up close, contained a patchwork of newer material where chunks of the original marble had been lost. Its size was best appreciated up close, but more distant views made it easier to imagine it as it must have once looked.

"And the sad part is that most of the damage could have been avoided," Markos replied, when I voiced these thoughts aloud. "For some unknown reason, the Ottoman Turks thought it would be a good idea to store ammunition here. It's possible they supposed their enemies would not fire upon a building of such importance to the history of Western civilization, but if this was the case, they made a tragic miscalculation. The Venetians fired on it—no one knows if they struck it by accident or targeted it deliberately—and almost completely demolished it, then looted what was left. What you see here has been reconstructed from the rubble."

I looked up at the jagged roofline, putting up a hand to shade my eyes. "It's a pity so many of the statues along the roof are missing."

"Oh, they aren't missing," Markos said drily. "Some of them are, of course, but most of them are safe and sound in the British Museum."

"Removed by Lord Elgin, you mean." I recalled something of this from my reading. "But he had permission from the Greek government, didn't he?"

"First of all, there was no 'Greek government,' since Greece was still part of the Ottoman Empire at that time. Aside from that, he had permission to build wooden scaffolding for the purpose of measuring, drawing, and making plaster casts. Somehow he ended up with twenty-one figures, fifteen metope panels, and chunks of the frieze that totaled seventy-five meters in length. Lord Byron called him a vandal to his face, and wrote about it in one of his poems."

"*Childe Harold's Pilgrimage*," I said. I'd thought the lines were moving when I'd read them in college, but never dreamed that someday I would actually see the ruins Byron described. " 'Dull is the eye that will not weep to see thy walls defaced, thy mouldering shrines removed by British hands.' "

"You are familiar with it, then."

"I majored in English literature," I reminded him. "There's more, but I don't remember the rest. Still, I'd never really thought much about what it meant to the Greeks. There's a difference between reading something and seeing it for yourself."

Having looked our fill at the ruined beauty of the Parthenon, we picked our way across the uneven, rocky ground (mere rocks, I wondered, or more antiquities just waiting to be discovered?) to the Erechtheum, a temple dedicated to Poseidon and Athena, who according to Greek mythology had competed for patronage of the city. Along the wall nearest the Parthenon, a porch jutted out, its roof held up by five caryatids, women in Grecian draperies that appeared flowing even though they were made of marble.

"Oh, how lovely!" I exclaimed.

"It's called the Porch of the Maidens," Markos told me.

I dug out my camera and snapped a couple of photos. "I like this better than the Parthenon. It isn't as large, but there's a grace and beauty about it that the Parthenon lacks. Although," I added charitably, "I'll admit I was hardly seeing the Parthenon at its best."

"You're not seeing the Erechtheum at its best, either," Markos said. "There was originally a sixth caryatid."

"Was there? What happened to her?"

"What else? Lord Elgin, of course. He actually tried to take two, and when he had difficulty with the second, he instructed workmen to saw her into pieces. The pieces smashed, and he abandoned the fragments where they lay. The lady you see here has been reconstructed, and the missing one may be seen in—"

"The British Museum," I finished for him. "I see now why you went to England to study archaeology."

He grinned at me. "There is a legend here in Athens that says the five remaining caryatids may be heard at night, wailing for their lost sister."

"If you're about to suggest we wait until dark and listen for them, let me tell you that climbing up the side of a moving ship is not an experience I care to repeat!"

"No, no, I think once was enough," he conceded, although I thought he sounded a bit regretful.

We turned away from the Erechtheum, and Markos took my arm to steady me as he led me toward a spot from which we could look down over the remains of the agora, the marketplace of ancient Athens. When I caught my toe on one of the many rocks strewn about the ground, Markos put an arm about my waist to steady me—and didn't remove it, even after I'd regained my balance. The agora was to the northwest of the Acropolis, and from where we stood we couldn't miss the sun sinking lower in the sky.

"I suppose we'd better start back down if we don't want to miss the ship."

His arm tightened about my waist as he spoke, and I regarded him suspiciously. "I don't suppose there happens to be an 'old tradition' regarding sunset atop the Acropolis."

"No," he said with a sigh, and this time there was no mistaking the regret in his voice. "But I wouldn't mind starting a new one."

15

To give each figure in the photograph his living name.
ROBERT TRAILL SPENCE LOWELL, *Epilogue*

I *wouldn't mind starting a new one.* Was he suggesting that our shipboard romance—if one could call it that— might continue after the voyage ended?

Even as I pondered the question, it was answered for me—and the answer was a resounding *no.* "I'll be glad when the ship docks in Venice and you go back home," Markos said.

I'd heard all about the fleeting nature of summer romances. Still, his words stung more than I cared to admit. I gave a little grunt that was supposed to pass for a laugh. "Well, that's flattering!"

"I'm serious, Robin," he insisted, and when I saw the intensity in his dark eyes, I believed he meant it. "I want you well out of this."

There it was again, that vague reference to some unknown danger—something to do with Devos and very likely Sylvia as well, but nothing specific.

"Don't you think it's time you told me what 'this' is?" I demanded. "You keep telling me to be careful, but it's difficult when I don't know what I'm supposed to be looking out for."

Markos regarded me curiously. "I should have thought you would have figured it out by now."

"I know it has something to do with Devos, and something to do with my camera, which probably means the photos I took in Pisa."

"It's impossible to talk privately in this crowd," Markos grumbled, glancing around impatiently at the mob of tourists poking about among the ruins. "Still, it might be safer here than on the ship, where we don't know who might be listening. I wonder—yes, I think we are two lovers exchanging secrets that could not possibly be of interest to anyone else."

Before I could ask for an explanation, he put his arm around my waist and pulled me close to his side, bending his head until it rested against my hair and gazing soulfully out over the ancient agora. "Yes, it has to do with the photos your aunt took in Pisa. The camera shop—or rather its storage room—was broken into while we were on Mykonos."

"Markos!"

"Sssh! Nothing seems to be missing, but someone rifled

through the drawer containing the envelopes of photos waiting to be picked up. Several of them were no longer in alphabetical order, and one or two had fallen to the floor. Yes, that will do very nicely."

"What will?" I asked, bewildered by the sudden change of subject.

"That look of wide-eyed wonder. Just the thing for a young woman receiving a declaration of love. As I was saying, nothing was taken—he could not have taken them in any event, for they aren't there. I had already given them to you, remember?"

"And he'd already searched my stateroom, and hadn't found them," I deduced. "So when he didn't find them among the recently developed photos either, he assumed the film must still be in my camera—which is why he tried to grab it in Istanbul. I'm assuming, of course, that 'he' is Devos." Markos confirmed this assumption with a nod. "But *why?* What's so special about them?"

He was silent for a long moment before answering in a low murmur. "Over the last year or so, there has been a dramatic increase in antiquities sold on the black market."

"So Mr. Hollis was closer to the truth than he knew!"

"Mr. Hollis?" Markos echoed sharply. "What does he have to do with this?"

"Nothing that I'm aware of. I don't even know yet what Devos has to do with it," I pointed out with some asperity.

"When Devos tried to steal my camera in the Grand Bazaar—although I didn't know it was him at the time—Mr. Hollis guessed someone hoped to sell it on the black market."

"I see," Markos said with a shrug, seemingly dismissing Mr. Hollis's involvement as being of no importance. "As I was saying, over the last year, more and more artifacts are ending up in the hands of private collectors who purchase them through less than legal means. Over the course of a long and no doubt tedious investigation, one common factor has emerged: In every case where an artifact's provenance can be identified, the cruise ship *Oceanus* has been in port a very short time before."

"How short?

"Usually a few days, but sometimes a matter of hours."

"As if a buyer were already waiting," I observed.

Markos nodded. "And in each case, there was among the *Oceanus*'s passengers a man whose physical description roughly matched that of Konstantin Devos. Always his name was different, and his passport was issued by a different country—sometimes Italy, sometimes Greece, once Bulgaria, and once Macedonia. Sometimes he wore a beard or moustache, while at other times he was clean shaven. Sometimes his hair was long, or short, or gray. Once he was bald. Sometimes he wore glasses. Still, there was one characteristic he could not change."

"A tattoo on his right forearm," I guessed.

"Precisely."

"But these artifacts—Markos, I think I might have seen them! Or at least some of them. I went to Devos's cabin last night—no, the night before—"

"You *what?*" Markos demanded, looking thunderous. "Didn't I warn you to avoid the man?"

"You threw out a lot of ambiguous warnings, yes. But Maggie wanted to invite him to participate in a shuffleboard competition she and Paul were putting together, and she could hardly hobble all that way herself, so when she asked me to stop by and deliver a message—well, I couldn't refuse without telling her things that I suspect you'd rather she not know."

Markos conceded the point, but didn't look happy about it. "All right, then, what did you see in Devos's stateroom?"

"First of all, I wasn't 'in' his stateroom—I'm not that stupid! I was standing just outside the door. But I could see the bed reflected in the mirror on the wall, and it was littered with objects—pottery, statues, that kind of thing. He said he'd bought them as souvenirs for his nieces and nephews, and I remember thinking they weren't the sort of things you should give children to play with."

"How many were there?"

"Children?" I asked, baffled by the sudden *non sequitur*. "He didn't say."

"Not children," Markos said impatiently. "Artifacts!"

"Oh. I didn't count, but maybe a dozen or so."

"Could you identify them if you saw them again?"

I thought back to the little collection, all seen from a distance and backwards, given that I was actually seeing their reflection—all, that is, except one. "I know I could identify one of them. It was a figurine of a woman in flowing draperies." Actually, she'd been half out of them, but that was beside the point. "I'd asked Devos for a closer look, and he let me hold it. I asked him if he would sell her to me—I even offered to pay him something for his trouble, over and above what she was worth—it's a good thing he didn't take me up on the offer!"

"Interesting," he murmured thoughtfully, and I knew he wasn't thinking of my trying to cut a deal with Devos. Nor, for that matter, was he thinking about the ancient Greeks, although no one seeing him staring out over the remains of the ancient agora would guess as much.

"There is one more thing I'd like to know," I said.

Markos came abruptly back to earth. "Yes, what is it?"

I cocked a knowing eyebrow at him. "Just how does a ship's photographer manage to know all about an international smuggling ring?"

He blew out a long breath. "Because I'm not exactly a ship's photographer," he confessed somewhat sheepishly.

"Now, why does that not surprise me?" I wondered

243

aloud.

"A little more loverlike, if you please, or all these good people will think we're quarreling. What I mean is, I am the ship's photographer, of course—you should know that, you've seen me with my camera often enough. But that's not the only thing I am."

"I knew it! You're with Interpol!" Remembering his warning, I gazed soulfully up at him. "Is Markos Rondo your real name?"

"Yes." His breath was warm against my face. "That is, no, I'm not with Interpol—I told you that once already —but my name is Markos Rondo. *Dr.* Markos Rondo, in fact, for I have a Ph.D. in Archaeology. I'm with the Ministry of Culture. You need not look at me like that, flattering though it is," he added hastily. "I don't have a very exalted position there—undersecretary to an undersecretary, in fact—but I'm sufficiently well-versed in the field to recognize genuine artifacts if I should stumble across them, and yet I still look young enough to be convincing as a member of the *Oceanus*'s crew."

"How old are you?" I asked irrelevantly.

"I'm thirty."

"And when I saw you at the museum today?"

"I had a meeting—a debriefing, you might say."

"I thought you'd been fired for missing the 'all aboard,' and were interviewing for a job."

He nodded. "I know you did. It is very kind of you to worry about me getting in trouble with the captain."

I didn't miss the hint of amusement in his voice, but a fresh thought drove it from my mind. "But you didn't get in trouble with the captain, because you don't answer to the captain."

"On the contrary," Markos protested, "everyone on board his ship answers to the captain. But no, he could not dismiss me without creating a great deal of ill will between the cruise line and the Ministry of Culture. The last thing the *Oceanus*'s parent company wants is for word to get out that one of their ships has been involved, however inadvertently, in the smuggling of artifacts. They have been very cooperative thus far—and as far as the captain knows, my tardiness in leaving Mykonos was purely for professional reasons."

"You mean he thinks you were wooing me in the hopes of determining whether or not I was an international smuggler."

He grinned at me. "Well, yes. But if he should ask, I will assure him of your innocence."

As I sputtered for words to express my indignation, two boys came running up to the edge of the outcrop, calling to the middle-aged couple who followed them, "Mummy! Daddy! Look at *this!*"

Without hesitation, Markos caught me to his chest and

kissed me passionately.

"Larry! Frank! Come back here," their mother called, glaring at us and muttering something under her breath how young people these days had no shame.

"Some of them don't, anyway," I scolded, freed at last from Markos's embrace.

"I didn't think we needed an audience," he said defensively. "I suspect you're not done asking questions yet."

"Darn right I'm not! What's so special about those photos, and why does Devos want them so badly?"

Markos shrugged. "I confess myself at a loss. I thought the photos would show something incriminating, but other than making it appear you and he were a couple, I saw nothing that might—"

"Oh, but there was another one!" I exclaimed, suddenly remembering the one I'd tucked away in my bag the night before we'd docked at Mykonos. So much had happened since then that I'd forgotten all about it. I fumbled in my bag for the glossy black-and-white square—now somewhat the worse for having spent the last three days in the bottom of my bag—and handed it to Markos, who frowned over it. "It's not as clear as the others," I said, "but you can see Devos on the left, over my shoulder. He's turned away from the camera, so you can't see his face, but I recognized him by his shirt. It's the same one he's wearing in the other photos. I'd thought at the time that it was odd, his wearing long sleeves on such a hot day—not only in Pisa, but two days later in Pompeii as well. Hiding that tattoo, I suppose."

But Markos wasn't interested in Devos's wardrobe. "Do you happen to know what he was holding here, or whether he was giving or receiving it?"

I shook my head. "I didn't know he was there at all until I got the photos back from you."

"Do you still have the negatives? You didn't throw them away, did you?"

"Yes," I said. "That is, yes, they're still in the envelope with the photos. I didn't throw them away, although I probably would have tomorrow, to lighten my bags as much as possible for the flight home."

"Thank God for that, anyway! Come on." He grabbed my hand and picked his way as quickly as he could through the large stones toward the path.

"Where are we going?" I panted, trying my best to keep up without tripping.

"Back to the ship," he said. "To the darkroom, in fact. We're going to enlarge this photo and find out exactly what is in Devos's hand."

The ship's atrium was practically deserted when we arrived. I supposed most of the passengers were enjoying their last few hours in Athens, or else were already in their staterooms dressing for dinner. To my surprise, Markos didn't wait for me at the photo counter as I'd expected, but insisted on escorting me to my stateroom to fetch the negatives.

"I'm taking no chances with your safety, Robin. You know too much." And having delivered this warning, impossibly, he grinned. "Besides, you're much less likely to be waylaid by your charming aunt if she thinks you have a date."

I could hardly argue with his reasoning. I gave him a rather nervous smile of acknowledgement, then unlocked the door to my stateroom. It had been straightened up by the cabin steward since I'd left that morning, but other than that, I saw nothing out of place. I crossed the tiny room to the nightstand where Pooping Pedro stood guard, pulled open the top drawer, and removed the envelope containing the photographs I'd taken in Florence and Pisa. I dug out the flimsy negative strips, being careful to handle them by the edges to prevent smudging, and held each one up toward the light streaming from the window. Even the innocent photos looked weird and difficult to identify with their black and white hues reversed, but at last I came to one that showed two black-faced women who could only be Maggie and me. My aunt's red hair appeared gray in the negative, making her appear older than she actually was, and our light summer dresses looked more suited to a funeral than to a Mediterranean holiday. In the background, a rather sinister-looking black tower tilted ominously to the left, while in the middle ground over my shoulder, a white-haired man in a dark long-sleeved shirt handed something to—or received something from—a companion.

"This is it," I said, giving it to Markos. "I'm sure of it."

He held the negative up to the light, peered through it, and apparently reached the same conclusion. "Let's go, then. I'd like to be safely shut away in the darkroom before the passengers start returning to the ship, all wanting to drop off their Athens film before dinner."

I saw nothing to argue with in this plan, so I followed him to the midships staircase and down to the atrium on Europa Deck. We had a bad moment at the foot of the stairs, when an elderly lady caught at the sleeve of Markos's suit coat.

"Excuse me, young man, but aren't you the one who's developing the film? I wonder if I can just give this to you now."

As she fumbled in her big patent leather purse for the exposed film, Markos put his arm about my waist and pulled me close to his side. "I'm sorry, ma'am, but I'm off duty at the moment," he said, with a leering grin that left her in no doubt as to how he intended to spend his off-duty hours.

"Oh. Oh yes, of course." She blinked at him, as if noticing for the first time that he was out of uniform—and that he had female companionship. "I beg your pardon. I

only hoped—well, it's a long walk to my stateroom, and—
but I don't want to interrupt anything. After all, I was young
once myself. I'll just turn it in tomorrow when I come down
to breakfast."

"I'll tell you what," Markos said impulsively. "Just
leave it at the purser's desk right over there, or put it outside
your cabin door tonight with a note, and the steward will see
that I get it."

After that, we were hard pressed to escape the woman's
effusive thanks. After we'd finally shaken her off and
reached the photo counter, I felt compelled to say something.

"That was sweet of you, Markos."

He shrugged. "She reminded me of my *YiaYia*."

"Did she?" I failed to see the resemblance. "From what
I saw of your grandmother, I can't imagine her being nearly
so apologetic."

"Oh, she wouldn't be. But this lady reminded me that
YiaYia would nail my hide to the wall if she saw me
brushing off an old woman in such a way."

"That does sound more like her," I agreed, smiling as I
recalled the elderly Greek lady who was Markos's
grandmother. "But couldn't she take the film to the photo
counter just as easily as she could take it to the purser's
desk?"

"Yes. But by the time she filled out the envelope with
her name and cabin number, there would be half a dozen

other passengers lined up behind her waiting to do the same thing, besides buying more film and flashbulbs for Venice, asking about the best time of day for photographing the Rialto Bridge—"

"I see your point."

We reached the photo counter and ducked behind it without further mishap, then dodged through the door into the storage room. Markos opened the darkroom door, ignoring the "DO NOT OPEN" sign, and shut it quickly behind us, flipping the lock to prevent anyone entering and ruining the undeveloped photos by exposing them to light. He switched on a bare bulb overhead that cast an eerie reddish glow over the tiny room, and in the faint light I could see a countertop with an array of shallow trays and what appeared to be a clothesline stretched a couple of feet over it from one end to the other. Against an adjacent wall stood a small table holding what appeared to be an odd sort of camera pointed straight down at the flat surface that formed its base.

Even in the dim light my curiosity must have shown on my face, for Markos, although engaged in stripping off his coat and tie, nodded in the direction of the strange contraption and explained, "That's the enlarger. I'm going to try and get a closer look at that package."

"You mean you really *are* a photographer?"

His eyebrows rose. "I took a crash course in

photography to prepare for my role in this operation. Does that surprise you?"

Actually, it did. Evidently a great deal of preparation had gone into what he called "this operation." I would have liked to know more, but I could tell Markos was focused on the task at hand, and was no longer open to questioning. He unbuttoned his collar and cuffs, then rolled his sleeves halfway up to the elbow. After filling three trays, each with a different liquid, to a depth of about half an inch, he set a timer and reached for the light switch.

"I'm going to have to turn the lights off for a few minutes," he said apologetically. "I have to make sure no light can get into the room. If you're uncomfortable in the dark, you can come and stand next to me."

Two weeks ago, I would have scoffed at the notion that I might be afraid of the dark. Now, however, I moved around the end of the counter without a word of protest. Markos took my arm with one hand and switched off the light with the other. We were instantly plunged into the *darkest* darkness I'd ever experienced.

"I would have thought you'd *know* no light could get in," I said, my voice sounding strangely loud in the blackness. "After all, it is a darkroom, and you work in it every day."

"Routine precaution," he said. "One of the things I learned in class. Besides, we're on a ship, remember? The walls are under constant stress from the sea. Who knows when one might shift just enough to admit a sliver of light? Even that little bit could ruin the film."

It seemed like we waited in the dark forever, although Markos later said it was only five minutes. At last, satisfied, he switched on the dim red safelight overhead. He fed the negative into the enlarger, affixed a sheet of photographic paper to its flat base, and adjusted the camera-looking part of the contraption up and down until he was satisfied that the image would fill up the paper, leaving only a narrow white border at the edges. He switched on a bulb within the enlarger, focused the light on the photographic paper, and started the timer again. When it went off, he removed the paper and plunged it into the first of the three pans.

"This is the developer," he explained, starting the timer once more. "Next is the stop bath, and the last one is the wash, which will remove the processing chemicals. Then I'll hang it on the line to dry."

"When will we be able to see something?" I asked, practically bouncing up and down with impatience.

Markos nodded toward the developing pan. "Take a look."

I couldn't see much of anything at first. Soon, however, contrasts between light and dark began to emerge on the paper, followed by vague, blurry shapes.

I pointed toward the lower right-hand corner. "What's

that big white blob?"

"That's your shoulder," Markos said, and although it was too dark to see his expression, I could hear the laughter in his voice. "I'm not enlarging the whole photo, you know, just the part with Devos and his friend. Anything in the foreground of the original photo will be blurred. I can assure you, your shoulders are much more attractive than they will appear here."

"Flatterer," I muttered, and turned my attention back to the emerging photograph. I could see Devos clearly now, although his image appeared grainy.

"Do you know the man with him?" I asked, looking up at Markos.

He shook his head. "Not personally, no."

"But you know who he is."

"I think I might. There will be others who will be able to identify him, though."

I suspected those "others" were his superiors at the Ministry of Culture, or else Interpol; in either case, he probably couldn't tell me even if I asked. I returned to my examination of the photograph, now clearly visible in its pan of developing fluid. "Markos!" I exclaimed, leaning closer for a better look. "It's Pedro!"

The brightly colored cardboard box was reduced to shades of gray, and the lettering was too blurry to be legible, but there was no mistaking the picture on the side of the box—a picture of a log with stubby legs, bright eyes, and a wide smile.

"But that's impossible! I saw him throw his *caga tió* overboard only the night before. Unless," I added doubtfully, "he changed his mind yet again, and his friend is buying, or giving, him another one."

"The night you saw him throw it overboard," Markos said thoughtfully, transferring the photo from the developing fluid to the stop bath, "was it in the box, or out of it?"

"Out of it," I replied without hesitation, shuddering at the memory of that happy, smiling face disappearing into the foam churned up by the ship's propellers.

"In other words, he kept the box."

"I suppose so. That, or put it in the wastebasket in his cabin. But if he was going to do that, why not put the whole thing in the trash? Why dispose of the box one way and its contents another?"

"Unless he never disposed of the box at all."

"But that doesn't even make sense!"

"Doesn't it? Tell me, Robin, when you saw the, er, souvenirs scattered on the bed, did you see any boxes?"

"No, but that's not to say they weren't there. After all, my vantage point wasn't the best. Markos, what are you thinking?"

"Suppose for a moment that you are a customs official. Someone is returning from a cruise, and he declares the value of certain items he is bringing back to his home country as souvenirs. If you ask to see them, he produces the sales receipts showing the purchase of these items, and he has safely stowed away in his luggage the boxes or bags they came in. The baggage handlers at the dock and the airport can even attest that his suitcases weigh just as much as they ought, neither being so heavy nor so light as to arouse any suspicion that he is not carrying exactly what he claims to be. Would you have any reason to search his luggage and look inside those boxes?"

"Is *that* how the smuggling ring works?"

"I think it may be."

"But he unloaded the *caga tió* box in Pisa, long before he disembarks in Venice," I pointed out.

"Even better, for in such a case he avoids customs altogether. We can only suppose that in this case he had a buyer waiting, and that this buyer is apparently Italian, and so runs no risk of having to remove his purchase from the country."

I leaned closer for a better look at the photograph. "Poor Pedro! I never realized he could be put to such illicit purposes."

"Robin," Markos said seriously, tucking a strand of my hair behind my ear before I accidentally dipped it into the stop bath liquid, "I wish I could accompany you to Venice tomorrow, but I can't. Everyone will want their photos ready before they disembark the next morning, and I'll be busy in the darkroom all day. Promise me you will stay with your aunt and her doctor friend tomorrow. You know too much—you are in more danger than you realize."

I might have made some sort of a joke just to lighten the moment, but the intensity in his eyes, glittering black as onyx in the dim safelight of the darkroom, caused the words to stick in my throat, and suddenly I could hardly breathe.

"I—I promise," was all I could manage.

16

I stood in Venice on the Bridge of Sighs,
A palace and a prison on each hand.
GEORGE NOEL GORDON, LORD BYRON,
Childe Harold's Pilgrimage

I awoke the next morning to sunlight streaming through the gaps between porthole and curtains, and eagerly arose from bed. I flung back the drapes, and gasped in delight at the sight that met my eyes. The ship had entered the Venetian Lagoon, and now glided past islands bristling with pointed *campanili* and cupola-topped domes. The sun sparkled off waters teeming with every kind of boat imaginable, from utilitarian barges to luxurious private yachts to water taxis and *vaporetti*, the waterbuses that ferried passengers to and fro on regularly scheduled routes. It was difficult to believe that evil could exist in such an enchanting world, much less that any of it might be directed at me personally. Still, I had promised Markos, so—

A light tap on my door interrupted this thought, and I crossed the tiny cabin and opened the door to admit Maggie, already dressed for the day in crisp seersucker.

"Good morning," she said cheerfully. "We missed you at dinner last night."

"I was—with Markos," I said noncommittally. It was no more nor less than the truth.

"I thought you probably were, which is why I didn't try very hard to track you down. I thought the two of you would *not* appreciate company." She plopped down on the foot of the bed and lowered her voice to a conspiratorial near-whisper. "And now I'm going to ask you to return the favor. I think Paul may pop the question today."

"Maggie!" I exclaimed. "That's wonderful! But—well, are you sure you should marry him? I mean, Paul's a great guy, but you haven't really known him very long."

"Maybe not," she admitted. "But long acquaintance is no guarantee of lasting happiness, you know. Paul and I have both been married before, so we know what it takes to make a marriage work." A shadow crossed her face. "We've also both lost a spouse to a long illness, so we know, too, that we're not promised a certain amount of time on this earth—so sometimes you have to seize the day."

"I think Uncle Herman would approve," I said warmly. "I know I do, and I hope you and Paul will be very happy together."

"I'm sure we will," she said, smiling up at me like the cat that got the canary. "which is why I'm going to ask you if you can explore Venice with Markos, and give Paul the privacy he needs for a proper proposal."

Markos. I'd promised him I wouldn't go off on my own today, that I would stay close to Maggie and Paul. But this—surely this was different. Tomorrow we would disembark and head for the airport, and Maggie and Paul would have missed their chance. I couldn't do that to her, not after seeing her grief a year ago at the loss of my uncle. Surely my aunt's happiness trumped my impulsive promise to a man I'd only just met—didn't it? But somewhere between Barcelona and Venice, Markos had become more—much more—than a chance-met stranger on a ship.

Fortunately, there was a third option. Markos might not be available, but that didn't mean I had to explore Venice on my own. I'd look for the Hollises instead, and ask if I could join them.

"I wouldn't dream of imposing on you," I assured her.

"Thank you, Robin," she said, and I could see the glint of joyful tears in her eyes as she hugged me close. "But don't say anything to him at breakfast, for heaven's sake! I would hate to be mistaken."

"Oh, I don't think you're mistaken. Anyone can see he's crazy about you. You'd just better be sure to invite me to the wedding," I added with a smile.

I was still smiling half an hour later when I reached the dining room. Maggie and Paul were there before me, looking for all the world like they were already an engaged couple. I ate a quick meal of juice, Danish pastry, and fruit, then made my excuses and left the two lovebirds alone.

"There's no rush, Robin," my aunt said. "We won't be cleared to disembark anytime soon."

"It may be hours," Paul agreed. "The captain will have to file all sorts of paperwork with the port authorities before they'll let us go."

"Unless you're in a hurry to get to the photo counter," Maggie added coyly.

"Maybe," I said, matching her tone.

Better, I thought, to let her think I was spending the day with Markos; otherwise she would feel obligated to invite me to join her. In fact, I needed time to find the Hollises; if I hadn't located them by the time passengers were given clearance to disembark, I would never find them. And so I didn't go to the photo counter at all, but to the Promenade Deck, where my fellow sightseers were gathered in one of the ship's nightclubs. It hadn't yet opened for the day, but it was here that we were to wait for clearance to leave the ship.

I recognized the nightclub at once—it was the same one where Markos had plunked me down at a corner table and plied me with ouzo—but it looked very different in the light of day. Sunlight streamed through the wide picture windows, replacing the dim yet intimate lighting of evening. No one tended bar, and no jazz combo occupied the raised dais at one end of the room—and even if they had, no one would have been able to hear them: The room was crowded with passengers, all jockeying for the best position for leaving the ship once the word was given. Staticky announcements crackled at intervals from the ship's intercom, incomprehensible over the snatches of conversation from the crowd.

"—don't know how much to tip the gondoliers—"

"—looking for the nearest currency exchange—"

"—were here back in '48, not long after the war—"

I scanned the crowd, looking for the Hollises. Mr. Hollis was a tall man, although a bit stooped; still, the top of his head should be visible—unless, of course, he and his wife had arrived early enough to snag one of the little tables. I squeezed through the crowd, muttering apologies to the people I unavoidably jostled, until at last I caught a glimpse of them seated at a table very close to the one where Markos and I had sat. I started to make my way toward them, but at that moment another announcement came from the intercom, and although this one was no clearer than the previous ones had been, someone must have understood something. In the manner peculiar to crowds, everyone in the place surged to their feet as one, and began moving toward the entrance. I was swept along with them, trying to keep Mr. Hollis's head of thick wavy salt-and-pepper hair in view. We moved down the passage to the midships staircase and flowed down the steps, where a bottleneck formed as we reached the open hatchway that crossed the gangplank. I managed to squeeze past an elderly lady without knocking her down, and a couple who stopped in their tracks to snap photos, but my efforts were futile. By the time I stepped off the gangplank, the Hollises were already being bundled into one of the launches that would convey passengers to the Piazza San Marco.

I thought of my promise to Markos, and glanced about. There were a few people I was on nodding terms with—the couple who'd won the dance competition, and a pair of elderly women I recognized from the lifeboat drill on our first day at sea—but no one I felt I knew well enough to invite myself along with their party; I remembered how Sylvia Duprée had latched onto us in Rome, and didn't want to be guilty of doing the same thing to someone else. The thought of Sylvia not unnaturally reminded me of her fate, and made me all the more determined to find the Hollises. Frustrating as it was, my best course of action was to wait in line for a launch and try to catch up with them at the Piazza.

This, as it turned out, was easier said than done. Three more launches filled and departed before I reached the front of the line and clambered aboard. At last we drew up alongside the Piazza, and I forgot my dilemma long enough to be charmed by the long black gondolas bobbing on the water between barbershop-striped poles, and the twin columns framing the Piazzetta, one topped with a statue of St. Theodore and his dragon (which looked remarkably like a crocodile) and the other with the winged Lion of St. Mark. I left the launch and wandered about the Piazzetta, searching for some sign of the Hollises as I passed booths selling everything from postcards to elaborate Carnival masks adorned with sequins and feathers. I wouldn't mind buying a mask or two later—besides making lovely wall decorations, they might be useful teaching aids when my classes read "The Masque of the Red Death"—but for now I had a more urgent task at hand. Unfortunately, the Piazzetta was even more crowded than the ship had been, and after half an hour of crisscrossing the square looking for them, I was forced to admit that they weren't there. My hasty breakfast had long since worn off by this time, and I located a charming little *osteria*, where I parted with far too many of my carefully hoarded *lire* for a Caprese salad, a glass of the house wine, and an umbrella-shaded table on the Piazza where I might keep a weather eye out for the Hollises while I ate.

By the time I'd finished, I still had seen no sign of them. Where could they possibly be? I decided the domed and multi-spired Basilica San Marco might be a likely possibility; besides being hard to miss, dominating the eastern perimeter of the Piazza as it did, it was just the sort of thing Mrs. Hollis might want to photograph in order to share with her friends. I stood in line and bought a ticket, and stood in yet another line to gain admission. While I waited, I decided to take a few photos of my own; it would be a pity to spend a day in Venice and be blind to anything but the back of Mr. Hollis's head. I snapped a shot of the basilica's western façade, and a couple more of the four bronze horses mounted on the loggia overlooking the Piazza. Here was another representation of the Lion of St. Mark, this time a mosaic showing the winged creature holding an open book with one paw. It occurred to me that he and his twentieth-century namesake had something in common: Markos was apparently no stranger to books himself, but he could be bold when the occasion warranted—and he would certainly do some roaring of his own if he discovered I was wandering around Venice on my own when I'd promised him I wouldn't.

"I'm trying, I'm trying," I muttered aloud, eliciting a funny look from the young man, apparently a college student, in front of me.

Once inside, I gazed about the cavernous space, my search for the Hollises momentarily forgotten. The interior was built on a Greek cross design, and the upper walls and bowl of the dome were covered with colorful mosaics and lavishly adorned with gold. I snapped a few more photos and then resumed my search for Mr. and Mrs. Hollis, the soles of my shoes clicking loudly on the tessellated marble floor. My shoes were not the only sounds that echoed in the vast room;

voices did as well, and my heart leaped as I caught a snatch of a deep voice speaking in a Midwestern twang. I couldn't understand any words, but I set out at once in the direction of the sound. I located the speaker, but it wasn't Mr. Hollis. Instead, the college student who had stood in front of me in the line had been joined by three friends, all with knapsacks slung from their shoulders and all engaged in lively debate over where they should go for dinner. Upon seeing me, one of them smiled appreciatively in a way that might have been highly gratifying, had I been in a mood for flirtation. Instead, I mumbled an apology (although I wasn't quite sure what I was apologizing for) and turned away. I gave the presbytery and the treasury each a quick look and even climbed the stairs to the loggia, thinking Mr. Hollis, being a farmer, might be interested in giving the bronze horses a closer look, but saw no sign there of either him or his wife.

Discouraged, I retraced my steps down the stairs and exited the basilica. *What next?* I wondered as I scanned the square. The Doge's Palace was the next most likely place, I decided, so I bought another ticket and stood in another line. At any other time, I would have been delighted to discover what lay beyond the pink and cream façade with its arcade and delicately arched loggia, but I was too aware of the fact that my time was running out; if I couldn't locate the Hollises soon, I would have no choice but to return to the ship. I wouldn't want to be alone in Venice after dark, even without the threat of Devos hanging over my head.

And then, just as I reached the front of the line and entered the palace, the bells of the many *campanili* across the city began to toll. I'd been hearing them at intervals all day, but for the first time it occurred to me to wonder just how long I'd been searching. I checked my watch, and was shocked to discover that the afternoon was already far advanced. Determined to speed up my search, I did little more than stick my head into each chamber, looking in vain for a glimpse of Mr. or Mrs. Hollis before moving on to the next room.

The place was so vast that I wondered more than once if I were simply going around in circles. Then, without knowing exactly how I'd gotten there, I found myself on the famous bridge dubbed by the ubiquitous Lord Byron as the "Bridge of Sighs." Made of white limestone and completely enclosed save for two stone-latticed windows on each side, it connected the Doge's palace to the prison on the opposite side of the canal. The "sighs" were supposedly the reaction of convicted prisoners getting their last glimpse of the outside world as they were taken to their cells. Instinctively, I crossed to the nearest window and looked out through the latticework just in time to see a gondolier in traditional striped shirt and straw hat steering his sleek black craft beneath the bridge—a craft bearing a beaming Mrs. Hollis and her husband, who gave her a quick peck on the cheek as they disappeared from view.

I didn't hesitate. I turned and retraced my steps as quickly as I could, glancing into chambers occasionally to make sure they were the same ones I'd passed on my way in. The palace was enormous, and my wrong turns were just frequent enough that it was some time before I finally emerged onto the sunlit Piazza. I hurried toward the edge of the lagoon, startling a flock of pigeons strutting about the square in search of handouts, and reached the place where tourists waited in line for gondola rides. I stood there for a quarter of an hour watching for the Hollis's gondola to return. Surely it shouldn't take this long; the Bridge of Sighs wasn't far from this spot at all. I waited another ten minutes, but there was still no sign of them. Clearly, they had returned while I'd been lost in the maze of the Doge's Palace. They were gone, and I'd lost my last, best chance of catching up with them. With a sinking heart, I turned away, prepared to catch the next launch back to the ship.

On the other hand . . .

I glanced back at the line of tourists waiting for gondola rides. The sun was low in the sky by this time, casting the twin columns of the Piazzetta into stark silhouette and turning the curved bronze prow ornaments of the gondolas to gold. It would be a pity to leave Venice without ever having had the ultimate Venetian experience. I'd been here all day, searching in vain for the Hollises; surely if Devos were anywhere nearby, I would have seen him. And even if he did happen to be lurking about, he couldn't get anywhere near me if I were on a gondola in the middle of a canal . . .

I wasn't even aware of having made up my mind, but suddenly I found myself counting out my *lire* into the gondolier's outstretched hand and stepping off the pier and into the long, graceful craft. It bobbed crazily beneath my weight, and I collapsed, not so gracefully, onto one of the two red velvet upholstered seats in the middle of the boat. The gondolier took up his position on a platform at the stern, from which point he plied his long oar. Soon we had left the lagoon behind and headed up one of the canals.

"This is the Rio di Palazzo," the gondolier informed me in lilting English. "See the enclosed bridge ahead of us? That is the Ponte dei Sospiri, the Bridge of Sighs."

He went on to recount its history—some of which I already knew, but I couldn't deny it sounded much more romantic when he said it than it had when I'd read it in the guide book. We passed beneath the high arch that formed the bottom of the bridge and made our way further up the canal, my gondolier pointing out sites of interest along the way while I returned the friendly waves of passengers in the gondolas we met coming back from the other direction. As we left the popular tourist sites behind, the gondola traffic grew thinner, the canals narrower, and the elegant pedestrian bridges that spanned them smaller, sometimes so low that my gondolier had to duck as we passed beneath them. The buildings close along each side blocked out most of the sunlight that remained, casting us into an early twilight and creating so romantic a mood that I began to wish for Markos for reasons entirely unrelated to safety or smuggling.

"The *signorina* would like a song, yes?" offered the gondolier, apparently sensing my mood.

"I would love it," I assured him, and he obliged by launching his very fine tenor into a poignant melody in a minor key.

It was quiet along these backwaters; the noise of tourists had faded to the point where there was nothing to compete with the melancholy song of my gondolier except the lapping of water along the walls of the buildings that clung to the canal on each side. Some of them had back exits with tiny private jetties where a small motorboat was tied; others had doors that opened directly onto the canal, with only a couple of moss-covered steps between the floor and the water. Baskets of colorful flowers hung from some of the windows overhead, while others were tightly shuttered, their secrets locked away inside. All had an air of elegant decay, with paint in shades of cream or pink or terra cotta peeling from the plastered walls.

Then my gondolier turned a tight corner, and I saw up ahead a crush of boats pulling up to a dock that formed one side of a paved square. Several dozen people milled about, all wearing elaborate masks similar to the ones I'd seen for sale in booths along the Piazza, and all dressed in clothing more suited to 1761 than 1961. The women's hair was piled high on their heads and coated with a thick layer of white powder, and their dresses had wide, panniered skirts of satin brocade, with foaming lace cascading from the elbow-length sleeves. The men wore gold-laced swallow-tailed coats, silk stockings, and breeches with knots of ribbon at the knees. Their hair was powdered as well, or perhaps they wore wigs, as no one but a beatnik would wear his hair so long—and anyone further from a beatnik than these elegant "macaronis" would have been hard to imagine. It was almost as if I had stepped back two hundred years in time, and I was utterly captivated, if a little confused.

"It isn't Carnival, is it?" I asked, turning to address my gondolier. "I thought that was earlier in the year."

"The *signorina* is correct," he assured me. "Carnival marks the last chance for revelry before the beginning of Lent, so it usually falls in February, or perhaps late January. But the wearing of masks is such a great part of Venetian history that private masquerade parties are popular any time of year. This is very likely such a party. But all these boats, they block the canal, *sì*? I know another way that will be, what do you say, a cut of a shortness."

"A shortcut," I said, suppressing a smile. His excellent English, contrasting with a rather charming failure to grasp colloquial speech, reminded me a bit of Markos. The thought of Markos was enough to make my smile fade, as I wondered what, if anything, would happen to us after Maggie and I disembarked in the morning for the last time. Meanwhile, I had to make sure my bags were packed by the time I went to bed tonight, so it was just as well that the gondolier steered us around the crush of boats and turned into another, still narrower, canal. We had gone a short distance along this canal when it opened onto another small square, this one lined with what appeared to be shops catering to the locals rather than the tourist trade. And in front of one shop window, with their backs facing the canal, stood a tall yet stooped man with thick wavy salt-and-pepper hair, and a woman wearing a flowered cotton dress and sensible shoes.

"Stop!" I cried, startling my gondolier. "That is, you can let me off here, if you don't mind. I was separated from my traveling companions earlier today, and it looks like I've found them at last." Seeing he was torn as to whether or not to obey this request, I added, "I know this isn't one of your usual stops, but if you'll make an exception for me, I would be *so* grateful." I gave him what I hoped was a charming smile, and made a subtle gesture in the direction of my handbag to make it clear to him just what form my gratitude would take.

He didn't hesitate. He plied his long oar, and the

gondola came smoothly to rest against the steps that formed one side of the square. He offered his hand to assist me out of the vessel, and I took it. I stepped up onto the square, and when I released his hand, I didn't leave it empty. He thanked me profusely, wished me a "*Buonasera*," and rowed his way back out into the canal. I gave him a little farewell wave, then joined the couple looking into the window of what I now saw was a shoe store.

"I'm so glad to find you at last!" I told the Hollises. "I've been looking all over for you."

The couple turned to me with friendly yet puzzled smiles, and I found myself looking into the faces of two strangers.

"Oh! I—I beg your pardon. I thought—" I could tell by the courteous yet blank expressions on their faces that they couldn't understand a word I was saying. I shrugged my shoulders and raised my hands in the universal gesture of helplessness. "*Mille pardons*," I said, hoping my schoolroom French would express the same sentiment in Italian.

They smiled and nodded, then turned back to the store window. Clearly, there were no hard feelings, and yet now I was left with the task of finding my way back, on foot, to the place where I could catch the launch back to the ship—no easy task even if I knew where I was. Which I didn't. I thought of asking the Italian couple for directions, but rejected the idea; even if I could communicate the question in a way they could comprehend, it was unlikely that I would understand the answer they gave me. I looked up at the deepening shadows cast across the canal by the buildings hugging its sides, and was able to determine by their direction which way was west. The lagoon, I knew, formed the southern edge of the Piazzetta, so if I could just work my way southward, I should come upon it eventually.

Fortunately for me, not every street in Venice was a canal, as I'd always believed. The major thoroughfares certainly were, and not a few of the minor ones. But there were also narrow pedestrian passageways—some of which crossed the canals at intervals, which explained the graceful little bridges spanning them. I chose one of the walkways that seemed to head south, and set out on foot.

I don't know what made me suspect I was being followed, or what made me look over my shoulder. But at some point I glanced behind me, and saw a figure dressed in a long black cloak and black tricorn hat, a figure whose face was covered with the long-beaked white mask of the medieval plague doctors. One of the masqueraders, I told myself, who was either leaving the party early or who had gotten lost trying to find it. There was no reason for me to panic, or to think of Markos's warnings about Devos. Still, something about that bizarre face that was no face made me walk a bit faster. I turned right, away from the canal, and had gone perhaps half a block when I looked over my shoulder again. The figure was still there. Probably an ardent young Italian man in search of a flirtation, I told myself with increasing desperation; after all, my bottom had been pinched more than once during our stops in Florence and Rome by too-aggressive Latin lovers. Still, I cut back to the left, trying to lose my unwanted admirer without losing my bearings completely. After all, it would be dark soon, and I would no longer have the shadows to judge direction by.

I walked straight for about a city block and looked again. He was still there, and perhaps it was my imagination, but he appeared to be closing the distance between us. I picked up my pace still more, made another left turn, and this time when I looked behind me, he was no longer there. The sound of lapping water came to my ears, and I realized the canal was only a short distance in front of me. It was too narrow to be on a regular *vaporetto* route, but I might, if I was lucky, be able to flag down a water taxi. Letting out a long sigh of relief, I walked toward the canal, reaching the edge just in time to see another figure, this one dressed in regular street clothes, step out from the shadows.

"Good evening, Miss Fletcher," Devos said. "Or should I say, *Buonasera?*"

17

How cheerfully he seems to grin,
How neatly spreads his claws,
And welcomes little fishes in
With gently smiling jaws!
LEWIS CARROLL,
Alice's Adventures in Wonderland

M r. Devos," I said, wishing my voice didn't sound so wobbly. "What a pleasant surprise." It wasn't, of course, but I refused to give him the satisfaction of seeing how frightened I was.

"Yes, isn't it? But you should not be wandering about Venice by yourself. It is not safe for a young woman alone. Some of the canals are quite deep. One might—fall in—and never be seen again."

"I didn't intend to 'wander about Venice' on my own," I said, suppressing a shudder at the picture his warning—or was it a threat?—evoked. "I've been searching high and low for the Hollises ever since I got off the launch."

"Is that who you were seeking? I thought you were looking for—someone else."

"Oh, you saw me searching?" I wasn't quite sure how I felt about that. Whatever his motives for not making his presence known, they couldn't be good. "I never saw you."

His teeth gleamed in the fading twilight. "I did surveillance in the war, Miss Fletcher. For someone trained to elude the Nazis, avoiding the gaze of one young woman presents no particular difficulty. Although you did give me a bad moment or two when you exited your gondola so abruptly. I congratulate you."

"Never mind the congratulations," I said sharply. "If you can't tell me where the Hollises are, I won't trouble you any further."

I started to turn away, but he grabbed my arm. "Not just yet, Miss Fletcher. We have unfinished business, you and I."

"I can't imagine what you're talking about." They were brave words, but my voice betrayed me, and my arm trembled in his hold.

He stepped nearer, and I could feel his fingers biting into my arm, bruising me. "You have something in your possession that I want very much."

"I—I don't know what you're talking about."

"I think you do. Let us not play games, Miss Fletcher. You possess certain photographs taken in Pisa. They are not in your cabin, else I would have found them, or in your aunt's, else Sylvia would have."

"Then it *was* you in my stateroom! I suppose that was

why you insisted on escorting me back to my cabin—to discover my room number, and my aunt's."

He continued as if I hadn't spoken. "Nor are they in the photography shop. Therefore the film must still be in your camera. Do not try to tell me you have left your camera in your cabin; I have seen you taking photos with it all day." His breath was hot and fetid in my ear as he added, "I am prepared to do whatever it takes to get those photos. The history of Venice is long and violent. What is the disappearance of one rather foolish young woman against so much bloodshed? If you doubt my sincerity, you have only to look to Sylvia. She could tell you I mean what I say—if she were alive to do so."

"Sylvia—" A lump formed in the pit of my stomach. He would not be telling me such things if he thought there was any chance of my repeating them.

"It was I who killed her—but you already suspected as much, did you not? The stupid woman had one task: to get that camera from your aunt while your group was in Rome. Yes, I admit to a mistake there: I thought it was Mrs. Watson's camera at first, for it was she who had been taking photos with it in Pisa. But Sylvia failed, and when I ordered her to search your aunt's cabin for it the next day, she failed again. She had clearly become a, what do you say, a liability, and so she had to go." He leaned nearer, his lips all but touching my ear, and I shuddered in spite of myself. "Why should I balk at ridding myself of a meddlesome stranger, when I did not hesitate to eliminate my own wife, hm?"

"Your *wife?*" The lump in my stomach began turning somersaults, and I thought I was going to be physically ill. Still, I had one ace up my sleeve that Sylvia hadn't. "Markos Rondo knows what you're up to," I said, drawing courage from speaking the words aloud. "If any-thing happens to me, he'll know where to look."

To my dismay, Devos began to laugh, a rumbling chuckle under his breath that was far more terrifying than his threats had been. "Is there anyone more trusting than a young woman in love? My dear Miss Fletcher, who do you think is behind the whole enterprise?"

"No!" I shrugged off his hand and backed away. "It isn't true! I don't believe you!"

Devos was lying. I knew he was. And yet . . . And yet there were certain things Markos had said, certain things that, in the light of Devos's accusation, could be interpreted in an entirely different way than they had first appeared. His supposed suspicions of me could have been nothing more than an attempt to discover how much I knew, his romantic interest in me no more than a ploy to make me lower my guard sufficiently to confide in him. Was that why he'd offered to show me about Mykonos before Sylvia's body was even cold? Had I been playing right into his hands all along?

"He's with the Ministry of Culture!" I insisted, not quite sure if I was trying to convince Devos or myself.

"Of course he is. Who would be in a better position to arrange such an operation than a highly-educated insider? And who would have greater reason than a lower-level bureaucrat who feels his talents are being wasted?"

Not very impressive, I fear, Markos's voice rang in my head. *Undersecretary to an undersecretary* . . .

With a sinking feeling in the pit of my stomach, I realized that while he'd let me keep the photos, he'd never returned the negatives to me, nor said exactly what he intended to do with the enlargement he'd made. A simple oversight on his part, or was there something else, something more sinister, at work here? Had the purpose of that enlargement been, not to identify Devos's activities, as I'd thought, but to determine exactly to what extent the smuggling scheme had been compromised?

Suddenly I felt as if I'd stepped into one of those negatives with their weirdly reversed colors. Black was white and white was black, and nothing was as it seemed. My heart cried out that Markos was innocent—but what if I was wrong? In that case, I had only to tell Devos that Markos already had the photos, and I would be out of danger. But no, Devos had told me too much. I would have to be gotten rid of either way, and in the meantime, if Markos was as innocent as I believed him to be—as I wanted so desperately for him to be—I would have put him in mortal danger. Right now, as far as Devos was concerned, my supposed possession of the photos was the only thing keeping me alive.

"By all means, believe whatever you wish." Devos was talking again, but I could hardly hear him for the conflicting thoughts clamoring inside my head. "Only give me the photos."

"And—and what will happen to me if I do?" I asked, stalling for time—time to think, time to plan. Time for Markos to come to my rescue? I had better not count on that. At best, Markos was hard at work in the ship's darkroom. At worst—but I couldn't think about that, not now.

"You will be free to return to the ship, of course," Devos said smoothly. "You may report me to the captain— or to Dr. Rondo, if you prefer—but with no proof to back up your outrageous claims—" He shrugged.

No proof, I thought, but certainly enough to make things very uncomfortable for him. And for Markos as well? I rejected that thought at once, or at least pushed it aside for consideration later. Outrageous they might be, but my accusations might result in the search of Devos's cabin by the port authorities, who would find the artifacts he hadn't yet had time to pass on to their buyers. No, whatever his assurances, Devos would not allow me to survive this encounter.

"And all you want is my camera?" I didn't have to fake the fearful quaver in my voice.

"That is all." His voice was soothing, placating. "Only give it to me, and I will escort you back to the Piazzetta myself." Of that I was certain, although I doubted very much if I would ever reach it alive.

I took a deep breath, and came to a decision. "All right, then. Here it is." I fumbled in my bag and withdrew my camera, the new one I'd bought just for this trip. As he reached for it, I hurled the camera over his shoulder, and heard it land in the canal with a splash. "Swim for it!"

The film was certainly ruined the moment the camera entered the water, but in the split second it took for Devos to realize this, I had dropped my cumbersome bag and was running, running as fast as I could down the narrow thoroughfare, cutting first down one side street and then another in an attempt to escape my pursuer. And that he was pursuing me I had no doubt; I could hear the ringing of his footsteps on the flagstone pavement somewhere behind me—and I was sure he could hear mine, even if he could no longer see me in the dark passageway. I rounded the nearest corner and kicked off my shoes, leaving them where they fell as I ran silently ahead on stockinged feet. Night had fallen by now, and the occasional pool of yellow light cast by the lamps overhanging the street provided the only illumination. I wasn't quite sure whether to be sorry or glad; the darkness would make it more difficult for Devos to see me, but it also made it impossible for me to read any street signs or recognize any landmarks.

I had no idea how long I ran, but eventually my side ached, my stockings were in shreds, and the soles of my feet were cut and bruised. I had lost any sense of direction long ago, and had no idea where I was or whether I was any nearer to the Piazza San Marco, where I might lose myself among the crowds. I ducked around another corner and paused, listening. My breath came in labored gasps, making it difficult to hear much of anything, but I thought—yes, I was almost certain I could hear the plaintive song of a gondolier. And, nearer at hand, the slower but unrelenting footsteps of Konstantin Devos. Ignoring the screams of protest from feet and lungs, I ran again—and came to an abrupt halt on the very edge of a canal, windmilling my arms to keep from falling in. I glanced wildly to left and right, but there was no sidewalk, no passageway—nothing. I'd reached a dead end, and Devos was even now rounding the corner, slowing to a leisurely pace when he realized there was nowhere else I could run.

"For shame, Miss Fletcher," he chided, and even though he was fully twenty years older than I, it seemed to me that he wasn't even breathing hard. "All that running, and where has it got us?"

He reached into the pocket of his jacket, and my blood

ran cold as the light from the streetlamp glinted on the blade of a knife. He was nearly upon me, but what could I do? Running was no longer an option, for I dared not attempt to dodge past him when he held a knife in his hand, while behind me lay nothing but the dark, oily waters of the canal.

The canal . . .

And suddenly I realized I *did* know what to do, that I had known ever since the lifeboat drill on our first day at sea. I put one hand over my mouth and pinched my nostrils shut with thumb and forefinger, then closed my eyes and stepped off the edge of the pavement.

My last thought before entering the water was that I would feel an awful fool, and would very likely be a dead one, if the canal was only four feet deep. But in the next moment, the water closed over my head, and my skirts, filled with air, billowed up around me like a balloon. I broke the surface a moment later, gasping from cold and shock, to the sounds of Devos's cursing.

"You can't stay in there forever, *skýla!*" He waved his knife threateningly, and for a moment I thought he meant to fling it at my head. But apparently he didn't trust his aim, for he satisfied himself with hurling abuses instead, and ending with a threat. "You'll have to come out eventually—and when you do—" He stroked the blade of the knife almost lovingly. "—I'll be waiting."

He was right, damn him. Besides being cold, the waters

of the canal weren't the cleanest or the healthiest place for a swim. Devos had only to outwait me, and when I finally emerged, waterlogged and shivering, the best speed I could manage would be no match for his—and even if I somehow succeeded in eluding him, he had only to follow my dripping trail. Unless, of course, I could swim across the canal to the opposite bank—but no, a low bridge arched across the canal less than a hundred feet ahead; Devos could run across to the other side in less time than it would take me, hampered by wet skirts, to swim there. I could, perhaps, swim underwater long enough to lose him in the dark, and then cross at some less easily accessible point, but my light-colored skirts shone beneath the water like some phosphorescent sea creature. The best I could do was play for time until my aunt realized I was missing and sent out a search party—but if all went well between Maggie and Paul, that might not be until morning, by which time it would be too late.

And then, just when my last hope was fading, rescue arrived, just like the cavalry coming over the horizon. Somewhere in the back of my mind, I'd been conscious of a gondolier singing in the distance, but I hadn't noticed the sound growing louder until the vessel emerged from around the corner like a great black swan, the light from its prow lamp bobbing across the water with each stroke of the gondolier's oar.

I didn't hesitate. I swam toward the middle of the canal,

reaching it just as the gondola drew abreast. With the last bit of strength I possessed, I grabbed onto the side of the craft and hauled myself up, no doubt looking like the Creature from the Black Lagoon.

"Help me," I croaked, and collapsed, hanging half in and half out over the side of the boat, at the stunned gondolier's feet.

"I hold myself entirely responsible," Maggie fretted, not for the first time. The last hour or two had passed in a blur, but I now stood with my aunt on the deck of the *Oceanus* where, having washed and changed into clean and dry clothes and given a statement of the night's events to the proper authorities, I leaned against the rail, letting the breeze off the lagoon dry my freshly shampooed hair. "If I hadn't run off with Paul and left you alone—"

"It isn't your fault," I insisted, also not for the first time. "Anyway, did he propose?"

"He did, and I accepted," she said with a smug smile. "But don't change the subject! If I'd had the least idea that I was putting you in danger—"

"I know you didn't, and I didn't think I would be alone, at least not the whole time. I'd thought to catch up with the Hollises, but I couldn't find them anywhere, and—and then when I thought I *had* found them, all of sudden *he* was there," I recalled, shuddering.

"I can't believe I ate dinner every night with that man, and never suspected a thing! Robin, why didn't you tell me?"

My gaze slid away from hers. "I—well, it's hard to explain." A movement beyond her shoulder caught my eye, and I saw Markos approaching. I had a vague memory of seeing him in uniform, his face almost as white as his starched shirt, when I had been brought back onboard the ship earlier that evening filthy, dripping, and exhausted, but now he was dressed in street clothes and looked more self-possessed than anyone had a right to look.

Maggie followed the direction of my gaze, and arched one eyebrow. "And unless I'm very much mistaken, here comes the explanation now. Don't mind me, Markos. I was just going to pack Robin's bags."

"I'll do that—" I began, but "No, you won't," Maggie and Markos said in unison. Yielding to the inevitable (in fact, I was too tired to do anything else), I acknowledged my aunt's departure with a little wave, and braced myself for the scold I knew would be forthcoming.

"Devos has been taken in for questioning by the port authorities," Markos said, taking the wind out of my sails. "The last I heard, he was singing like a canary, as your American gangster movies would say."

"He killed Sylvia," I said. "He told me so, when—" I broke off, not wanting to relive that harrowing moment when Devos had stepped out of the shadows and plunged me into nightmare. "She was supposed to steal my camera, and when she didn't, he killed her. 'A liability,' he called her. Markos, she was his wife!"

"Yes, I know."

"It's true, then? But Mr. Grimes said she'd been married to a hero of the Resistance!" And so he had. But I'd assumed by her surname that he was talking about the French Resistance. Until I'd met Markos, I hadn't realized that the Greeks had had a resistance movement of their own. "Tell me," I said thoughtfully, "was Sylvia actually Greek, by any chance?"

Markos nodded. "Now you're catching on. Devos married Sylvia during the war—she had ambitions even then, and both of them fully expected that he would be able to parlay his wartime heroics into a position of influence within the new Greek Communist government. But the Communists lost, and instead of being lavishly rewarded, Devos was lucky to avoid execution. Still, he came up with a way to bleed his country for what he thought was rightfully his, by stealing her treasures and selling them to the highest bidder. He later extended his activities into Italy, since he considered, perhaps with some justification, that they owed him something as well."

"And Mr. Grimes?"

"As far as I can tell, he was perfectly innocent. But it

takes money to set up an operation such as the one Devos had. The right people have to be bribed, besides the unlawful digging itself."

"But—but that must have taken years!"

"I can assure you, this operation has been years in the making. Devos and Sylvia had to learn something about antiquities, then Sylvia had to recreate herself as a French-woman and find a wealthy man to seduce—"

"And having lost his wife years earlier, Mr. Grimes was ripe for the attentions of an attractive woman," I concluded. Mr. Grimes had never pretended Sylvia was the love of his life, but I found myself hoping he would never know to what extent he'd been taken in. "He knew she was interested in him for his money, but I'll bet he never guessed the half of it. I hope not, anyway. I suppose it's a mercy, as far as Mr. Grimes is concerned, that she died before the whole thing blew up in her face."

"It's certainly blowing up in Devos's, even as we speak. The port authorities have searched his stateroom, where they found some very interesting items that you won't see in any of the souvenir shops." He laid his hand over mine, where I held onto the railing. "I would have been here sooner to see about you—God, I was never so scared in my life as when I saw you being brought in!—but I was called in to identify Devos's little trinkets."

"And?"

"And they were—what is the word?—the real McCoy? Is that it?" Receiving a nod from me, he continued. "The two larger vases and the statue you described to me are Greek, from the first or second century before Christ; the rest are Etruscan, and are even older—I would put the pieces at the fifth through the sixth centuries B.C., although that is just a guess. An expert in Etruscan art will be able to date them more exactly."

"So you were right about everything!"

"Not just me," he demurred hastily. "A great many people have been working on this for a very long time— although we might never have been able to prove it, had you not decided to wander about the deck at midnight." Turning away from me, he gazed out over the lagoon and added diffidently, "This habit of wandering about on your own is going to get you in trouble someday—even more than it has already. If that fiancé of yours is wise, he will put a stop to it once you are married."

"Believe me, I've learned my lesson." Following his example, I looked away, staring with great intensity at the lights dotting the far side of the lagoon. "In fact, I've learned a lot on this voyage."

He turned back to me abruptly, with an arrested expression lighting his dark eyes. "Like what?"

"Like trusting my instincts. If something seems a bit 'off' to me, then it probably is—whether it's one man throwing a log overboard, or another man refusing to set a wedding date."

"Meaning?" prompted Markos, moving nearer.

I took a deep breath. "Meaning I've come to realize that the reason Gene won't set a date is that deep down inside, he really doesn't want to marry me. And the reason I've let him get away with it for so long is that deep down inside, I don't really want to marry him either." I gave a shaky little laugh. "A very educational trip, wouldn't you say? My only regret is that I lost all the photos I'd taken of Venice."

Markos grinned. "You can take new ones on your honeymoon."

Suddenly it was all too much, and his laughing at my broken engagement was the last straw. Tears welled up in my eyes, although I couldn't have said exactly why I was crying. "*What* honeymoon? I just said I'm not going to marry Gene!"

"I'm not talking about Gene," Markos said, and pulled me into his arms.

"Well?" he said when at last we broke apart, breathless. "Do you think you could bring yourself to marry a minor bureaucrat who dabbles in art and photography on the side? What do your instincts say to that?"

I started to protest that we hadn't known each other long enough, but the words stuck in my throat. I'd known Gene forever, had dated him for almost ten years, but as

Maggie had said, long acquaintance hadn't been enough. On the other hand, I'd met Markos only a couple of weeks earlier, and yet when Devos had pointed out the seemingly indisputable evidence against him, I'd known—*known*—that I could trust Markos with my life. I could put that knowledge to the test and marry him, or I could play it safe, could walk down the gangway of the *Oceanus* in the morning and out of Markos's life forever—and, perhaps, could spend the rest of my life regretting the opportunity I'd lost. I remembered what my aunt had said about seizing the day, and suddenly there was only one answer.

"My instincts say I'd better start learning Greek," I said, and we kissed again.

Author's Note

As a teenager in the mid-1970s, I was a voracious reader of the romantic suspense novels of Mary Stewart, Phyllis Whitney, and others who wrote in a similar vein. To this day, I attribute my love of travel to a steady diet of these tales of love and danger set in exotic locales. When my husband and I went on a Mediterranean cruise in 2015, I decided to try my hand at writing such a book as a way of sharing my experience with readers, and as a tribute to the women whose works brought so many hours of enjoyment and served as a window on the wider world to a girl growing up in rural Alabama.

So, how much was real and how much was a product of my imagination? First of all, if there was any sort of skullduggery going on amongst our fellow passengers, I never knew of it. There *was* a couple onboard that I dubbed the Mistress and the Sugar Daddy, however, who looked very much as I've described them here. We caught glimpses of them on the ship from time to time, as well as ashore in Pompeii—so like any good fiction writer, I came up with several wholly speculative explanations as to the nature of their relationship. When I decided to write a book based on some of the places we'd seen, it seemed only natural to include them.

Speaking of Pompeii, it was hot the day we visited, so I

bought a cheap plastic fan from a vendor just outside the ruins, a purchase I've attributed to Mrs. Hollis here. (It was the best five euros I ever spent, and more than one of my fellow passengers expressed envy.) Like Robin, I found the aggressive salesmen in Istanbul's Grand Bazaar too overwhelming to do much shopping there—and unlike Robin, I had my six-foot five-inch husband along to discourage them. (It didn't seem to make much difference; they simply tried to sell him a "genuine leather jacket." Whether it was genuine leather or not, I have no idea, but thirty-five years of experience in buying his clothes has taught me that the sleeves would almost certainly have been two inches too short.)

I was the one who bought a pair of shoes in Rome at a shop near the Spanish Steps when the sandals I was wearing rubbed blisters on my feet (probably the only thing Sylvia and I have in common), and I awoke one night to choppy seas and the soft clicking of the unused hangers in my closet—an incident I decided would make a spooky "false alarm" for Robin, thus making her less likely to trust her own judgment even when she had good reason to be concerned.

Of course, not all of the real-life incidents I borrowed for this book took place on the cruise. The "tuna fish" episode Robin recounts from her college days actually took place in my own French class at the University of South

Alabama.

As for the other ports of call described in this book, my husband and I visited every one of them, although we didn't necessarily have as much time to spend in each one as Robin did. (We didn't get to climb the Leaning Tower while we were in Pisa, for instance; the line there, as well as the ones at St. Mark's Basilica and the Doge's Palace in Venice and at Rome's Sistine Chapel, made those at Walt Disney World look short by comparison!) I've tried to draw word pictures for you, but if you'd like to see actual photographs from my trip, as well as pictures of early 1960s fashions and a real *caga tió*, you can find them on the Pinterest board I created just to go along with this book, https://www.pinterest.com/cobbsouth/moon-over-the-mediterranean.

About the Author

Sheri Cobb South is the author of more than twenty books, including the critically acclaimed Regency romance *The Weaver Takes a Wife* and a historical mystery series featuring idealistic young Bow Street Runner John Pickett. The latter was recently included in a *USA Today* book blog piece on historical mysteries with strong romantic elements. Her works have also been released in large-print and audiobook editions, translated into half a dozen languages, and recorded by the Library of Congress as part of its Books for the Blind program.

For more information on Sheri and her books, visit her website at www.shericobbsouth.com, or "Like" her author page at https://www.facebook.com/SheriCobbSouth.